"THIS BOOK IS PURE MAGIC!" —HELEN HOANG

# SCANDALIZED

# IVY OWENS

**$9.99** U.S.
$12.99 CAN.

ISBN 978-1-9821-9985-2

**$9.99 U.S.**/$12.99 Can.

50999

# PRAISE FOR *Scandalized*

"This book is pure magic!"

> —**Helen Hoang**, *USA Today* bestselling author of
> *The Heart Principle* and *The Kiss Quotient*

"I strongly suspect that Ivy Owens has smashed my skull open, inventoried every single thing I adore about romance novels, and then used the knowledge to write the most steamy, scorching, smart, sweet, exhilarating, passionate, swoony book I could ever imagine. I will literally need everyone to read *Scandalized*, so that when I quote by heart my favorite scenes, they can quote theirs to me, and we can bond over the magnificent experience of being swept away by Ivy Owens's magical writing."

> —**Ali Hazelwood**, *New York Times* bestselling author of
> *The Love Hypothesis*

"I wish I could express how much unfiltered joy and pure 100 proof escape I've gotten from this book. I don't remember the last time I reread a book this many times. Alec and Gigi are a romantic fantasy that feels so viscerally real, it's nothing short of magical."

> —**Sonali Dev**, *USA Today* bestselling author of
> *Recipe for Persuasion*

"*Scandalized* is a delicious, unputdownable romance. Sizzling chemistry, with a tremendous amount of heart, it's the oh-hey-that's-my-friend's-brother-and-wowza-has-he-grown-up book that we all need in our lives right now."

> —**Susan Lee**, author of *Seoulmates*

"Blistering hot chemistry and an edge of suspense that demands a one-sitting read!"

> —**Tessa Bailey**, *New York Times* bestselling author of
> *It Happened One Summer*

# Scandalized

## IVY OWENS

**POCKET BOOKS**

New York   London   Toronto   Sydney   New Delhi

Pocket Books
An Imprint of Simon & Schuster, Inc.
1230 Avenue of the Americas
New York, NY 10020

This book is a work of fiction. Any references to historical events, real people, or real places are used fictitiously. Other names, characters, places, and events are products of the author's imagination, and any resemblance to actual events or places or persons, living or dead, is entirely coincidental.

First Pocket Books paperback edition August 2022

POCKET and colophon are registered trademarks of Simon & Schuster, Inc.

For information about special discounts for bulk purchases, please contact Simon & Schuster Special Sales at 1-866-506-1949 or business@simonandschuster.com.

The Simon & Schuster Speakers Bureau can bring authors to your live event. For more information or to book an event, contact the Simon & Schuster Speakers Bureau at 1-866-248-3049 or visit our website at www.simonspeakers.com.

Interior design by Esther Paradelo

Manufactured in the United States of America

10  9  8  7  6  5  4  3  2  1

ISBN 978-1-9821-9985-2
ISBN 978-1-9821-9986-9 (ebook)

*For CH and KC.*
*When I was little,*
*I dreamed of having friends*
*like you someday.*

# Author's Note and Content Warning

This story includes a plotline related to sexual assault. Specifically, the heroine is an investigative journalist uncovering a related group of crimes. While no assaults happen on-page, character testimony and video evidence are described briefly.

The National Sexual Assault Hotline, 800-656-HOPE, is free and confidential. For resources related to sexual assault, please visit rainn.org.

# One

I am great with names, terrible with faces.

But I know I've seen this one before.

He's alone at the end of a row of seats and nose deep in his phone. I've lived in LA long enough to read his posture as respect-my-bubble rather than absorbed-in-reading, but I've also worked in journalism long enough to know this is a man doing his best to try to blend in.

It isn't working. Even his haircut—precise and combed neatly off his face—looks expensive. And I know I know him from somewhere. Jawline that could cut steel, cheekbones carved like stone, and a mouth in a perfect candy pout. His face is like an itch in my brain, a teasing tickle.

I hear my mom's voice, encouraging me to make the polite choice, to get up and say hello. But it's the airport and I'm tired, having spent the last thirteen days in London, hounding strangers for information they don't want to give and knowing no one except for one chain-smoking UK colleague with the alcohol tolerance of a rhino and whose bat-out-of-hell London driving had me praying to a God I don't believe in several times a day. I've been on a plane for eight hours and sitting at this gate for another four, waiting out a storm, waiting on the connecting flight to LA that has been delayed and then delayed again and again.

To be fair, this man's face doesn't feel like one I've seen in the past two weeks. The feeling I get goes deeper than the hit of chase-the-story-related adrenaline that dumps into my bloodstream; this adrenaline corkscrews into my bones. The glimpse I got of his full face—when he looked up, when he squinted at the monitors and then seemed to let out a tiny grunt of frustration—was like a song that I haven't heard in forever. Something about his posture makes my heart ache with nostalgic pain.

Paradoxically, he's both upright and slumped, so refined in his tailored navy pants, polished brown shoes, and white button-down shirt still crisp after our long flight from London to Seattle. He's gorgeous.

I pull my scarf up over my mouth, burying my face in it, but it smells like stale airplane and I tug it down again. The urge to scream in petulant exhaustion pulses through me. I want to teleport myself home to my bed. I want to skip all the self-care things and just crawl in unshowered, in my clothes. I don't even care how disgusting I am: after a fourteen-hour day of tracking down an elusive nightclub bouncer who didn't want to be found, then eight sleepless hours on a flight, I am reduced to my most feral self.

I look around and see a few people stretched out across four chairs, sleeping, while others have to find space on the floor. My skin is shouting at me to lie down somewhere, anywhere. And yet I don't, knowing that even if we board and depart in the next five minutes, by the time I grab a cab and make the long trek home, it'll be well past midnight, and I'll need to get working as soon as I can. I've been given the chance of a lifetime with this story, and as of this minute, I only have two days to finish writing it.

Near the gate, the airline employees have carefully avoided stepping behind the podium. If they so much as hover nearby, an irritated line forms. Instead, they shift around in the background, staring gloomily at each other every time the Jetway phone rings with an update on the torrential storm outside. Finally, one bravely steps toward the intercom, and from the sag in her shoulders and the way she stares down at the monitor as if she needs to read from it, I know.

"I'm sorry to announce that United flight 2477 has been canceled. You have each been rebooked onto a flight departing tomorrow. Tickets will be reissued to the email address linked to your reservation. Please contact our customer service line or go to the customer service office in baggage claim with any questions. We will not be able to rebook you here. We're sorry for any inconvenience."

On instinct, I look up to watch his reaction to the news.

He's already lifting his phone to his ear, nodding. Our eyes meet briefly as his gaze passes unseeing across the room, but his attention freezes, eyes quickly drawing back to mine, focusing with the same unknowing recognition. It's only a beat, but in that time heat spreads through me wild and unchecked, and then he blinks away, frowning.

And now I wonder how he knows me, too.


In a perfect world, I would be home already. I would have been booked on a direct flight from London to LAX, instead of this route via Seattle. In a perfect world, I would be well rested and already at my computer, downloading the torrent of information from my brain and my phone and my notebook into a cohesive story. I would not be standing behind this perfect man in the lobby of a Seattle hotel, feeling like a run-down bridge troll.

There is a line of three people in front of me, another four behind. We all came from the same canceled flight, we all need rooms, and I have the unsettling feeling that I should have ventured out farther into the city than I have. This feels a lot like a race I didn't know I would be running, one that I will most definitely lose.

The man whose name I still can't remember has his neck bent as he appears to text in a flurry, but at a brief commotion at the hotel entrance—a horn honks, a woman shouts out a name—he turns in alarm, and I get a close-up view of his profile.

All at once it hits me, where I've seen his face.

I've seen a younger version of it looking back over his shoulder as he skateboarded away on a heat-warped Los Angeles street in the dead of summer. Laughing with friends on a living room couch, oblivious to me passing behind them through the room. Ducking around me in the hall at his house late at night as I went to use the restroom and he was finally heading to bed.

"Alec?" I say out loud.

He turns in alarm, eyes wide. "I'm sorry?"

"Aren't you Alec Kim?"

A laugh works free of his throat and the smile reveals a perfect set of teeth. He has a face that continually reveals new, fascinating angles. Dimples. An Adam's apple that moves in a masculine tease when he laughs. Skin like silk. I've been around beautiful people for the past two weeks but he's something else entirely. If he isn't a model, it's a crime.

"Yes—I'm sorry." He frowns, searching. "Do we know each other?" I haven't seen him in fourteen years, and his words are wrapped up in a new, delicately complex accent.

"I'm Georgia Ross," I prompt, and he turns to face me fully, tucking a hand into his pocket. The effect of his full attention is like having a powerful suction inside my chest, pulling air directly from my lungs. "Your sister, Sunny, and I were close in school. Your family moved to London at the end of eighth grade."

Alec was six years older than us. My crush on him was intense almost to the point of painful. For years he'd just been my best friend's brother. Occasionally present, always polite, mostly unremarkable. But then one night, only a couple weeks after my thirteenth birthday, I'd gone downstairs for a glass of water and caught him digging in the refrigerator for a midnight snack: nineteen years old, shirtless, and sleep rumpled. I could think of nothing but his naked torso for weeks afterward.

I think back to the muscled bodies wrestling over game controllers on the couch, the shirtless boy-man kicking at the street, pushing away on his skateboard. Halfway through his time at UCLA his family moved to London for Mr. Kim's job, and Alec went, too. Sunny and I each sent about three letters before dropping our well-laid plans entirely. She'd been my closest friend from second to eighth grade, but once she moved, I never saw her again.

He lets his gaze move over my features, clearly trying to connect the face in front of him with the one on the kid he used to know. Good luck to him. The last time he saw me I had braces, unsupervised eyebrows, and arms as thin as toothpicks. I'm still on the petite side, but I'm not the scrawny kid I once was. Even though I was at his house nearly every day after school, I'd bet a wad of cash he won't remember me.

Still, he's putting in a real effort to recognize the little Gigi Ross inside the grown-up Georgia. I've never been particularly insecure about my appearance, but under his inspection I could not be more aware of how desperately I need a shower. Even my eyes, which are arguably my best feature—wide-set, thickly lashed, hazel green—are probably bloodshot and squinty. Let's not even imagine my hair. It was already so greasy fifteen hours ago that I used up the final dregs of my expensive dry shampoo and twisted it into a bun. Standing in front of a man like this, looking like I do, is mortifying.

"Georgia. Right." He doesn't exactly light up in recognition. It's fine. These things are always one-sided. To a nineteen-year-old, I'd have been so uninteresting as to be practically invisible. But then his expression clears. "Wait. *Gigi*?"

I grin. "Yeah, Gigi."

"Wow," he says. "It's been a while. I haven't been called Alec in . . ." He thinks. "Fourteen years?"

"What do you go by now?"

He regards me with a beat of surprised hesitation and then, eyes twinkling, says, "Alexander. But Alec is just fine."

I reach to shake his hand and he wraps long fingers all around mine, squeezing firmly. "It's good to see you again."

He doesn't immediately pull away. My sleepy body reads it as foreplay and immediately gets hot all over. When he finally releases me, I curl my hand into a fist, shoving it into the pocket of my jeans. "How is Sunny?"

Alec's face breaks into a heartbreakingly perfect smile. "She's great. Living in London. Modeling. Maybe you—"

The hotel clerk leans forward to grab our attention. "I can help whoever's next."

Alec gives me a small nod, indicating that I can go first, but I'm still feeling the handshake sex. My wallet is in my backpack, my neck feels like it's about to scorch from this blush, and I really just need someone to drop me in a bathtub and give me a scrubbing with a giant scouring pad.

"Go ahead." I wave him on, pretending to need to find something. Which I guess I do. Namely, my composure, which must be somewhere in this bag with my wallet. But after only a few seconds, a woman steps out from behind the counter and approaches the remaining five of us in line.

"I'm so sorry to say that we are fully booked for the night," she says, wincing. "Unless you have a reservation, we're unable to accommodate you. I know there are a lot of groups in town, but our concierge might be able to offer some alternatives."

Before I can even react, the other guests have jogged over to the concierge's desk and formed a line in the reverse order from this one, all clamoring for attention. Great.

Looking down, I send an email through the work travel portal, letting the help desk know the hotel I went to is booked solid. But it's almost ten now, and I have no idea how long it will take someone to see it. I try calling, too, and get a voicemail. The surfaces of my eyes burn with frustrated, exhausted tears and I squeeze my lids closed, thinking. What are the odds I could just nap on a couch in the lobby and no one would notice? Or even return to the airport and curl up on a row of seats there? I've been rebooked onto a flight tomorrow morning at eight; it's not like I need anything elaborate.

I'm startled back into awareness when a hand comes around my elbow, gently guiding me away from where I stand alone in a line that now leads nowhere.

"Do you have somewhere to go?" Alec asks.

"No. I'm trying to figure it out."

He gazes down at me. "Do you need me to make some calls?"

I shake my head. "I'm just . . . so tired and need a shower more than I need my next breath."

Tilting his head, he studies me with disarming focus for a few quiet seconds. "If you'd like, you can do that up in my room."

Surely he's kidding. "I—no, really, it's okay."

"If you're uncomfortable, I understand," he says quickly, "but you're a family friend. You look like you might drop where you're standing. If you want to take a shower upstairs, it's really okay with me."

Two more seconds of eye contact and then I break it.

I've been whittled down to my barest self. Even my hands feel grimy.

I nod, totally defeated and lifting my chin for him to lead the way. "Thank you."

■ ■ ■

Inside the elevator, we stand as far apart as we can and fall deeply, heavily quiet. The realization lands like a tarp thrown over my head: No matter how badly I need to shower, this is a terrible idea. I'm five-foot-four, heading upstairs with a guy who easily has eight inches on me, and I've just spent two weeks tracking down scum-of-the-earth men all over London. I know better.

I wonder if Alec is having the same thought, or if not the same—surely he doesn't worry about me physically over-powering him—then wariness about who I might have be-come in the years since we knew each other. The quiet is so absolute that it feels like some cosmic force has put the world on mute. I stare at my sneakers, scuffed and dusty on the gleaming polished floor of the elevator.

I don't realize he's been watching me until he speaks. "You can text a friend if you're feeling uncomfortable," he says. "Or—God, sorry this is obvious—I can stay downstairs until you're done."

Making him stay out of his room until I'm done feels . . . un-necessary. He isn't a stranger, not really, and he's probably just as exhausted as I am. I knew his family for six years—spent at least half of my weeknights across the dinner table from him, eating his mother's Korean home cooking. He was soft-spoken, playful, attentive. God, eighth-grade Georgia would have kissed him until she passed out if she'd had the chance.

Still, a text is a good idea. If I was better rested, fed, and clean, it might have occurred to me to do this before even getting into the elevator.

My voice creaks out of me. "What's your room number?"

He slides a hand into his pocket and pulls the envelope out, blinking his eyes down to it. "Twenty-six eleven."

I text my best friend, Eden. Met an old friend. Using his room to shower because hotel situation is a mess. Seattle Airport Marriott. Room 2611. He's a good guy but I'll text within the hour to let you know I'm okay.

Immediately, she replies with a shocked-face emoji followed by a simple Okay.

"Thanks," I say, pocketing my phone. Just the fact he suggested I text someone makes me feel better. He's poised, has such a gentle presence. I try to imagine him turning menacing and . . . I mean, anything is possible. It's astonishing how well the world hides viciousness. "How'd you manage to snag a room?"

He smiles as he holds the elevator door for me to exit first. "I was lucky to have someone call ahead of the crowd."

After swiping his key against the door labeled PRESIDENTIAL SUITE, Alec gestures for me to step in ahead of him, and I'm so caught up in the view before me that I'm halfway down the long entry hall before I remember my manners. Of course, he's still by the door, stepping out of his shoes. I'm blurry and wiped, and few things make me feel more graceless than the way he glances down at my feet as I trip out of my Vans.

He carefully wheels his glossy carry-on past me into the room.

Or rooms, really. I knew hotels had suites—I've stayed in them once or twice on very extravagant girls' trips and have been in my share of them for interviews with important people—but this is different. This isn't just an apartment, it's a luxury apartment. An apartment villa. One entire wall is just floor-to-ceiling windows with a view of the Seattle skyline. There's a living room, a full kitchen, a separate dining room, and a door leading down a hall to where there seems to be multiple other rooms. "Wow."

He watches me with a hint of a smile. "You look exhausted, Georgia."

"I am," I admit, meeting his eyes. "I'm so grateful for the shower. I'll head downstairs after and figure out the rest."

"Are you sure I can't call someone while you're in there?"

I shake my head. "We have a travel department."

"'We'?"

"My work."

"Ah." He looks like he wants to ask, but his attention slides to the sag in my shoulders. Alec lifts his chin. "Go ahead. I'll be right out here."

Even though he's so refined, he seems to give each tiny gesture deliberate forethought; after the darkness I've seen in London over the past two weeks—after the stories I've heard over and over—I'm grateful for the reassurance.

And for the lock on the bathroom door.

I lean back against it once it's shut, exhaling. Even though I'm exhausted, I can't deny Alec Kim still has a real presence. Masculine and composed and stern. Gently arrogant in a way I find intensely sexy but, wow, what a contrast between the two of us. Looking the way I do right now, I feel like I'm stealing something by even thinking about him in a vaguely sexual way.

I haven't had these kinds of thoughts in so long. Months, to be precise, and Alec is a sharp contrast to the other, more recent man in my sex-brain. But in the span of eleven months, Spencer lost all the Best Boyfriend points he'd gained over our six-year relationship. Men, sex, and the complex dance of being vulnerable with someone lost all the shine it once had.

And talk about being vulnerable: in the twenty minutes since our reacquaintance, Alec Kim has looked at me so squarely, as if he can see all of me in a glance.

Spence had stopped looking at me directly, but I realized it only in hindsight. At some point, he started offering only the briefest flickers of eye contact even when he gave me his trademark dazzling smile. His smile would crack wide open, but his eyes would angle over my shoulder or down to the side, like he was delighted by something out the window or charmed by the cat curled up in the corner. That alone should have tipped me off; when we first met, he would stare. Whether I was naked, clothed, it didn't matter. He once told me he wouldn't ever stop being surprised that I was his. We were the envy of our entire group of friends, all of us close since college. While our friends were chaotic and messy, Spence and I were the solid heart of our social circle. We were playful, affectionate, down-to-earth.

But over six years together—two of those spent sharing an apartment—somehow a switch was flipped. One day we were Spence-and-G, one word, the next day something was off. I'd get a quick peck at the door before he rushed out for the day. Gratitude at night for whatever I'd managed to throw together for dinner—over-the-top gratitude that seemed to expand until it became something desperate and off-putting. That should have tipped me off, too.

But by then I'd been hustling so hard to advance my

career I barely looked up. I thought that's what we were supposed to do in our midtwenties. I thought reaping the rewards came later: disposable income, vacations, weekends. I worked eighteen-hour days. I scraped for every freelancing gig. When I was hired under Billy at the *LA Times* foreign-news desk, I felt like I'd been given a golden egg. During all of it, I didn't really have time—didn't really *take* time—to notice how Spence had changed.

I'd changed, too, I guess. I'd always been ambitious, but those first few months at the *Times* had simmered off the weak, diluted parts of me that didn't know how to go after what I wanted. I grew hardened mentally, having to battle for every story, every inch of copy. The grueling hours, skipped meals, and sprinting all over town left me hard physically, too. Sometimes I get why Spence did it. Sometimes I get why our friends took his side. Sometimes, I want to forgive them all just to be done carrying it around alone.

When I shove away from the door and step in front of the mirror, I'm horrified to catch a glimpse of my haggard reflection. My eyes are deeply bloodshot. Skin sallow and shiny. My lips are chapped, and my hair holds its shape in the bun even when I take out the clip.

Good God I smell.

Shedding my clothes, I imagine tossing them into the trash can, stuffing my jeans and socks and even my underwear in the small brass receptacle. I could leave my suitcase in Seattle and never have to see any of these things again. Alec probably wouldn't even wonder why I'd done it—everything I had on is now crumpled on the floor and looks like it wouldn't last another day anyway.

Naked, I turn on the shower and look around while the water heats up. The bathroom counter is a massive slab of granite, the sink a raised and gleaming blown-glass bowl. The complimentary toiletries are full-size and housed in a plush leather case. It's disorienting to enjoy such luxury when I feel barely human.

When I step under the showerhead, I can't help the moan that escapes. I have never had a shower this good, but especially in the past two weeks, every shower has been rushed and distracted. A quick rinse before shoving an apple in my mouth and bolting out the door. Some days it was only cold water splashed on my face and a fresh application of deodorant.

But this is bliss. Water pressure for the gods. Foamy body wash, expensive shampoo, and a conditioner that smells so good I don't want to rinse it out. I'm aware that Alec is out there waiting, probably wanting to go to bed himself, so I do rinse, but only after using the small razor to shave myself clean and the body scrub to make my skin tingle all over. The towel is plush and enormous. I brush my teeth with one of the toothbrushes in the vanity kit, then turn to grab my suitcase.

Which I have left out in the hallway.

Of course I have. Because of course the flight was canceled, and there are no more rooms available. Of course Alec is here, and he goes by the much fancier name *Alexander*, and he's a god and I'm a monster, and of course he has an enormous suite and he let me shower here, so of course my suitcase is out in the hall.

There are two robes on the back of the door, and I pull

one free from its hanger, sliding into it. Soft, thick—it smells like lavender. I have never felt so clean and refreshed in my entire lifetime; for the first time in several days I'm hopeful that I can get home and find the strength and energy to write the story that's been haunting my sleeping and waking hours.

Out in the hallway is my bag, and I catch a glimpse of Alec in the living room—facing the window, hands tucked into his pockets as he looks out over the skyline. He turns at the sound of my suitcase wheels on the marble floor and our eyes meet. Electricity spirals through my torso and he takes in my clean face, my wet hair, now free from the grubby bun. It's spread halfway down my back and is darker from the water. And then his gaze trails down my neck and widens—

I clutch the robe closed where it's gapped open. Oh God.

Jerking my suitcase in with me, I call out a mortified "Sorry!" and slam the bathroom door closed again. I don't know how much boob he saw, but it definitely wasn't no boob.

Suitcase open. Hair towel-dried and brushed, lotion applied, and now comes the hard part. Nothing is clean, but the question is, what is the least dirty? Packing only a carry-on for a two-week trip means wearing things multiple times, but even having washed some things in a sink at the hotel in London, everything at this point is crumpled and worn— horrible, really.

I pull out a bra and a red three-quarter-sleeve jersey dress. Forgivingly wrinkle-resistant. Comfortable. Cute. I take a sniff and decide it smells fine. Maybe too dressy for a cab ride over to another hotel, but unlike pants, it doesn't require me to put on a pair of dirty underwear.

Truly, I am a mess.

Packing everything back up, I move out into the hall.

"Alec," I say with gratitude, and he turns. His expression tightens, and he looks me over in surprise. "Thank you. Seriously, I feel like a new person after that shower."

He nods. "You're welcome. I'll walk you down."

"You don't need to do that."

"I don't mind. I'm not tired anyway. I'll probably get a drink downstairs."

Inadvertently, my attention darts across the room to the fully stocked bar in the corner. "Oh. Okay."

"I spend a lot of time alone in hotel rooms," he explains, giving me a new and devastating grin. This smile is different. It's flirtatious and oddly knowing. It feels like fingertips slowly dragged down my arm.

I turn and move toward the door, suddenly aware how close we are. I mean, not really—I don't think he's moved from where he stood near the window, but an odd silence has fallen over the room and the force of his presence shrinks the cavernous suite down to a shoebox. Even with my back to him, I sense that his eyes have scanned my body, that he's figured out I don't have underwear on. And maybe in reality he's looking at his phone behind me and the last thing he would think about is what's under my dress, but somehow it doesn't feel like it. I feel the press of his attention like a hot iron against every part of my body he can see. The back of my legs, the small of my back, my shoulders. My hand as I brace against the wall to balance and put on my Vans—shoes that absolutely don't work with this dress, but I'm beyond caring. Alec Kim probably dates women who only wear four-inch heels or higher. Who roll out of bed fully made up and who never run out of clean underwear.

But I'm too tired to worry what I look like from the back right now. If thirty-three-year-old Alec Kim wants to check out grown-up me in the cleanest article of clothing I currently own, I'm not going to stop him.

# Two

He follows me out into the hall, to the elevator, and the strident chime announcing its arrival startles us both. I catch a hint of his similarly aware smile as he reaches forward, pressing the button for the lobby with a long finger and then stepping to the far side of the car—giving me space again. I pull out my phone and text Eden that I'm okay before looking up at him. A familiar ache hits me right in the center of my chest, radiating out. It's wild how quickly our bodies remember infatuation.

"Do you come to LA often?"

He gives the slightest shake of his head. "It's been a few years since my last visit."

"Is this a work trip?"

Alec gives me his disarming attention again, but this time, something in his expression reads as oddly . . . tickled? "Yes."

"What will you be doing there?"

He turns to face the doors as they open and holds his arm out to keep them from closing as I pass. "Endless meetings."

It's a weirdly bland answer for someone who looks like he was God's pet project in the human-design studio. But if he was in the entertainment industry, it would have been the first thing out of his mouth. I've met more businessmen than I can count in the past couple weeks and my curiosity about his job is now officially flaccid. I send a silent prayer out that Alec Kim isn't like any of the executives I've spoken to and heard about in London. He's gorgeous and polite, but I've learned that means nothing. Evil loves to hide in pretty packages.

"What's that face?" he asks. Both the exit and the hotel bar are in the same direction off the elevator, and we move together down the hall, two of my strides for every one of his. I am eager to leave and get a room, but also dreading losing this warm, vibrating feeling I have being so close to him.

"What face?"

He lifts a hand, amusement shining in his eyes, and gestures to my head. "You have a thing against meetings?"

"I'm sure there are great businessmen out there. But I haven't met many in the past few weeks."

We stop near the hotel exit. He'll go left. I'll go straight. "I hope I've been the exception," he says quietly.

"You have been amazing." One . . . two . . . three beats of eye contact before I look away. My crush is back, hot and persistent.

"What were you doing in London?" he asks just as I open my mouth to say goodbye.

"I was there researching a story."

"Fiction?"

I shake my head. "I'm a journalist."

His expression changes almost imperceptibly but I clock it. "Ah. Which outlet?"

"*LA Times*."

One eyebrow performs a quick, impressed flicker. "What's the story about?"

I smile, chewing my lip. Looking at him, it's easy to tell that he's well connected, and being a well-connected businessman in London means the odds are good that he's heard of Jupiter. Maybe he's even been a guest there. I tread carefully: "It's about a group of people doing very bad things."

Alec squints at me, and what he says next isn't what I'm expecting. "That sounds like a grueling assignment. Are you sure you're up for hotel hunting?"

"I promise I am." I adjust my backpack strap on my shoulder. "Though thank you again for letting me use your shower. I feel like a new human." I nod toward the exit. "I'm going to grab a cab."

"Take the bedroom, Georgia," he says abruptly. "The one upstairs, I mean."

"In your suite?" I cough out a laugh. "No way. I couldn't."

He exhales slowly. "Come on." That quiet *come on* changes everything in his demeanor. He's the same man as he was a second before but gentler, somehow more real. "You haven't booked a room yet. It didn't sound like there were a lot left around here."

"I emailed from the lobby," I say, adding without conviction, "I'm sure our travel department booked one for me."

He lifts his chin like, *Well, take a look, then.* And when I do, I see a missed call and voicemail from Linda in Travel Services.

Alec watches me as I lift my phone to my ear, and his expression changes in tandem with mine. Eyes widen in hope, brow drops in defeat.

I slip my phone back into my backpack. "There's some big science conference in town. Airport and downtown hotels are full."

"Everything's fully booked?"

"Everything close by, at least. They've booked me at a motel in Bellingham."

"That's nearly two hours from Sea-Tac." He pulls back his sleeve, glancing down at a visibly expensive watch. "And it's almost eleven."

I groan at the ceiling. "I know."

"Are you on the eight o'clock flight?" I nod, and he frowns again. "Seriously, Georgia."

I deflate. What he's offering sounds convenient but so very awkward. "It feels like a huge imposition. I'm not comfortable saying yes."

He glances to the side, jaw clenched, and it looks like he wants to argue with my personal boundaries but won't. "Okay. But come have a drink in the bar while you look for something closer. How can I send you off in search of a hotel this time of night?"

"That's exactly what cabs are for!" I protest, but follow him anyway.

He leads me to a dim, far corner and gestures to a low table with couches circling it. "Maybe, but you're small and it's dark out." He watches me sit and adjust my skirt around my legs. *And not wearing underwear*, it seems he wants to add.

Or maybe that's just me.

There's a small oil candle in the middle of the table, and I stare at him as subtly as I can while he reads the cocktail menu. His hands are a love sonnet to masculinity. His neck is pure filth. And even though the person in front of me is a full-grown man now, the contours of his face are so familiar, it's almost like I saw him yesterday and not fourteen years ago. I spent so much of my childhood at his house that I understood about half of what his mother would say to her children in Korean. I wonder what Sunny is like now, whether she ended up loving London like I promised she would. Whether my shy best friend had someone she trusted to talk to about her first kiss, her first heartbreak, her worries and victories.

Alec clears his throat as he checks his phone, and my attention refocuses on the sight of him in front of me. He's a treat I want to savor. I want to take long pulls of the view of him, hold it in my mouth, slowly swallow him down. I can see his parents in his face: his mother's dimples and cheekbones; his father's height and long neck. And then I remember I'm supposed to be looking for lodging, not studying the bulge of his Adam's apple or the thoughtful fullness of his mouth. I pull out my phone, but as soon as I get my travel app open, he reaches across the table and gently lowers my hand.

"Hey," he says. "You've seen the suite. It's huge. Let this go. We're talking about a few hours of sleep in separate rooms."

I reach up, rubbing my face. "It's not weird?"

"You're the one making a big deal out of it." He blinks over my shoulder, surveying the room behind me. There are a handful of people at the bar, a few people at tables, but no one immediately next to us in this tiny, dark corner. Alec settles back into the sofa.

"Okay," I say, "but I insist on splitting the cost with you."

He gives me a delightful shot of both dimples. "And of course I will refuse. Besides, you're a journalist. Isn't this how a great story begins?"

"What kind of stories do you think I write?" I ask, grinning at him. "Stuck-in-a-strange-city, there's-only-one-room-left-at-the-inn? I don't write for *Penthouse*."

He stares at me, expression straightening in surprise, and my words slowly reach my own ears.

"Oh my God." I press my hands to my face. "I can't believe I said that."

Across from me, he bursts out laughing. "I mean, you wouldn't tell me what you were writing, but I did not mean to imply *that*."

"I know you didn't," I say through horrified laughter. "Now I really can't sleep upstairs."

He drags a hand down his face, pulling himself together. "No, come on, let's start over."

"Let's."

We stare at each other, eyes shining. Finally, we both break again, and oh my God, what is happening? My brain is too fried to successfully drag us out of this.

Thankfully, the waitress comes for our orders—Zinfandel for me, whiskey neat for him—and when she leaves, he leans back and stretches his arms out across the back of the couch. "That was fortunate timing."

"We needed the reset," I agree.

"Tell me more about your job," he says. "Am I right that you and Sunny used to pretend to be detectives?"

I laugh. "How on earth do you remember that?"

"You two were always hunting around the neighborhood with notepads, looking for clues for mysteries." He gazes at me with amusement. "I guess I shouldn't be surprised you ended up working for the *LA Times*. But that's a big deal."

"Thank you." Pride warms my chest.

"How did you end up there?"

"I only started about a year ago," I say, "but I really love it so far. I went to USC for journalism and then hustled my ass off just trying to get any story anywhere I could. I did some crime reporting for *OC Weekly* for a while. Freelanced for every website that would take me. But when I wrote a pet project about a man in Simi Valley painting monthly portraits of his wife as she succumbed to Parkinson's disease, and it got picked up by the *New Yorker*, I got a job offer from the *Times*."

"The *New Yorker*?" He stares at me like he's seeing me for the first time. "How *old* are you?"

"I'm the same age as Sunny."

Alec gives an amused flicker of an eyebrow. "That's an impressive résumé for a twenty-seven-year-old."

"I am," I admit with a small smile, "occasionally a bit intense about work."

A dimple makes only a brief appearance. "I'm getting that."

"What kind of business are you in?" I ask, changing the subject. I've gone from feeling proud to feeling like I'm bragging.

The waitress returns with our drinks and he thanks her, raising his glass to toast mine. "I work in television."

Ah, there it is. But also: Yawn. I look at his outfit, remember his sleek suitcase. "Let me guess: business development at a new streaming service?"

He laughs and lifts his glass to his lips. "Nope."

"Contracts attorney?"

"God, no."

I study him, eyes narrowed. "BBC exec coming here for meetings with American networks about a show?"

Alec pauses with his glass halfway back down to the table. "That's shockingly close, actually."

"Really? That's wild. My roommate, Eden, lives and breathes BBC."

A tiny grin as he sets his glass down. "Does she?"

"I realize how shameful it is in this day and age to not watch TV," I admit, "but I've been so wrapped up in work that I've missed most of what everyone has been obsessed with the past couple years. Tell me what you've worked on so I can remedy this. Eden tells me this is where creativity lives and breathes these days and I'm missing out."

He waves this off. "Television isn't for everyone."

"If you work for the BBC," I say, "she'll lose her mind." Alec laughs. "Which show? I'm going to text her. I'm sure she's seen it."

He gives me a wry smile. "It's called *The West Midlands*."

I type a quick text. The old friend I ran into? Yeah he said he works on The West Midlands for BBC. You like that one right?

Eden replies immediately with a string of unintelligible all caps. I turn my phone around to show him. "See? She knows that one. How cool." I tuck my phone back into my purse and sip my wine. "I bet that's a fun job."

"It is." He pauses. "What's the story you're writing? Two

weeks is a long time to go to London on assignment, I'd imagine."

"The original plan was a week, but it took an intense turn, I guess. I asked to stay."

In fact, I begged to stay.

"Intense how?"

I do the internal calculation. I could tell him about the story, gauge whether he might be useful after all. He's a businessman, clearly well connected. It's a long shot, but wouldn't it be wild if this inconvenient layover actually broke the story open for me somehow? The prospect makes me feel more alert. "Okay, let me ask you: Have you heard anything about a club called Jupiter?"

I watch him closely, searching for signs of a mask slipping into place. I get only a tiny thoughtful frown and, after a beat, a little shake of his head. "A nightclub, right?" he says carefully, and I nod. "There was something in the news about it recently."

"Right." I take another sip of my wine. "You probably heard about the bouncer who was beat up in an alley behind the club the same night he'd reported incidents of workplace harassment to his superior. He tweeted all about it and detailed how the police did nothing."

Alec nods. "Okay, yeah, I think I saw something about that."

"So, that's all the London news outlets reported about it. Everyone moved on. No one seemed to notice that, about a week later, the same bouncer shared screen caps that someone sent him of a few of the club owners sharing sexually explicit videos in an online forum." I pause, gauging his reaction. "Videos, allegedly, of those owners having sex with women in the club VIP rooms. But next day, the screen caps were gone. He deleted his entire Twitter account."

No overt reaction passes over his features. So, Alec isn't aware of all of this and . . . actually, I'm relieved. The story isn't being talked about very much in London, and if he'd heard any of this about Jupiter, it likely wouldn't reflect well on him. "So, I went over there to cover a really dry international meeting on pharma law, but I volunteered to be the one to go because of this Jupiter story. After I saw those tweets, the whole thing had been hovering in my thoughts for a couple weeks. I thought there was a chance this bouncer knew about some shady stuff happening at the club and got beat up for reporting it to his boss. It felt like he was trying to alert the mainstream media."

"Right," he says carefully. "But . . . you don't think that anymore?"

Setting my glass down, I work to keep the anger from my voice, remembering the way the bouncer, Jamil, staunchly refused to speak to us once we tracked him down. "Oh, I still believe it. In fact, I know in my bones that someone is threatening him now. It's why my boss let me stay longer. And the more I learn about what happens in those VIP rooms—the more terrible it becomes—the more I can't seem to stop digging."

Alec looks at me for a long, quiet beat. I expect him to ask what I mean, to explain what "terrible" looks like in this context, but either his manners prohibit him from pushing, or he sees the exhaustion ripple through me, because he says only, "Well, then it's good that you're working hard on this."

I need a track change. "We never finished talking about Sunny."

His expression flickers. Apparently, sex-scandal-to-sister-update is an abrupt transition. I need to get my social skills back in place. "How—?" he starts, and then frowns. "Oh. Yeah. She's good. You should have looked her up when you were visiting in London."

I pull my wineglass closer. "Would she even remember me?"

"Of course she would. You two were inseparable."

"We were." I frown a little in memory. "It's true."

He leans forward, picking up his glass to take with him as he settles back into the couch. "I remember when you two cut up her clothes for the talent show and Umma lost her mind."

I laugh, wincing at the memory. "She was . . . not happy with us. But she could have called my parents and didn't. We had to pull weeds for a month in her garden every day after school."

"That was a minor punishment," he says, smiling wryly. "I took the car without permission *once* and had to rebuild our back deck out of my own savings. We moved only a week after I finished it."

Grimacing, I manage only, "Oof."

"The transition to the UK was hard for Sunny," he says.

"I bet." This presses against a bruise I didn't know I still had. "It was hard for me, too. Turns out making a new friend group in ninth grade is rough."

He laughs. "Who knew?"

I grin at him, taking another sip. "Everyone?"

This makes him laugh again. I love the sound. His voice is

deep and smooth; I bet he's never yelled a day in his life—his laugh has that same calm resonance.

"She's doing okay, though?"

He swallows, nodding. "She's modeling. It's a hard career, and I swear, fashion in London is brutal, but she's doing well. You may have seen her in some print advertisements?"

"I wish I'd known to look for them." I shake my head. "She's working under her name? I should look her up."

"Her given name, yes. Kim Min-sun."

"And your parents?"

"They're retired, just outside of London. They're doing well." Alec's smile comes in so many forms, and this one is sweetly polite. It's the one he would give when I'd pass him something at the dinner table, when he was instructed to say good night as I was leaving. "I'll relay that you asked after them."

"Thanks. Tell your mom I'm a great weed puller thanks to her." We fall into a few beats of silence where we both stare into our glasses. "What did you do after you moved?" I ask.

He takes another sip of his drink before answering. "I moved to Seoul after graduating and returned to London . . ." He pauses, thinking. "Let's see, a bit over three years ago now."

I realize that's what I'm hearing in his accent; it's beautiful. "Oh, wow. You lived in Korea?"

"I did." He smiles, and then it dies away. It's the death of small talk: inquiring about family, doing the easy update, reaching the end of our knowledge about each other's lives. Sexual innuendos have been awkwardly played out. I dig around for something more engaging to ask, but everything that comes to mind seems deeply inappropriate.

*Are you married?*

*Are those hands as strong as they look?*

*What do you look like naked?*

Finally, I string words together. Unfortunately, he's doing the same thing and our questions burst out in overlapping awkwardness:

"How long will you be in LA?" / "How are *your* parents?"

"Sorry," we say in unison.

"Go ahead," also in unison.

I clap a hand over my mouth and point to him with the other. "You," I mumble against my palm.

"I'm in LA for a couple weeks," he says, laughing. "Actually, some of my colleagues left for Los Angeles two days ago. I was delayed but will meet them there." He sips his drink. "And now your turn. How are your parents?"

"They're fine," I say. "They're in Europe until next week."

He narrows his eyes, nodding. "They traveled a lot? Wasn't your dad a diplomat? Am I remembering that right?"

"Close. He works for the State Department. Mom travels with him as much as she can." I don't add that this is Mom's first trip since Spence and I broke up, that she basically put her life on hold to help me pick up my pieces. I wash the weird catch in my throat down with a sip of wine. "Did you ever meet them?"

"Once or twice when I was picking Sunny up at your house. If I recall, your father is very tall, and your mother is—"

"Very *not tall*?" I nod, laughing. My father is six-foot-four. My mother is well over a foot shorter. "I was always hoping to get his height, but . . ." I gesture to myself. "I'm the person who always makes sure the doctor writes down five-foot-three and a *half* on my chart."

He smiles at me and licks his lips distractingly. So distractingly, in fact, that it takes me a second to process his next question. And then my heart takes a nosedive off a cliff.

"No," I finally manage. "I'm not married. . . ."

The way I've said it—trailing off, with a grimace—clearly leaves the impression that there's a story there. Shit. Why did I do that? The last thing I want to do is talk about Spence tonight, not with Alec sitting across from me looking the way he does.

He nods, brows slowly rising, and I guess I have to explain my weird answer. "I'm about six months out of a long-term relationship. Rough breakup, and he took most of our friends with him."

"Ah." He sips his whiskey again. "I'm sorry."

"It's okay." Fidgeting, I pull my hair up and he watches my fingers quickly twirl it and tuck it into a bun. My hair is stick straight and dry now, and I feel a few strands escape and brush against my neck. He tracks that movement, too. "It really should have ended sooner."

Alec watches me, his gaze unswerving. "What happened?"

We stare at each other for a few wordless moments before my smile breaks free.

"Are we really doing this?" I ask. "The below-the-surface catch-up?"

"Why not?" His answering smile is sly and playful.

"We've covered work and family. Will we ever see each other again?" He's talking about sharing our stories, but I sense another dare below the surface—a heated one.

"He fucked up," I say baldly.

Alec's expression shifts. "With you?"

I like the way he says this. Disbelieving, like he can't fathom it.

"Not in the way you're thinking," I tell him.

I've only really talked about this with three people: my parents and my best friend, Eden. Not only because our mutual friends all decided I was overreacting and should give Spence another chance, but also because it's deeply mortifying to realize that I'm a journalist whose boyfriend buried the lede every day for nearly a year. It seems weird to launch into the story with a near-stranger. But I am. Because I'm here with Alec—whom it oddly feels like I know, even though I don't, and I've seen, even though I haven't—and I'm tired but don't want to go to sleep yet now that he and I are talking about something real.

"He lost his job because he got caught stealing company clients for his own freelance business and undercutting his firm's rates. But he never told me. He kept leaving every morning, dressed for work, and coming home every night feigning exhaustion. He made up stories about drama between coworkers, gripes and promotions that I totally believed. Slowly drained his savings until he had nothing, then started dipping into mine."

Alec goes still. "And your friends took *his* side?"

"He's very charismatic," I explain. Spence's eye-crinkling smile appears in my thoughts, his infectious laugh echoes in my ears, and I feel the familiar urge to climb out of my own skin. "The quintessential good guy, you know? I'm sure he gave them a bunch of shiny half-truths, made himself out to be the victim. I cut him out completely; they didn't. But they weren't living with him. He wasn't lying to their faces every morning and every night. I guess it was easier for them to find sympathy."

"How did you find out?"

"I realized something was off when my bank statements seemed low. I followed him to work. He was going to the park and sleeping. At home, while I slept, he was up all night gambling, trying to make money."

Alec laughs incredulously. "Is that a thing?"

"Not the way Spencer was doing it."

He laughs again, but this time it turns sympathetic at the tail end. "I'm sorry, Georgia."

"Yeah." I finish my wine and nod when he signals for another round. "It sucked."

I watch his neck when he downs the last sip of his whiskey. His throat is long, his jaw so sharp I want to sink my teeth into the pulse point just below it. "What about you?"

"Not married." He scratches his cheek. "Not dating anyone at the moment."

"That seems . . ." I'm not sure how to finish the sentence. What I want to say is that it seems like a goddamn tragedy for women. Or men. Or all of humankind. Balance in the world seems like it should depend on people who look like Alec Kim getting laid regularly. "Hm."

"What's 'hm'?"

"A bummer," I say as wine and fatigue suddenly settle like a narcotic in my blood. "You're a hot guy. You should be dating."

"You're a beautiful woman. You shouldn't be lied to."

Thank God it's dark in here, because I'm sure I'm blushing like a maniac. "Thanks."

"And anyway, it's hard for me to date." He pauses, going still like he's taken an impulsive step down a hallway he isn't sure he's supposed to explore. "I'm under a lot of"—he stops again before settling on—"professional pressure."

"That sounds deeply intriguing, Alec."

"It's not. Or maybe it is." He waves this away. "But for once I don't feel like talking about work. It's all I'll be doing for the next two weeks."

"Fair enough." I raise my glass when the fresh ones are delivered. "No work talk then."

He nods firmly. "No work talk."

"No ex talk, either."

Alec laughs. "Agreed, no more ex talk." He stares at me. "And what else is there?"

"Hobbies?"

"*Hobbies*. Sure."

"Do you still skateboard?" I joke.

His face goes flat in disbelief. "Really?"

Laughing, I say, "Remember, you used to skateboard all the time down your street?" I definitely remember. I would sit on the sofa by their front window, ostensibly doing my homework with Sunny but really watching Alec and his trio of friends do ollies and kick flips and pop shoves over, and over, and over.

"Oh, I remember." He laughs again and shakes his head. I feel like I'm missing something. "You're a trip."

And then Alec studies me in that gentle calculating way of his.

"What?" I ask after a long ten seconds of hyperaware silence.

"I think it's because I'm tired," he says, blinking to clear his trance. "And have had a drink—now another—on an empty stomach."

I wait for the rest of it. "You think *what* is because you're tired?" I finally ask.

"I remember you as this sweet, scrawny kid. Not this . . ." He gestures to my body, and I don't miss the way his eyes trip over my breasts. "Woman."

"I already said I'd sleep upstairs; you don't have to seduce me." I expect him to laugh or backtrack, explain in his polite way that no, no, he only meant it's surreal to see someone after so long. But he doesn't say that. He gazes at me patiently.

I blink down at my glass, bringing it to my lips. "But seriously, Alec. If I'm going to your room, I insist on using the pullout." My eyes go wide. "The sofa bed, I mean." I bark out a laugh. "Oh my God."

Alec fights a smile. "Does that mean what I think it means?"

"Strike it from the record."

"I can't." He grins. "It's already out there."

I bend, burying my face in my arms.

"It's great." Alec laughs. "Honestly, it's refreshing."

Sitting up, I gulp my wine. "In my defense, I haven't slept in . . ." I calculate. "Well over thirty hours. You have no idea the stuff that's reeling through here." I press my index finger to my temple. "I really should just go to bed."

He glances over my shoulder and then pulls his sleeve back to check the time. "Try me."

"You're asking to be scandalized."

He laughs, a round, open-mouthed sound. "I promise, you can't shock me."

*Is that right?* I grin at him. "Are you daring me?"

"Absolutely."

Swirling my wine, I stare at him over the rim of the glass. There's a dark, playful gleam in his eye, and I'm tempted by it but also wary of it. What if I'm thinking this is a flirtatious moment, but he actually thinks I'm just going to tell him about an oddball scrapbooking hobby?

"Georgia, hello," he whispers, and points to his chest. "I'm waiting to be scandalized."

So I blurt it out, "Sitting this close to you, I am intensely conscious of the fact that I'm not wearing any underwear."

He nods slowly, gaze heating but—to my surprise—not showing any sign at all of being scandalized. "I am also intensely conscious of this."

"You knew?"

"Of course I knew." He sips his drink again. "You took only a carry-on for a weeklong international trip that extended for another week and were planning to be home tonight." He leans back and adds in a quiet rumble, "Besides, Gigi, I've studied every inch of you in that dress."

My skin is engulfed in heat. His frank, unruffled reactions throw me. Alec isn't nervous in the slightest. I have to bite my lip to keep from letting an embarrassed laugh burst free.

"Pervert," I whisper, grinning and secretly loving that he called me by my familiar nickname. It tunnels me back almost a decade and a half to watching him, shirtless, throw a football to his friend jogging away down the middle of the street. But now—here—it rolls out of him differently, like a filthy promise.

Laughing, he leans forward to set his glass down. "*Pervert*? Says the one who can't stop staring at my hands."

I open my mouth to protest, but his eyes shine with amusement. "True," I say instead. "But they are indecent, Alec."

"Indecent?" He smiles around the word. How many women must he get into his bed this way, simply by being sweetly playful and forthright?

He lifts a hand, holds it palm up, and slowly turns it, wiggling those long, graceful fingers. "How is this indecent?"

"Watching you play a piano would be like watching porn."

This makes him smirk. "Is that what you'd like to watch me do?"

"Frankly I'd watch those hands flip through an encyclopedia if it was my only option."

"It's not your only option." These words land seductively between us. "But sure." He lifts a finger, pretending to flag down the waitress. "They probably have a book behind the bar somewhere."

I lean over, smacking his shoulder, and he quickly catches my hand. Leaning forward, Alec props his elbows on his thighs and turns my hand over in both of his, trailing a fingertip along the inside of my wrist. I swear my heart-beat is centered right there, being dragged like a magnet beneath my skin wherever his touch goes. He loosely grips each of my fingers, squeezing down the length of them in turn before pressing both thumbs to the center of my palm, massaging in firm circles. With just this touch, he's coaxing nearly six months of tension from my entire body.

I don't think I realized how much I needed physical contact until he did this, but suddenly I'm starved for it. It's all I can do to not scoot around the U-shaped couch and climb into Alec's lap. I feel him look up and take in my reaction as he rubs my hand, but I can't stop looking at what he's doing. His fingers are strong, his touch firm. His hands are huge around mine, but he's not treating me as delicate. He's giving a goddamn amazing massage.

"Do you by chance work for the massage office at the BBC?" I mumble.

"No." He laughs. "Give me your other one."

Without hesitation I offer my left hand up and he takes it, repeating the actions almost identically. I imagine those fingers kneading the tense muscles of my shoulders, walking down the ridges of my spine, gripping my hips. It's impossible to not extrapolate this feeling and imagine it on my breasts, my neck, between my legs.

"Is that nice?" he asks quietly.

"You have no idea."

"I have some idea," he says, "going off your expression."

I look up, meeting his eyes. "What are we doing, Alec?"

A few seconds pass before he answers, "Whatever you want."

He turns his face back down, watching what he's doing to my hand. I want to suck on his fingers.

"Do you do this every time you go on a business trip?"

He laughs again. His dimples are genuinely obscene. "Absolutely not. I'm never alone like this on a trip."

I try to decipher this as his hand moves up my forearm, squeezing, massaging. "What does that mean?"

"It means I usually travel with a number of people who are very nosy."

"Right." I am in a trance. "You mentioned that already, sorry. Your team came early."

He's watching me again, waiting, I presume, for me to tell him what it is I want.

So I do. "I think we should go upstairs now."

# Three

While I'm digging into my backpack for my wallet, he's already dropping a handful of crisp twenties onto the table.

"I've got it," he says.

"Thank you." I'm hyperaware of every movement I make as I stand up and smooth my dress down my legs, because I know he's watching me from behind. Before I can, he grabs the handle of my suitcase and then pulls my backpack from my shoulder, stacking and wheeling them between us as we make our way out of the now-empty bar and back to the lobby. He keeps a weird distance all the way to the elevators. Like we're two strangers, coincidentally moving in the same direction. I don't question it; I can't really devote much conscious thought to anything but breathing and walking. The edges of my vision blur with wine and lust and fatigue.

Alec's expression is distant, too, as he holds the elevator door for me and follows me into the empty car. And as soon as the doors close, I expect him to crowd closer—after all, we have twenty-six floors to climb and an ocean of sexual tension lapping at our toes. I expect him to back me into a corner, tease me with those long, silent looks, but he leans against the opposite wall instead, crossing one foot over the other, and pulls out his phone to type something. He hits send, and slides the slim phone into his pocket, but then tilts his face to the ceiling, taking a deep breath.

Confusion makes me mute. Maybe I wasn't clear as to why I wanted to go up to his room. Maybe he thought that was me putting the flirting on ice? God, I hope not. The power of his physical presence is suffocating—the unreal length of his legs, his strong hands reaching back and gripping the handrail running the perimeter of the car, the lean bulk of his chest beneath his white dress shirt. He exudes sex and confidence but seems paradoxically hyperaware and unaware of it. The idea that I might be told to go to bed alone after all that sexual tension is like being told to cut off a sneeze, mid-sneeze.

I guess he senses the thick silence, too, because he clears his throat. "Cameras," he says quietly, pointing a finger at the ceiling. "I don't want to get caught on video being naughty in an elevator."

"Oh." Relief adds to the intoxicating mix simmering under my skin and I tilt my face up, slowly sucking in a lungful of air.

"Your neck is so flushed," he murmurs.

I look back at him, and when our eyes meet, heat streaks through my chest so abruptly that I feel a weird swell of emotion rise. This is crazy. And I don't care.

Have I ever wanted something physical the way I want this? I remember being attracted to Spence—especially in our early days—but I never felt like I was choking on a tangible need for him. I dig my teeth into my lower lip, working to keep a cry from escaping my throat. He hasn't even touched me yet and my thighs already feel warm.

He angles his body toward me, nostrils flared. "Do you blush like this when you come?"

"I don't know," I admit with a fragile edge to my voice. "I feel . . ."

"I know." The elevator dings, the doors open, and Alec bursts forward, catching my wrist in his grip and pulling me out after him. I want him to wheel on me here, shove me against the wall. I want his hungry hands to dive under my skirt, bunch the fabric in his fists. I want to drag his zipper down, pull him free, and watch his face as he first feels me.

I am nothing but hollow ache; my skin feels prickly and tight.

He wordlessly marches me down the hall, almost like I'm in trouble, his long legs pulling my shorter ones into a jog behind him. With his free hand, he swipes his keycard, pushing the door open and propelling me inside. The door swings closed with a heavy thud, and my suitcase collides with the wall at the same moment he grabs my waist with both hands, turning me into him. His body comes up against mine and he pivots us, trapping me against the wall.

Alec's mouth comes to my neck, hot and open, sucking right where it seems my heart beats the wildest. I finally feel the broad expanse of his back, sliding my hands up to his neck and into his hair.

He speaks into my skin. "Where do I start with you?"

I want to start at the end, with his body inside mine, but I want, too, to slow time and get there in tiny increments. We haven't even kissed yet and I'm sharply aware that I get this only one time in my life. Not just this night with Alec Kim but this kind of night ever, this kind of sex where there aren't rules, there's no emotional fallout, there's only the intensity of need that seems to expand now that we're touching.

I turn my head, urging his mouth to mine. He groans at the contact and my legs nearly give out. His soft candy lips, firm touch, that cherry-pout mouth sucking at my bottom lip, nudging me open with a sigh. He tastes like whiskey and kisses like he's already fucking, with growl and heat. Alec Kim isn't here to mess around.

He reaches down, bunching the hem of my dress in his hands and drawing it up my body and over my head, tossing it into a red puddle at our feet. Reaching back, he flicks the clasp of my bra and slides it down my arms before discarding it somewhere to the side, his eyes fixed on my naked skin.

I have nowhere to go, but when he takes a step back to look down the length of me, naked and pressed against the wall, I wouldn't move even if I could. I've never seen this degree of unmasked lust on a man's face before.

He braces one hand on the wall beside my head and with the other reaches forward, gently pulling my hair loose from the makeshift bun. It spills, soft and cool, over his hands, over my shoulders. Alec slowly draws his index finger down my throat, between my breasts, and along my stomach. My nipples are hard, a blush crawling down my neck and across my chest. Biting his lip, Alec watches his fingers slide up over my ribs, cupping my breast, and then he bends, opening his mouth and closing it around the peak.

At the wet slide of his tongue, I feel the first sound tear

out of me, my hands going to his hair, fists forming around the silken weight of it. He sucks and then drags his teeth over my nipple, sending his other hand down my back and around the curve of my ass.

Digging my hands between us, I tug the hem of his shirt from his dress pants and unbutton it from the bottom up, pushing it away from his chest so I can get my hands on him. He's warm and solid under my palms: his smooth chest, ribs that contract and expand under the pace of his breathing, the lean line of his waist. When he pulls my body into his, the first sensation of his skin on mine is obliterating. Whatever patience he was able to muster is gone as he wrestles his arms out of his shirt, throwing it onto the floor.

Alec grasps my hips, turning and walking me backward with his mouth working up my neck until we collide with the arm of the couch. Laughing against my throat, he lifts me up, wrapping my legs around his waist.

"Bedroom?" he asks.

I nod, sending my arms around his shoulders, kissing the sweet heat of his neck, biting down the unreal length of it, sucking my way back up.

He walks us down the hall, into the bedroom, holding me until my back hits the mattress and he rests over me. Pulling my leg higher up over his hip, he dry-fucks me with slow, hard thrusts, his mouth working along my jaw and collarbone, hand finding its way from my waist to my breast where he squeezes, plumping me for his tongue, his body bending to suck me deep. I have too many thoughts to sort and let them fly through me unfiltered. The wet slide of his tongue around my nipple. The heat and suction of his full lips over my breasts. The hard press of him between my legs and how wet I am and how it's going to be all over his clothes.

He slows his tongue into lazy circles; his hips slow, too, and he finally pushes up onto his arms, looking down at me. "You okay?"

"I'm perfect." My exhaustion fell away with my clothes. Sleep is the last thing I want right now. I run my hand up from his stomach to his chest and can feel his heart under there, pounding. "Are you?"

"Yeah, I just—" He nods, dropping his head. "I never get this."

I laugh, drawing spirals on his chest. "Alexander Kim, I have a *very* hard time believing that."

"No—I mean—like this," he says. "I should take my time." He studies my mouth. "Three hours ago I wanted to just be at my hotel in LA. Now I want tonight to last a week. It's never like that anymore. Being with someone—it's always so loaded."

Sinking my teeth into my lower lip, I stare up at him. I think I know what he means; it's true for me, too. For the first time in a long time, sex can just be sex, but that doesn't make it meaningless, either. Sliding my hand around his neck, I pull him down for a kiss.

It's slower this time, deep and claiming, and he cups my jaw with his hand, his thumb stroking just next to where our mouths move together in such a natural way. Now that we're in bed, it feels like we have an eternity. I sense the cocktail of giddiness and devastation brewing in my blood; I know what he means when he says he wants this night to last a week.

Alec pulls back, kneeling between my legs, pushing my knees apart, and resting back on his heels. In any other lifetime I would be conscious of the fact that we've spent barely two hours together, that I'm naked and he's staring down at this part of my body that only two other men have ever seen. Neither of them ever really *looked* the way he is right now, too. But his expression wipes away any question I have that he wants this just as much as I do. I feel him shift his attention to my face while I watch his hand slide up my shin and over my knee. Silently, I send a quick thank-you to the universe for hotel razors. He smooths his palm up my thigh, and everything inside me grows tight in anticipation. With a quiet groan, he glides the pad of his thumb between my legs, from where I'm wet, up over the small rise that makes me want to scream in pleasure.

He exhales a curse, circling my clit with his thumb. Looking down at what he's doing, he whispers, "You're so soft."

I lift my hips, seeking, needing more than this glancing touch, and he grins, twisting his wrist and slowly sliding two fingers into me. I nearly go airborne, surging from the bed, back arched, reaching down to grip the sheets in my fists. He rises over me, sliding his mouth over mine, his tongue teasing in time with his fingers, and I feel drugged, like I'm in the middle of a wildly realistic dream and any second I might wake up coming. When I reach for his belt, he grunts into a kiss, pushing his hips into my hands.

His belt falls to the side, and I work the button and zipper free before greedily digging in, moaning at the solid weight of him, distractedly shoving his pants and briefs down his thighs. He kicks them down and off and, struggling to keep his fingers from leaving my body, laughs into a preoccupied kiss.

When I open my eyes to gauge his expression, I find him already looking down at me. The spontaneous smile that takes over both our faces makes my chest squeeze so tightly I lose my breath. I watch the same overwhelmed relief I felt earlier pass over his face when I wrap my hand around his cock, stroking up and back down.

His lips offer silent encouragement as he nods, nostrils flared.

*This is mine,* I think. *For tonight at least, you're mine.*

Alec is so hard the skin stretches impossibly tight around the tip; it makes my mouth water. He swallows thickly, Adam's apple bobbing, lips parted as his breathing grows sharper, more broken. With someone new I'd normally be questioning everything I'm doing—*is the pressure right, are we going too fast*—but tonight there's none of that. I'm not sure if it's the way he looks like he's already struggling to hold on or how hard he is in my hand, but everything about this feels like it's happening exactly the way it was meant to. His body is defined and smooth, skin glistening with a hint of sweat. I want to feel him moving in every part of me, want the salt of him on my tongue and the entire length of him shoved deep in me, but just imagining how his hand looks on me and *in* me makes pleasure rise like steam beneath my skin.

I fuck his hand; he fucks my fist. Our kisses grow messy and distracted by pleasure. I keep thinking we'll stop this and move on to the next thing—if we only have one night, shouldn't I taste him? Shouldn't he kiss me between my legs?

Maybe we'll transition to actual mind-bending sex. But even with only our hands it's better than any sex I've had before; I'm so close to the feeling of falling, of coming so hard I worry I'll wake everyone on the twenty-sixth floor.

"I want to feel you come on my hand," he says, gasping when my body seizes around him. "On my fingers."

I'm not far off, and neither is he, I don't think. My eyes fall closed and he rests his lips on mine, telling me, *I'm close, I'm close*, and then his words break into filthy, broken phrases that send heat streaking up my neck.

It's like having pleasure uncorked inside me, spilling every-where into my blood, and the way my heart is beating, it im-mediately spreads to every single part of my body, down every fingertip. With a relieved cry, I come on his fingers, clenching around the deep shove of them. He tells me he knows—*I can feel you coming*—and my desperate unraveling seems to turn everything over in him. With a deep grunt, he follows in a warm pulse against my hip, his teeth bared against my jaw.

I grow aware of how quiet the room was otherwise, and how much noise we were making with our breathing and the frantic movements of our hands and bodies. The air seems to settle in a soft blanket over us, stilling.

"Holy shit," he says, carefully dragging his fingers back. I shudder, overstimulated, and he whispers an apology into my mouth, kissing me with unbelievable sweetness. With the frenetic energy temporarily quieted, we kiss deeply until it feels like his mouth is a part of mine, until I wonder how it is that we've only ever done this tonight.

Alec kisses down my neck to my chest, trailing his wet fingers up my body, where he draws circles over my nipples, following with his tongue, telling me I taste as good as I feel. I am split open and bare for him, on decadent display. I want this man to take me apart, piece by piece, with his hands and mouth and cock. I want him to eat me and fuck me and own me. I dig both hands into his hair and he presses his face squarely between my breasts, stilling there, catching his breath.

"I'm dizzy," he says, laughing.

"Me too."

"I don't think I've ever been so turned on in my life," he admits. "We didn't even make it past third base. Is that amazing or tragic?"

"Amazing," I say on an exhale. His words echo around inside my head, inflating my pride. *I don't think I've ever been so turned on in my life.* "It wouldn't have mattered where you touched me," I say. "Even if you'd just kept looking at me the way you were downstairs, I would have come just as hard, probably."

Alec laughs sleepily, and then his inhales grow deeper, his exhales transition from forceful to exhausted. He falls asleep all at once, like a gas flame extinguished, his mouth slack against my breast, arms wrapped all the way around my waist. I close my eyes and don't have another thought until they drift back open again, nearly an hour later.

I stir in the tight confines of his embrace. We haven't moved. It's 2:37 a.m., and his skin under my hands is smooth and warm. I only mean to send a sleepy palm down his back, but he feels so good, and a little moan escapes. On instinct, his body makes a slow, deep thrust as he drags his cock against my leg. Alec pulls his face away, blinking sleepily up at me.

The intimacy of seeing his eyes open and the relieved smile he can't help pulls a breath out of my chest. When our eyes meet, it's like I'm a tuning fork that's been struck—everything in me vibrates. It's wild how immediately I want him again.

With a quiet, relieved, "Yeah?" he climbs up my body, coming over me, sliding hard and ready against where I am wet.

I'm just about to ask about protection when he kisses me once more and rises up. "Let me get something."

I watch him leave, hear the sharp zip of his bag being jerked open. Frantic rustling. A tearing of foil, and I imagine a long snaking strip of condom packets spiraling from a box. I absolutely do not think about him traveling to LA with a full box.

Tension eases in me as soon as Alec returns, kneeling on the bed between my legs.

He curves a hand around my knee. "You good?"

I nod, reaching for him, and he tears the wrapper with his teeth. Gripping himself with practiced assurance, he rolls it on with a loose fist down his length.

It's so erotic I have to look away, up to his face and the lip-biting focus he has as he shifts closer, leaning so he's there, right there, just the tip of him in and out. He drags his gaze up my body, and it stalls at my mouth. But I need all of him, deep, as far into me as he can possibly go. With both hands I pull at his hips, but he comes into me in tiny increments, an inch forward, an inch back, teeth still tightly trapping his candy bottom lip. His brows are a portrait of focus as he moves barely deeper and then away.

He whispers a guttural "Oh, shit" the next time he shifts forward.

It is an absolute torture, and when he tilts his head up in a tiny gesture of hard-won restraint, the light catches a hint of sweat on his upper lip.

I don't know why it's this tiny detail that ruins me.

"Please," I say.

He drags his attention back to my face, and then groans, closing his eyes. "I can't look at you or I'll lose it. I don't want this to end."

I laugh out a tight, hysterical sound. "I might actually lose my mind."

His laugh is breathless, disbelieving. "I know. Me too."

How? How is it like this? Is it because we know this is the only time, and it isn't worth hiding? I grip that truth as tightly as I can; imagining that this is something more meaningful will only lead me to a dead end.

"I want you deep."

Alec lowers to his elbows beside my head, sliding his kiss-swollen mouth over mine. "I know you do."

I bite his lip, reaching for his ass to pull him deeper but he's still set on taking his time getting started and makes me wait. Still teasing. Barely in. Barely out.

I want it so much it's nearly painful. Dragging my eyes open, I catch him gazing heavy-lidded and desire-drunk down at me. And then his eyes fall closed as he pushes his entire body forward, going so deep into me that his chest rises over my face, his hand grappling for the top of the mattress for leverage.

I leave my body. Or maybe I am more aware than I've ever been that I am just a bright collection of a billion nerve endings, a mass of tissue and bones made to feel this kind of pleasure. Crying out, I work my hips up as he works deeper and deeper in, in a slow grind that quickly grows frantic, almost wild. I'm so wet, so ready for it, that I come within only a handful of these perfect thrusts, gasping for air and sanity, sending my hands up his body and into his hair.

He lets out a laugh of triumph, of disbelief, before covering my mouth with his.

I'm kissing him with everything I have, like he's my anchor to this room and this world, and for a flash I wonder if something terrible has happened to me and this is my heaven, my salvation: in this bed with this man over me, working his body in and in and in and in.

His breaths go from jagged to rhythmic to not just breaths but grunts and then louder, harsher moans, pressed right into my temple and delivered through gritted teeth. He's so hard, so tense all over, I think he's close, hear his sounds change to an abrupt, almost shocked cry—

but then he pulls himself all the way out—

a sharp, unexpected loss,

"Not yet," he gasps tightly—

deftly rolling me to my stomach and lifting my hips to enter me from behind in a single perfect slide.

I scream into a pillow at the feel of him, and he laughs breathlessly, bending to press his sweaty forehead between my shoulder blades. "Holy shit, what is this sex?" he whispers. "Holy shit, Gigi."

I laugh, too, biting the pillow as he starts to move long and deep, giving me all of him, from the tip to the base, his thighs pressing to mine before he leaves space between us, only to return again hard and then harder and then harder, hitting a place in me that makes me want to shred the sheets with my fingers.

His breaths turn to sounds again. Groans, another disbelieving, overwhelmed laugh, and I look over my shoulder at him, finding his head thrown back, face tilted to the ceiling in an expression of total fucking bliss.

And at least for a moment, every bit of damage Spence did to my heart and self-esteem is wiped away. How can I be unworthy of trust and transparency when a man like Alec can show me this so readily, so openly?

It isn't just that it's sex—like he said it's *this* sex; it's unreal, whatever this is. I'm going to need a few days to come down from it. I'm going to have to work to not think about this over and over. If Alec Kim told me he wanted something I'd never done before, I would give it to him without question. He could fuck me anywhere. Does he want me to crawl? I'd do it. I want to feel his relieved exhale against the back of my neck, the dig of his fingertips in my hips. I want to be depraved for him.

He looks down, angling his head to watch his body work in and out of me, but he catches my eyes over my shoulder and smiles wickedly—knowingly—with that obscene bottom lip trapped tightly between his teeth. Alec leans forward and I twist to meet his kiss, hot and messy; he sucks at my mouth, my chin, biting and roughly tugging before he straightens behind me.

"Come here," he whispers, sitting back on his heels and pulling me backward onto his lap. Reaching up, he gathers my hair and slides it over my shoulder, exposing my neck to his mouth. He pushes up as I grind, and our bodies are so in sync I want to scream into the Seattle night sky how good this is, how it feels to have his hands come around me, one cupping my throat and the other between my legs, patiently coaxing another orgasm free. He holds me up when I start to collapse. It's fucking, sure, but it's not *just* fucking. Alec's mouth opens on my neck and I feel his breath start to shake, feel how quiet focus turns into desperation, and he angles me down again, moving with such solid strokes I can do nothing but marvel at the beauty of his uninhibited unraveling. Behind me, he whispers "It's good" and "God, so good" and that he's close again and again and then gasps my name with increasingly tight strain until he curls his hands around my hips and shoves in deep, coming with a sharp cry.

We collapse, his front to my back, his heaving chest pounding along my spine.

For minutes, we are paralyzed. Sweaty, entwined. He reaches blindly up, finding my hand, weaving our fingers together. His palm presses to the back of my hand, and then he does the same thing with the other, until I'm sweetly caged beneath him, and this time, I fall asleep without even realizing it.

# Four

In unison, our phone alarms go off at five, after only maybe an hour of sleep. It's like being heavily drugged, the way I can barely roll over, and then I realize it's because I'm still on my stomach with a full-grown, six-foot-one-inch man asleep on top of me.

He stirs, rolling to the side and groaning, covering his face with a hand. "*No.*"

"I agree," I mumble into the pillow.

"This must be what zombies feel like all the time."

It seems we're on the same page about the alarms: let them go until they time out in a few minutes. His chime sounds like the default setting on the phone, and I feel him laugh beside me at the Black Sabbath ringtone.

"I guess that would get me up, too," he murmurs, kissing my shoulder.

Laughing, I stretch to grab the bottle of water on the bedside table, offering it to him. He pushes up onto an elbow, unscrewing the cap and taking a long drink. After what we did, it should be awkward to stare directly at Alec in the weak light filtering in from the hallway, but it isn't. I watch him gulp down the water with primal satisfaction, and it is genuinely one of my favorite things ever to witness. Pillow lines crease his face. His hair is crazy. The fact that it's five and we have an eight o'clock flight means we don't have time for another round, but my body doesn't get the memo. Blood seems to rise to the surface of my skin in anticipation of his hands.

And when he passes over the water to me and I lift the bottle to my mouth, he takes the opportunity to slide his hand over my stomach, stroking back and forth, eyes closed and forehead pressed against my shoulder.

"I had fun," he says quietly. "I'm so glad you remembered me."

It is both wonderful and terrible when he says this. Wonderful because I know he means it; terrible, because—of course—this is how the goodbye starts.

"Me too," I say. "Really. I don't want to get too intense, but it's been a shitty year, and I needed this."

"For maybe different reasons, I needed it, too." He pauses, frowning. "But I just want to say—"

*Oh God.*

"Alec." I turn to smile at him, hiding the way my chest immediately tightens at this tonal shift. "You don't have to say it. You live in London. I'm in LA. I have no expectation of seeing you again."

"No, no. Well, yes, that is—unfortunately—probably true, but I meant something else." He gazes down at me. "This will sound weird, and you'll understand it later, I think, but I mean it when I agree this was exactly what I needed. And I'm just—" He swallows, neck flushing. It's weird to see him stumble over words. "I'm really happy to be here with you. Exactly how it was last night. Whatever happens after this, I want you to promise to remember that. Okay?"

Even a cold brick would realize that Alec Kim is saying something without saying it, but it's so carefully veiled I don't know how to probe deeper. He doesn't give me a chance, either, because he cups my jaw, offering up a kiss that is both sweet and passionate, gently coaxing me back onto the pillow.

"I wish we had time," he says against my mouth, and I know exactly what he means.

But we don't.

He stares down at me, exhaling, and then with a quiet groan pushes up and turns to sit at the edge of the bed. I want to roll over and wrap my arms around him because, oddly, it seems like he needs a hug, but it doesn't feel like something we'd do at sunrise. So I sit there staring at his back while he stares down at the floor. All of the ease and comfort of last night have started to fade, and I quietly hate it.

We both startle when the room phone rings, and then Alec lets out a mumbled "Oh" of recollection. Leaning over, he answers it with an instinctive "*Yeoboseyo*," and then, "Hello . . . Yes, thank you. Let's say fifteen. Thank you."

He hangs up and looks over his shoulder at me. "If you'd like, you can use the restroom right there to get ready." He lifts his chin to indicate where he means. "The concierge is bringing something up for me and will be here in about fifteen minutes. I'll shower in the other restroom."

The outside world is pressing back in, making us both adopt a level of formality that feels completely unnatural. Thanking him, I hold the sheet to my chest and avert my eyes as he stands fully naked, finding his clothes on the floor and carrying them out into the living room with him. With a towel around his waist, he returns just as I'm getting up, bringing me my suitcase, bra, and dress. I want to kiss him in thanks; it's what every cell in my body is leaning forward to do, but he just gives a polite nod and ducks back out. In only a few seconds, I hear another door close farther out in the suite and the sound of the shower turning on.

Staring down at my open suitcase on the bed, I decide the dress is still the cleanest thing to wear, and then debate the underwear situation. I could wash a pair in the sink and wear them—damp—on the plane. I could go without. I don't like either of these choices. This is a problem for post-shower Georgia. But after rinsing off quickly and wrapping myself up in one of the hotel's lush, thick towels, I hear a quiet knock land on the bathroom door. I open it, letting Alec in.

He's clean and dressed in a black T-shirt, black jeans, hair neatly combed, and with soft stubble on his chin. Instantly, my libido stands up, waving the white flag. He misses my ogling gaze because he's staring at where my towel is tucked closed between my breasts. A drop of water runs down my neck and he looks like he's considering licking it. My ego logs this moment for the mental scrapbook.

"Do you know what a thirst trap is?" I ask him.

He jerks his attention up to my face and I think takes a second to translate this in his head. "I'm thirty-three, not eighty. Yes, I do."

I point at his chest. "Lethal."

He laughs. "Is that right?"

My attention is caught on what he's holding in his hand. It's a small black shopping bag. Looks expensive. "What's that?"

Remembering it, he holds it out to me, dangling it on a long finger. "Oh. For you."

"You got me a present?" And then I amend: "*When* did you get me a present?"

"I asked my assistant to have something sent over." He lifts his chin for me to take it. "When we were in the elevator last night."

This feels vaguely *Pretty Woman* and I'm not sure how to feel about it. But I take the bag and peek inside. Whatever it is, it's wrapped in heavy black tissue paper, and when I pull it free, I am both delighted and horrified.

"The dress is fine," he says quietly, "but I didn't want you getting on a plane with nothing underneath."

I stare at him, strangling my smile between my teeth.

He winces. "It's weird, right? Am I being weird?"

"It's incredibly sweet," I say, laughing, "if not a tiny bit weird." It's simple, beautiful, and functional—as much as a pair of satin-and-lace underwear can be. "This is definitely a first for me as far as one-night stands go."

"Well . . ." His lips purse in a scowl as my words sink in. "How many have you had?"

He seems to immediately regret asking, but I tease back, "How many have *you* had?"

Alec stares at me, eyes narrowing. "All right."

"Thank you for this." I stretch to kiss his cheek. Cheek feels safe. *Not boyfriend*, my brain whispers. I focus on the gesture rather than the reality that his assistant had women's lingerie delivered to his hotel room during his unexpected layover. How standard is that kind of request? Did they even blink?

Whatever. It solves my underwear dilemma, and I'm choosing to be thankful for it. "I'll be a lot more comfortable on the plane now. I mean it."

"Speaking of comfort." He pauses and then nods to the bag. "There's something else in there." Alec reaches up, scratches the back of his neck. His skin is flushed again, his movements unsure.

I feel around, and my fingers find a stiff piece of paper.

It's a ticket.

The blood drains from my face. "Alec. This is too—*no*. You cannot buy me a first-class ticket for a flight from Seattle to *LA*."

"It's not a big deal, Gigi."

"It is to me. A very big deal."

He steps closer, cupping my face. "You haven't slept. Even before last night you were exhausted."

"Which is exactly why I could easily pass out in a coach seat!"

"If you don't want it, you still have your other ticket." He leans in, resting his lips on mine. It does something weird to my heart, this kiss. It's unquestionably our last one. "You've really given me a gift, just being here." Stepping back, he looks down at his watch. "I'll head to the airport separately. I have some things I need to do. But I've arranged for a car to get you at six."

My heart has fallen into my stomach. "Okay. Wow.

Thanks—thank you. For the car and the room. And the underwear and the ticket." I feel awkward the longer this list gets. "And the drinks," I say. The next words come out before I can stop them: "And the great sex."

He laughs. "It was great. Unbelievable, really." He backs out of the bathroom and closes the door only after giving me a final "Take care, Gigi."

As much as I think I won't, I look for him at the gate, growing increasingly worried when he fails to appear. Once I'm in my seat, I watch every person pass by and wonder, *Did you end up getting my coach seat? Are you making it home also thanks to Alexander Kim? Where is he? Did he give me his ticket?*

And in fact, Alec is the last person on the plane. He boards wearing a baseball hat, sunglasses, and with his phone pressed to his ear.

As he passes my seat, 1B, he gives me a tiny smile but doesn't stop to talk.

Of course, the first sign that I was missing something important was Alec's small speech in bed this morning. But the second is maybe more obvious: All three flight attendants come over to greet him within only a few minutes of him sitting down. Two rows behind me, on the other side of the aisle. *3C,* my brain screams. Which means, he can see me, but I can't see him unless I turn around to look.

I need a distraction and bend, pulling out my phone before they tell us to go into airplane mode, texting Eden.

hi. I'm finally headed home.

She replies instantly, as I knew she would: her phone is attached to her hand. Yes! I missed you. Can we hang tonight? I'm off.

It's a fair question. She's my best friend and roommate, but a bartender who works Wednesday through Sunday. I see the hot part-timer at the Coffee Bean and Tea Leaf more often than I see Eden. I might pass out midsentence but you have me until I'm comatose.

I hit send and then stare at my phone. I want to talk this out in person; no one else would understand how great last night was in the context of Georgia's Really Shitty Year. But Alec getting onto the plane in such a covert way and the fawning attention of the flight attendants leave a weird feeling of disbelief coating my memories. He's next-level hot, yes, but who *is* he? Did I miss something really important? I can't help reeling back through every moment we spent in the bar, catching up.

So, I type to Eden, and hit send to keep her attention on our text box and away from her Viki app. I'm sure she's lying in bed, watching kissing scenes from her favorite dramas, and it's almost impossible to snag her focus once it's gone that route. I had a one-night stand.

Because I am absolutely the last person she would ever expect to do such a thing, she sends back is a string of exclamation points followed by a W H A T

It was so wild, and I will tell you everything when I get home, but he bought me a first-class ticket home and got on the plane last this morning and the flight attendants went over to greet him and now I'm sitting on the plane going WHO IS THIS GUY

Yes who is the guy???

Do you remember my friend Sunny who moved when we were twelve? It's her brother. I recognized him. Teenage me is dead on the floor.

Omg I bet

He must have a million airline miles though lol because they love him

Was it good? she asks.

I stare at my phone. Saying only *yes* feels like a lie, because it wasn't just good. I can still *feel* him.

It changed me—God, so cheesy—but not in a way that means I'm desperate to see him again or need to have more of this. I mean that I think it changed *me* and my shitty post-Spencer thought pattern. It reminded me that real, genuine human connection isn't a fluke. I wish I had elaborated more on that this morning when I said last night was what I needed, because I like the idea that Alec might take that with him into whatever he finds next. After all, who cares if I made a fool of myself by being so bare and forthcoming? I'm never seeing him again, and at least he would know that his ability to show himself to me like that meant something.

I type one letter at a time—*it was really amazing, E*—and then delete it all, because it feels like I'm sharing something sacred. I try again, *It was exactly what I needed*, and then delete that, too. Too cliché.

I close my eyes, leaning my head back. I want to turn around and see if he's looking at me right now. It feels like he is. I just need one beat of eye contact to know that my memory isn't shit. But I can't look, not without feeling weird or making it weird. It was one night.

So I just type, Yeah, hit send, and then turn off my phone.

■ ■ ■

Alec bought me the ticket so I'd sleep, and it seems like the best way to thank him is to at least try. As soon as I close my eyes, I feel immediately woozy. It's the same feeling I've had the few times I've been drunk enough to be sick. The seat spins beneath me; blackness seems to bleed in from the edges of my lids.

But also, I think I'm still drunk on Alexander Kim.

I try to remember what it was like visiting Sunny's house as a kid. While my thoughts spin down into deeper and deeper drowsiness, I imagine her porch, her living room, the scent of her kitchen, the dark stairway. I tumble into a dream about it, and when the wheels of the plane touch down, my eyes jolt open and I have the sense of just having been there. I can taste the bright tang of Mrs. Kim's spicy tteokbokki on the very tip of my tongue, can feel the gentle spray of the lawn sprinkler on the soles of my feet; I can hear Alec yelling down the street to his friend.

The Kim family was very close, but not overt in their expressions of affection. Whatever life Alec lived after I knew him taught him to communicate with the emotional intuition he had in the hotel, and after the trip I had, it means something.

*I didn't want you getting on a plane with nothing underneath.*

*How many have you had?*

*You haven't slept,* he'd said. *Even before last night you were exhausted.*

In my experience, an asshole doesn't usually say these

things. I would know. Or at least I hope I would. I've had so many terrible interviews in the past two weeks. Interviews about men I now believe drugged women, raped them, and recorded the act on video to share with friends. I talked to the friends who'd viewed the videos without thinking anything of it. I've met with club bouncers, employees, and guests who saw it all happen and never thought to say anything at all.

I squeeze my eyes closed. I thought I'd built up my professional detachment, but it didn't survive the horrors I uncovered in London. And the sour kick of Spence's lies was a constant film at the back of my throat during my entire trip. Shitty men are everywhere.

I need one more minute with Alec. He was real with me. I thanked him for the ticket and wine and sex but never for that. I never said, *You're a good man,* and for some reason, calling it out when it happens feels important now.

The wheels touch down and I turn my phone on, texting Eden about my angst, needing to diffuse it somehow.

I think I'm being a weirdo.

How?

I want to tell him that what he did last night was great but what he did this morning was better.

The seat belt light goes off, and we all stand, stretching in the aisle. I bend, reading her reply.

Oooof, girl. What did he do this morning?

I'll explain later, I type. He was just a good guy. He took care of me.

Are you still drunk?

I pull my bag from the overhead bin and turn around to look at him. He's still in his seat, showing no signs of hurrying to exit the plane. Our eyes meet for only a second before someone steps between us, blocking my view. It isn't long enough for me to get any sense at all what he's thinking. No, I reply. I'm tired. And emotional. Maybe I should just get in a cab.

Get in a cab versus what other option?

Wait for him, I text.

Don't wait for him. This way lies madness.

Eden is right. If I even lean in the direction of hoping for more contact, I'm destined for disappointment. We both made it clear that last night was a onetime thing, and Alec has done more than enough for me. Up front in row one and already standing, I have no choice but to exit when the plane door opens. If he wanted to he could, with his long legs, catch up with me once we're both off the plane. But a glance over my shoulder reveals he isn't in the cluster of passengers making their way up the Jetway, and he isn't in the mass of people behind me as we make our way through the terminal. It's possible I lost track of him, but the terminal we flew into isn't very crowded, and it wouldn't be very easy to lose track of a man who looks like Alec Kim anyway.

Which might explain why, when I emerge out into the arrivals lobby, there are at least two hundred people—mostly women—standing with signs, banners, and clothing all bearing his name.

# Five

**Welcome to CA Alexander Kim!**
**SARANGHAE ALEXANDER KIM!**
**MARRY ME, DR. SONG**
**USA LOVES JEONG JINWON**

I blink in disbelief, feeling like I'm floating outside of myself as I stare at these cryptic signs, trying to figure out what any of them *mean*.

Finally, with my heart hammering in my chest, I wheel my suitcase behind a pillar and do what I probably should have done in the lobby of the hotel last night, before he carried me into his bed, before we had drinks in the bar, before I even followed him upstairs to shower.

I google Alexander Kim.

And holy shit.

My phone's browser immediately fills with photos and links to articles, interviews, fan sites in Korean and English. Photographs of him in Seoul, in London, in New York. And then, I see one image in particular and register that I am the world's biggest idiot.

Yes, maybe I recognized him because he's Sunny's brother and my first crush, but that wasn't the only reason his face was familiar to me. And the reason I felt like I'd just seen him was because I *had*. His face is on promotional posters in probably every other tube stop in London.

*BBC exec coming here for meetings with American networks?*

*That's shockingly close, actually.*

I fall back against the pillar, deflating. I am astoundingly stupid.

*It's called* The West Midlands.

If I could find a way to make the floor of LAX open up and eat me, I would.

In the background, pulsing frantically in time with my heartbeat, the crowd begins to chant, *Alexander Kim! Alexander Kim!*

The roar grows louder and then the entire terminal explodes into screams as four men in black suits step through with Alec just behind them. His security team keeps the crowd away with arms outstretched, creating a path to pass through to, I assume, a car idling at the curb. But Alec stops short, gaping in surprise at the scene waiting for him. Sure, he was able to move around Seattle largely unnoticed, but had he forgotten the way Los Angeles loves its celebrities?

With a winning smile, he accepts a few items to sign, pauses briefly for a couple of photos, and then tries to press his way through the crowd. Meanwhile, I'm stuck in place in an empty stretch of floor about thirty feet from where he's surrounded, realizing that I spent the night with a man I really should have recognized for the right reasons; realizing

I'm apparently so deep in my journalism niche that I didn't recognize one of Korea's, London's—and now the world's—biggest stars; realizing Alec could have told me a hundred times who he was but didn't even try, didn't bother to share that part of himself with me while I went on and on about my job and Spence and—

And I'd wanted to *thank* him for being real.

While I stare at this man whose face and mouth and body I kissed and touched and took pleasure in, I register this is exactly what he meant this morning.

*This will sound weird, and you'll understand it later.*

*I mean it when I agree this was exactly what I needed.*

*I'm really happy to be here with you.*

*Exactly how it was last night.*

*Whatever happens after this, I want you to promise to remember that.*

*Okay?*

Well, how nice for him that he got to have exactly what he needed, exactly how he wanted it.

I figured out who he is, I text Eden. There was a huge crowd waiting for him at the airport.

Good God, I bet she could have told me if it had even occurred to me to tell her his name.

Wait, what?? Who is he???

His name is Alexander Kim.

She replies immediately, a string of incoherent letters and symbols as if she's just crashed her hands down on a keyboard.

I look up from my phone as Alec's head turns and he gazes out in disbelief into the distance, scanning the size of the crowd. Our eyes meet. Betrayed, embarrassed tears rush up my throat, burning my eyes, and I break away first—just as his mouth forms the shape of my name—turning and exiting the doors just behind me.

My frantic rabbit-hole internet searching does nothing to calm me down on the congested drive home. I can't even reply to Eden's increasingly hysterical texts, because I'm apparently intent on punishing myself with how big an idiot I am.

For example: I knew he moved from London to Seoul when he was twenty-two, but I didn't know that he'd been scouted on the street there, hired by a management company, trained in acting, and cast at twenty-five in a romantic comedy about a group of professional skateboarders. His character, the street-smart second male lead, fell in love with the daughter of a chaebol family. ("Do you still skateboard?" I'd asked him in the bar, to which he'd only replied, "Really?" with a flat expression of disbelief that I can now, of course, translate.)

His second role was in a fantasy drama where he played a ghost that can only touch the woman he loves when she dreams about him. To get her to dream about him he—wait for it—plays the piano.

When I read this one, I audibly groan, earning an odd look in the rearview mirror from my Lyft driver.

I now know that when Alec turned twenty-eight he took a break from acting for his compulsory military service. His comeback was in a science-fiction-themed drama that received mixed reviews, but he followed it up with an indie film, *A Quiet Devastation*, which turned into an unexpected hit throughout Asia and for which he won nearly all of the main pan-Asian drama awards that year. After that, he landed the role as Jeong Jinwon in *My Lucky Year*, which is apparently the highest-rated Korean drama of all time.

Now he's in his third season as Dr. Minjoon Song in BBC's hit series *The West Midlands*. The *Hollywood Reporter* conveniently explains that the upcoming season focuses on the stoic Dr. Song's story arc and his uncharacteristically wild tumble into love with a woman he meets when she crashes into his car during a blizzard.

Sweet Jesus.

He was rumored to be dating his current costar, a French actress who, even if they both deny it and I believe that they really aren't romantically involved, is so beautiful that I want to punch my own face. Searching for information about the two of them together—a type of personal Google search I never in a million years thought I would do—leads me to a string of gifs of kissing scenes, scenes so hot they make me both turned on and mildly queasy, and are understandably setting the worlds of both K-dramas and BBC fangirls on fire.

In one gif, Alec pulls away from a scorching kiss and rises up on his knees to take his shirt off. In the back seat of the car, I watch it on a loop approximately seventeen thousand times. His abdomen is like a beautifully symmetrical rock garden, for fuck's sake, and there are so many links to YouTube edits of the scene that I have to put my phone down and cup my hands over my face.

When we pull up in front of my building, Eden is standing outside, shouting at me before I'm even out of the car. I catch a fair bit of what she's yelling while I pull my bag from the trunk—"How did you not know it was Alexander Fucking Kim? Why did you not text me his name the second you went into his room?"—but with the Alec-induced chaos in my head, and going on only a paltry handful of hours of sleep, I can't walk and listen to her freaking out at the same time. I really need to go upstairs, climb into my bed, and sleep for a hundred days.

Unfortunately, neither Eden nor my deadlines are going to let me do this. Every time I spoke to my editor, Billy, when I was in London, he grew more and more invested in the Jupiter story. He wants five hundred words but is willing to stretch it to an almost unheard-of fifteen hundred if I can, as he puts it, "break a bottle over my head with this one."

Eden follows me into my room and sits on my bed. "Start at the beginning."

I push my suitcase into the corner and decide to ignore it for now. Maybe forever. "E, I have a ton of work to do."

"Ten minutes," she says. "I just need ten minutes. I mean, you could have called me in the car to save time."

"I didn't want to talk about it in front of the Lyft driver."

"No," she counters, seeing straight through me, "you had to google the fuck out of him."

This is the one person who has known me at my best and worst. She was my college roommate, my postcollege roommate, my post-Spence roommate, and the only person in our circle of friends who never clicked with Spence, who warned me against moving in with him—*I don't trust him, George,* she'd said, *and I'm not sure how he'll fuck it up, but I'm worried he will.* She's the one who took my side and suggested the five who sided with Spence in the split "needed cult deprogramming."

Eden Enger has seen me heartbroken crumpled and rock-concert high and has never judged me for any of it. But right now, she's about to judge my complete obliviousness. I'm just going to have to absorb what's coming.

"Fine." I sit down at the edge of the mattress and fall onto my back. "Get it off your chest."

"Gigi Ross," she growls. "How did you not know who you were fucking? Alexander Kim's shirtless promo still from *Quiet Devastation* was my computer background for, like, six months."

"I was living with Spence," I remind her. "I didn't see it."

"Alexander Kim's face has to be all over London!"

I nod. "Practically every tube stop. He's everywhere. I have no good excuse, I just—" I drag my hands over my face. "I wasn't tuned into the television world. All I was thinking about was this tiny handful of terrible people in the night-club world. Be glad I didn't come across him when I was there, and trust me, I feel stupid enough without your help."

She pries my hands away and then lies down on her side next to me, propping herself on an elbow, head in her hand. "Start from the top." Her warm brown eyes soften. "Where did you see him first?"

"Airport." I tell her how I knew I'd seen him before—she

snorts at this and then claps a hand over her mouth, promising with a look to behave. I describe how I couldn't remember his name and how when I did remember at the hotel, I called him Alec.

"I think that's how he knew I didn't know him from TV," I say. "And he dropped hints a few times—seriously, I am so incredibly dense—but I didn't get any of them."

"I bet that's why," she says quietly.

"Why what?"

"Why he let you use his shower. Why he bought you drinks. Why . . . all of it."

"Because I knew Sunny?"

"Well, and because you didn't really know *him*."

I hate this sentence and have to work to not let the hurt pass over my face. The problem is that I did feel like I knew him. I felt like I showed myself to Alec and he showed himself to me, and we were real together. But obviously, that wasn't true.

"Oh. No, no, no, that expression doesn't work for me." She leans over, studying my face. "Let's move on from that."

"Yes, let's."

I describe going to Alec's room, the shower, the heavy tension afterward. "I felt him everywhere," I say, adding at her giggle, "I mean, even with my back to him, I could have probably estimated how far away he was to within an inch." I look at her and wince because I know this is going to absolutely shred her poor fangirl heart in the best way: "He has such an intense presence in person. It's honestly insane."

She screams, covering her face with both arms. "This is *terrible*."

I nod. "It really is."

"I can't believe my best friend had sex with Alexander Kim." She pauses, dropping her arms, eyes widening in renewed realization. "George, you had *sex*. With *Alexander Kim*."

I sigh. "I sure did."

Finally, Eden sits up and composes herself. "So," she says with forced calm after a few deep breaths, "the sex was good?"

The image of him moving over me, teasingly inching his way in, crashes into my thoughts. His face tilted to the ceiling, upper lip glistening with sweat. The recollection sends me spinning, filling my chest with a tight, uncomfortable ache.

"It was." I don't want to say too much because it feels so deeply personal, even still, but I'm sure she hears the way my voice comes out thin and shaky.

*Holy shit,* he'd said. *What is this sex?*

And I knew exactly what he meant.

"Actually, I'm ruined," I mumble in confirmation.

She smacks her hand down on the mattress. "I *knew* it."

I laugh. "Eden, don't be weird."

"You do realize you slept with my actual perfect man?"

I nod. "I admit I feel sort of guilty."

"You should! I've loved him for a decade! If I came to you and said, 'Last night I slept with that hot *New York Times* editor you love,' are you trying to tell me you wouldn't piglet all over my story and ask for every detail?"

I grin up at her. "I think we both know I am not the intrusive one in this relationship."

"Says the journalist!"

"Speaking of which . . ." I plant my hands on her back and roll her off my bed.

She looks up at me from the floor. "I hate that you're not more high-pitched and hysterical about all of this. I truly want to lose my mind that my best friend had sex with the man who is arguably on his way toward being the biggest BBC star of the decade and I can't even tell Becky or Juan about this, can I?"

"No." Her bartending team is a cluster of adorable, gossipy knuckleheads, and my experience with Alec would end up as a vaguely dishy post on Instagram within an hour. But I do know what she means. I don't feel giddy or deliciously slutty. I mostly just feel tired and a little sad. "I think I'd be more bubbly about it if he'd been honest about who he was."

"But maybe he liked that he could be anonymous with you."

I nod, chewing my fingernail and thinking about what he said again.

*I'm really happy to be here with you. Exactly how it was . . . Whatever happens after this, I want you to promise to remember that.* "I just feel a little used."

"I would let Dr. Minjoon Song use me however he damn well pleased."

I laugh. "I know you would. And I'm sorry to tell you, but it's everything you'd hope."

She falls back onto the floor, speaking to me from the grave, with her arms crossed over her chest. "He gave you underwear and a plane ticket, and you're not even going to call him?"

"That's the best part," I say, and lean over the edge of the bed to give her a wry grin. "We didn't exchange numbers."

For about an hour, my brain is too full for me to be very productive in writing anything up. The pharma meeting feels like a gray hum of boredom in the background. And Jupiter feels like a confusing jumble in my thoughts: too many faces and details and overlapping timelines. Alec penetrates everything—the sharp angle of his jaw, the heat of his body, and the quiet, deep rumble of his voice—but Spence is somehow there, too, his betrayal filtering in and out of my thoughts. It sends a confusing mix of anger and lust and horror creeping into my mood, making objectivity hard to find.

I know I should sleep some more before I dig into writing, but I now have just over thirty hours before I need to get both assignments to Billy for editorial. And one isn't just a "story" but the first big chance I've been given since I started working at the *Times*. I can't fuck this up.

I write the boring five hundred words on international pharma law, send the piece, and then work until nearly midnight on Jupiter. I sleep until four, when I drag myself out of bed to finish what I know is a very shitty draft.

With only half a day left to finish, I immediately begin edits.

But because journalism follows Murphy's Law, just as I get into a rhythm—with my notes compiled and organized, fingers flying over the keyboard reworking entire paragraphs, my mind slotting the myriad pieces together into a clear narrative—a text pops up from Billy with a request to meet a verified Jupiter source at a hotel on Wilshire at 9 a.m., which will eat at least an hour and a half of my deadline time. But he's marked it as URGENT, and I know what that means.

It means I don't have a choice.

# Six

A strikingly tall woman meets me in the lobby of the Waldorf Astoria and seems to identify me immediately. "Georgia?" Her clipped British accent matches the severity of her coppery-red hair pulled back in a tight knot at the back of her head. "Yael Miller. This way."

Before I can reach to shake her hand, she's already turned and taken two long strides toward the elevator bank.

I'm uneasy about the lack of information, but not overly so. Billy knows where I am, knows who I'm meeting. He wouldn't send me into a shady situation. And it's obviously important if he agreed to give me a twelve-hour extension on my deadline.

Yael Miller presses the button for the penthouse, and we ride in the elevator in silence. Finally, the elevator doors open and we step out into a small alcove with only a single door ahead of us. She swipes a keycard and opens it, gesturing for me to step inside.

I do, but she doesn't follow me in. The door sweeps closed with a heavy whoosh, sealing me inside.

And then my heart falls from my mouth and straight

through the floor. Standing in front of the windows, leaning back with his hands braced on the sill, and looking very much like he did on the elevator up to his room only two days ago is Alec Kim.

The first words out of my mouth are simple reflex: "You've got to be kidding me."

He straightens immediately. "Don't walk out."

My shoulders are angled away already, and I'm sure the instinct to flee is written all over my face. A sour thought hits me like a pill dissolved on my tongue. "Wait. Was that your assistant?"

"Yes."

"The one who got me the underwear?"

Alec nods.

"Well, remind me to thank her on the way out. I'm sure she loves running that particular errand."

"It was a first," he admits.

"She must have been pretty displeased," I say, looking around. "She didn't say a word to me the entire ride up."

"That's just how she is." His brows flicker up as he interprets my meaning another way. "There's no jealousy happening. I don't appeal to Yael in that way."

I exhale slowly, looking to the side. I now have no idea why I'm here. Does Alec really have something to tell me about Jupiter? And if so, why did he give no indication that he knew something when we were together in Seattle?

"Well," I say, staring at the art on the wall. It looks expensive. I don't remember even noticing the art in his last suite. "I'm here. What did you want to tell me?"

He inhales sharply through his nose, nodding slowly. "The

way you left the airport, I couldn't tell for sure . . . but it's hard to miss the anger in your tone right now."

"I'm not angry, Alec. I'm annoyed. I shared a really intense night with someone who lied to me about who he was, and now I've been summoned—while on deadline—and I have no idea why."

"It was intense for me, too," he says, ignoring the rest of what I've said. "But we both know it wouldn't have been anything like that if I'd told you more about myself."

He might be right but, "Still shitty," I say.

"You work for the foreign news desk at the *LA Times* and had no idea who I was, and I'm supposed to feel sorry for not telling you?"

My jaw drops. "You're an actor, not a diplomat," I say. "Is your ego really so huge?"

He groans, tilting his face to the ceiling. "Come on, you know that isn't what I mean. I just—either be angry that I didn't tell you, or be glad we had the night we had, but you can't be both."

"I can absolutely be both. But it's moot anyway: what we had two nights ago was bullshit."

He weathers this as if I've physically shoved him, and a thread of guilt tugs at my chest. "Why would I think I should clarify for you who I am?" he asks. "Why would it matter, at least at first? You were my sister's childhood best friend. I let you use my shower. I figured that would be it, and if you didn't recognize me as someone other than Sunny's brother, it made no difference to either of us. But then we started talking, and then we were having drinks, and then we were holding hands, and the longer I didn't tell you, the more I didn't want to."

"You asked me all about my life and then were deliberately vague about yourself," I say. "At least tell me, 'I want a night off from my reality,' or, 'I don't feel like getting into it.' Don't give me half-truths that make me feel like we're being equally forthcoming."

"I *liked* that I could just be a man with you," he says. "That I didn't have to live up to some expectation and that you weren't nervous with me. I liked that you were real. I never get real, ever." He stares at me for several tense seconds. "But I'm sorry I lied to you."

I don't know where we can possibly go from here. "Did you really bring me here to talk about what happened between us? You don't have anything to tell me about Jupiter?"

He takes a few seconds to answer this, and in the quiet, I watch his jaw clench and relax. "No," he says finally. "I had information to tell you."

Immediately, my brain changes tracks. "Wait. You *do* know something?"

This story is a powder keg. My UK colleague Ian and I spent the last two weeks scrambling to unearth what's really happening inside Jupiter. We found some bombshells, but without sources willing to speak to us, we also met a frustrating number of dead ends.

And Alec knows something important enough for him to call Billy and have me sent here? Stunned, I feel my jaw open and then close.

He reads my reaction in the silence. "I wasn't sure I could talk about it at the hotel." Alec doesn't break eye contact but winces very slightly. "Unfortunately, my source is having second thoughts."

An incredulous laugh bursts free. "You are so full of shit."

"I'm not. There's so much I want to tell you, but the story isn't mine to share. I really can't talk about it without this person's go-ahead."

The words slice out from between my gritted teeth: "If you end up somehow being involved in this disgusting—"

"*Gigi!*" Alec cuts in. Horror washes him out. "Are—are you kidding? That's not—" He closes his eyes, taking a steadying breath. "I'm not involved with Jupiter in any way—not as an investor or patron. That's not at all what I wanted to share with you."

Either he's an even better actor than I imagined or this one landed on an incredibly tender target. "Good," I say, more gently now. "That is a huge relief."

He opens his eyes and looks at me steadily. "I thought I had information to give you that could help you expose someone, but I don't."

The adrenaline drains in a cold flush, leaving me numb. "Okay, then we're done here."

I make my way to the door, but Alec cuts out a sharp, "Wait." I pause but don't turn to face him. "I . . . also realize we forgot to exchange numbers."

Now I turn to gape. "You're unbelievable."

"Come on. I'm trying to make things right."

Unexpectedly, my heart tightens in a painful pinch. "Why?"

"Because I've thought of nothing but you for the past thirty-six hours."

His words drop a black curtain in front of every other thought. I forget about the story and—for a scattered few seconds—I forget to be mad. All I see is his posture, with hands tucked tightly into his pockets and the heavy bob of his Adam's apple as he swallows again. I see his tongue as he licks his lips, anxious for my reply.

My "Why?" comes out much quieter this time.

"It . . ." He seems unsure how to answer this. "I needed to see you again."

Apparently I only know one word anymore. "Why?"

His disbelieving smile is fleeting. "Gigi, come on."

"For sex," I guess flatly.

"For whatever this is between us," he corrects. "I have a hard time believing it was just me. Did it feel like regular sex the other night? The kind of sex you've had with other people?"

"Not sure that's a fair comparison," I say. "I'm betting my list is much shorter than yours."

He sends a hand into his hair, looking away. I should feel guilty for that shitty jab, but I'm too distracted by the tight clench of his jaw, the way his neck flushes red in anger. This deep, ravenous feeling in the pit of my stomach shoves everything else aside.

"Right." Alec turns back to me. "Then you'd know if I just wanted sex, I could get it anywhere."

*Exactly,* echoes a chiding voice in my head. *The assistant who sends underwear to Seattle could easily find someone to satisfy an itch. It isn't about that, and you know it, Gigi. You're being a coward.*

I let out a shaking breath. "I'm sorry. I shouldn't have said that."

"Yeah." He blinks out the window, frowning. "Well, I guess we've answered that question."

"What question?"

"Whether it was only like that between us because you didn't know who I am."

I'm not sure why this raises a contrary, defensive flag inside me. "That isn't fair."

His surprised gaze flashes to me. "How is that unfair?"

"You have to let me be hurt that I was being real and you weren't."

"Is that really what you think? That I wasn't being real?"

And this, right here, is where he has me. He knows it, too.

We stare at each other, breathing fast and deep, worked up.

"If I acknowledge that I hurt you," he says quietly, and when he fights a coy smile, it digs a dimple into his cheek, "then what?"

I bite the inside of my cheek to keep from smiling back. "Then . . . I don't know."

"Come here," he says in a gentle purr.

Staying put requires pretending my feet are blocks of concrete. "I have to edit my article."

He stares at me, jaw tensing, and then nods once. "Right. You're on deadline."

And . . . that's it? He would just let me leave? I feel like a punctured balloon. My thoughts are a swirling storm of relief and lust and irritation and ambition and infatuation. Alec Kim has the wildest chemical effect on my blood.

I mean . . . technically, the article is written.

All it needs is editing.

And by calling me here, he's given me twelve additional hours.

Excuses line up in my mind, and Alec watches me with increasing amusement the longer I do not turn and walk toward the door. Finally, I say, "*You* come here."

With a quiet laugh, he walks over to me, standing so close I feel the heat of him all along my front. "And then what?"

Can he hear my heart? I swear it's the loudest thing in this room. "I still don't know."

Alec reaches down, threading his fingers with mine. Holding my hand. "This?"

"Maybe." I am unable to stifle this grin, and he sends his other arm around my waist, pulling me against him. He tucks me into his chest and squeezes.

A hug.

"And this?" he asks.

Emotion swells thick in my throat at the familiar feel of his body and the duality of the sweet seduction of his embrace. Every memory from our night together is sealed back into place. I wrap my free arm around his neck, pulling his head down until he rests his forehead against mine, and like this, with eyes closed, we breathe in jagged, charged tandem for a handful of seconds.

I open my eyes to find him looking at me. Fondness blooms in my expression before I can tuck it away.

Alec smiles, pulling back. "How mad can you be if you're looking at me like that?"

"Very mad."

He swallows a laugh. "Your 'very mad' is not very intimidating." He kisses his fingertip and gently rubs it over my heart.

"I felt stupid," I admit, finally. "I told you about Spence. About where I work."

"It wasn't fair." He presses his lips to my brow. "I'm sorry. I would have shared more but—it was selfish, I know. It was a perfect night. I worried it would vanish."

"What are we even doing?" I ask. "We barely know each other anymore."

"That's not true. We may have changed a lot in the past fourteen years but just as with renovations . . ."

I grin up at him as we both register that he's committed to the terrible metaphor. "We'll always be part of each other's foundations?" I guess.

He nods, laughing in self-deprecation. "That was bloody awful."

"No, it was surprisingly cute."

I take a minute to really look at him. It seems like his face should jolt me into a different kind of awareness, that his presence should now send me into shaking, nervous territory. He's my oldest crush and now he's an actual celebrity. But the electricity along my spine isn't nerves or insecurity; it's raw hunger.

Alec bends, hovering with his lips near mine, staring at my mouth. "You smell so good."

"Do I?"

He hums. "I didn't want to shower you off that morning. Wanted to feel you all over me a bit longer." He tilts his head, breathing in deeply beneath my jaw. "It's sugar and sex."

His words light a fire under my skin, and I send my hand up under his shirt, feeling this body that's immediately familiar, but with the new visuals in my head—the picture of him from Jeju Island with his shirt blown up off his beltline, exposing his tight abdomen; the way he's so tall he has to bend to kiss me and how every fan site has written an entire feature about his perfect proportions—*now* I'm jolted into a new hyperaware territory.

And the mouth that is the subject of a thousand close-up photos—it's sucking at my jaw, my neck—

I pull back, squeezing my eyes closed. "Okay. This is weird."

He reads my tone immediately.

"No." Alec tilts my face up to his. "Don't do that."

I slide my hands around his neck again. Dig fingers into his hair. His mouth hovers only a fraction of an inch away from mine and he tilts his head, waiting, letting me make the final decision.

I stretch, pulling his lower lip between mine, sucking. A helpless moan escapes his throat and he cups the back of my head, deepening the kiss with tongue and teeth, with his other hand sliding down my back to my ass, where he can hold me, grind into me.

"This," he says when he pulls away to suck in a breath. *It's still like this,* he means.

He walks backward to the bed, tugging me with him before sitting at the edge of the mattress and smiling as I straddle his lap.

Pulling back, I rest my fingertips beneath his jaw, holding him still and studying him feature by feature. Taking him apart and putting him back together in my memory, up close. The warm dark eyes. His perfect, straight nose. A soft, full

pout; his lips make my own mouth water. Sharp jaw, cheekbones from dreams.

"How long do we have?"

He moves his eyes without turning his head, glancing at
his watch on a lifted arm. "Two hours before I have an interview here."

Two hours isn't that much time away from work, I reason. I'll do this instead of eat or clean or reply to emails.

Setting my fingertip on his left cheek, I fit it into his dimple
when he smiles in reaction. He leans in for a kiss.

"Be still," I tell him, and he laughs soundlessly.

I draw a path from his forehead down his nose, across the
bow of his top lip. Alec sits patiently as his bottom lip gets
traced next. Cupping his jaw, I tilt his head up, looking at
his neck. I have a thing for masculine throats, and his is the
stuff of fantasies, of dreams I wake up from sweating and
hot with the urgency of unfinished business.

So it gets my attention first; I drag my tongue up the
length of it, sucking on his Adam's apple; it vibrates against
my lips as he moans.

I suck his lips next, licking them, sinking my teeth into
the bottom. Beneath me, he starts to move his hips, thrusting
up slowly, his hands sliding beneath my shirt at my back.

I kiss his cheekbones, his eyelids. I rest my mouth against
his temple, breathing in the clean smell of his shampoo.
His hand makes a slow journey up under my shirt, gliding
up my spine. With a quick flick of his fingers he unclasps
my bra.

When I pull back, his eyes drift open and meet mine. I feel

suspended in place, motionless, while it seems like he stares directly into my mind.

His gaze travels over my face as he reaches up to move a strand of my hair out of my eyes. "See? I was right."

"You're going to be smug now?"

"Mm-hmm." He leans in, and whatever patient energy we managed for the past few minutes is incinerated when he kisses me. Hot, open, his mouth slides over mine with the same vibrating desire I feel. His big hands go back under my shirt, sliding to the front to cup both breasts as he exhales something I don't understand.

"What did you just say?"

His lips move down my throat. "It's prettier in Korean, but essentially I'm saying I like these on you."

I laugh. "Boobs?"

He laughs, too, rolling me to my back so he can push up my shirt and put his mouth on my stomach, kissing his way up my body. "It's a nicer way of admiring your curves."

I fit my hips to his, rocking against the shape of him, hard, in his dress pants.

He grunts a quiet sound of frustration. "An unexpected oversight," he says, and nips at my bottom lip.

"What?"

"This isn't my room. It's the room we're using for interviews."

"Is that going to be really weird later?" I ask, laughing.

"I doubt it. We'll be out in the seating area." He frowns. "My present concern is that my bag isn't here."

His meaning doesn't immediately click. But then he flexes his hips up into me again, and . . . oh.

"No condoms?"

"No condoms."

"There are other things we can do," I say into a kiss.

"If memory serves," he says, "we did just fine during our first round last time." Alec takes my breast into his mouth.

I tug my shirt off and then his, and he settles over me, his skin warm and smooth. When he kisses me, the fever rises, overtaking my instincts to be slow and enjoy every second. I scratch down his back and know it'll leave a mark, but it just makes him more frantic. He pushes up onto his knees, tugging my jeans off and stilling at the sight of my underwear.

I grin up at him. "Don't worry. I did laundry yesterday."

He breaks into a smile, but it's distracted, singed at the edges by heat.

"You like them on me?"

He reaches forward, sliding a finger under the fabric at my hip. "Yes."

"They made me think of you."

"So," he says, stroking my skin, "you put these on today not knowing you were coming to see me?"

"Correct."

"And even though you were angry with me?"

I nod.

He glides the finger along the curve of the silk, over my pubic bone, and then down between my legs, over my clit.

His eyes fall closed. Alec circles his finger, dipping lower, and lets out a moan as he spreads the slick heat around and around.

He pulls away, guiding me up to the head of the bed, and then climbs down between my legs.

My brain goes haywire and I actually get a head rush just imagining what he's going to do. I need . . . I need more air before he does that.

"Wait."

He looks up at me. "What?"

"I'm almost naked."

He stares, waiting, breath impatient and hot against my stomach. "And?"

"And you're not."

With understanding, he backs up, standing at the foot of the bed, and reaches for his belt. I immediately realize my mistake. Watching him take his pants off in broad daylight isn't going to help me relax. The buckle clicks softly, metal on metal in the quiet room. The sound of his zipper lowering is obscene; I hear it tooth by tooth, and he bites his lip through a grin that is, I have to assume, related to whatever my face is doing while I'm watching him.

So, to retaliate, I slide my hand up my body, cupping my breast. Lightly pinching my nipple.

Alec lets out a little grunt, upping the ante in this game by hooking his thumbs under the waistband of his dark briefs, tugging them down, and freeing the hard length trapped there. And then, with his gaze on my face, he wraps his hand around it and strokes himself.

I'm moving on instinct, mouth watering, sitting up at the foot of the bed to run my hands up his thighs to his hips, pulling him one step closer so I can push his hand away and hold him steady for the long, wet draw of my tongue.

He exhales a surprised curse, steadying himself with a hand on my shoulder.

Over my tongue he's smooth and hard; he tastes like lust. I look up at his face to catch his expression when I spread my mouth over the tip of him, sucking.

With a moan he steps back and bends to kiss my jaw.

"Gigi?"

"Hm?"

His mouth slides over mine. "What're you doing?"

"What does it look like?"

"You tricked me into taking my clothes off."

I laugh. "And you teased me by touching yourself. You don't like being kissed here?"

"I like it too much," he says, and groans when I stroke him. Kissing me again, Alec pushes at my shoulders until I'm flat on the bed. His hand comes over mine around him and moves with me for a few strokes before he guides me away. "Not yet."

With his hands under my arms, he drags me up the mattress before climbing down between my legs again, planting wet and open-mouthed kisses down my torso.

Tugging the satin of my underwear to the side, he leans over, spreading me with his thumb and bending to press a soft, sucking kiss directly over my clit.

I don't know how I live through what comes next. It's his open hungry mouth, sucking me with full lips, exploring me with an expert, teasing tongue. It's fingers that are gentle at first, one, then two, and then three—when it's no longer teasing and seductive but fucking, his whole arm working those fingers deep and fast until everything in me is heat and light, until the pleasure is so intense it's the only thing I'm conscious of, until my own sharp cries penetrate somehow,

how loud I am, how I have to be quiet, I have to, and I'm pulling a pillow over my face to—

Alec reaches up, grabbing it and throwing it roughly to the side.

So my scream comes out unimpeded, aimed at the ceiling, filling the air.

I'm breathless, with an arm thrown over my face, chest heaving to catch my breath, but he doesn't immediately pull back. He kisses me there sweetly, close-mouthed, and it's like a soft landing after a long, hard fall. I have never even imagined oral sex like that. I never knew it existed.

Equally breathless, Alec crawls up my body, dragging his mouth as he goes, but stops at my breasts.

"Good?" he asks, and then licks a wet circle around my nipple.

I nod, letting my arm fall away.

"Look at me," he whispers. "Look at me and say it."

"I'm dead." I manage to drag my eyes open, but it takes me a few breaths to get words out. "No one has ever done it to me like that."

He points his tongue, circling it around and around. "Like what?"

A kink for the words, this one.

"So wild and—" I gasp up to the ceiling. "Hard."

I can feel him staring at me for a second longer before he turns his attention back to my breasts, licking and sucking, wet. The sound of his mouth pulling away, his low groans against my skin, make me shake with longing: how he makes me feel completely insatiable and greedy after coming so hard not two minutes ago is unreal. But I understand his intentions when he rises over me, shifting to straddle my ribs, and pressing my breasts together around his cock.

"This okay?"

I nod, but he shifts his gaze to my face, flicking up a playfully annoyed eyebrow. "I like it," I tell him, grinning.

He plays with my breasts as he starts to move, leaving me free to run my hands over his thighs, his waist and chest, scraping my nails gently over his nipples, making him hiss out a tight, hungry sound.

"Yeah," he says when I do it again.

And that single word becomes a whispered call and response, with his growing tighter, mine more encouraging; I have never in my life seen anything more erotic than Alec hungrily chasing pleasure.

My hands smooth over his skin everywhere and finally come over his fingers, wet and slippery, and he leaves me to hold my breasts around him as he reaches up, gripping the headboard.

"Gigi," he says, and then his throat bobs with a heavy swallow. "I'm coming."

He cries out sharply and then again, and I watch his face as his pleasure jets from him, warm and wet across my chest and neck. In the panting quiet that follows, I raise my fingers to it, watching him watching me.

"You okay?" he asks, gently dragging his thumb along my lower lip.

I nod. "You're ruining me. Sex won't ever be like this again."

"Was it before?"

"Please. Any man who goes down the way you do has had plenty of good sex."

"I don't think I've ever been quite like that. That wild, like you said," he adds. "I worried I'd hurt you."

I smile up at him. "Do I look injured?"

"No." He scoots back, settling over me, and speaks the next words against my lips. "You're beautiful."

And there it is, the entwined bliss and tragedy of this. He makes me feel beautiful, even sweaty and spent on a rumpled hotel bed.

He shifts back, stands, and walks to the bathroom. The water runs, and Alec returns with a warm, wet cloth, bending to clean my fingers, my neck, between my breasts.

"To think," I say, using my free hand to finger-comb his hair off his forehead, "I came here thinking I was getting information and we did this instead. I can't even be mad that I lost two hours of editing time."

Alec pauses as he folds the washcloth inside out and then carefully runs the clean side over my neck again. He lets out a quiet sound of acknowledgment, a rumble in his throat. "I promise I'll tell you if and when I can."

I tilt my head, looking up at him. "Actually, you probably couldn't tell me anything on the record anyway. We've sort of destroyed any objectivity."

Setting the washcloth on the bedside table, Alec lies down facing me on his side, head propped on a hand. "Well, I'm not sure I'd be comfortable talking to anyone but you about this."

"Alec, what is going on?" My question ends just as a single, sharp knock lands on the door.

He startles, glancing toward the door before his attention bolts to the clock beside the bed. I don't even bother to look. I'm sure we're out of time, but I'm made suddenly uneasy by his tone. He seems upset—devastated, really; it's the first time it occurs to me that this might not be as straightforward as Alec knowing someone who knows something. If he doesn't answer my next question, Yael Miller will actually have to drag me out of the room by my feet.

"Hey," I say, touching his chin, redirecting his attention to me, and trying to keep my voice steady, my hands from shaking. "At least tell me I don't have to worry about your safety."

"I'm okay," he says with convincing urgency. "I really am." His gaze drops to where his finger draws spirals on my collarbone. The knock lands again, twice this time. "But that's the best I can do before Yael walks in here."

# Seven

To say that I'm distracted when I get home is an understatement. Alec has information about the story I have been thinking about during nearly every waking hour for the past month, and I have no idea what it is, when I'm going to hear it, or if someone is going to get it before I do. I understand he had to clear it with his source, but will it change everything I've already written? I can tell it's not just a small bite, either, but something important. Something big enough to make his face remain tight and shuttered, even when he walked me to the door and kissed me goodbye.

It was a hesitant peck, but to be fair we both knew it would be: we were dressed, put back together—he as a polished actor, me as a hungry journalist—with the weight of a bombshell of unknown magnitude between us.

"Try to get some sleep," he said, adding, "Don't worry. I mean it."

"When are you done tonight?"

"Late." And then he pressed a sleek iPhone into my hand. "I promise to call tomorrow."

I stared down at it. "This isn't mine."

"I'd like us to use different numbers than our usual, if that's okay. I've put my private number in the contacts there."

I laughed at this—called him 007 Casanova, named the gadget my Batphone—but my smile faded as the truth sunk in: fooling around with Alec after knowing he had information created a slew of personal and professional conflicts. "Okay, yeah, good thinking."

He kissed me, quickly, letting Yael in, and they bolted into action getting him ready for his flurry of interviews while I took the elevator back downstairs.

Of course, I google him a second time as soon as I'm home, looking for something different now. Last time, I wanted to figure out why people might wait for him at LAX; this time I want hints as to who he spends time with, where he's been caught by photographers and fans, who he might know that's even tangentially related to Jupiter.

But when I do a deep internet dive, I'm relieved to find that Alexander Kim isn't seen in public very often at all. His social conduct seems completely respectable. Most of the places he's been photographed are airports, museums, red carpets, and on set.

There's not even a whiff of an association with Jupiter.

My stomach drops when my phone rings.

"Hey, Billy," I say, leaning back in my desk chair and squeezing my eyes closed.

"How's it coming?"

"It's done," I admit. "Just working on edits."

"With the new info from this morning?" he asks, his words distracted and clipped. I imagine him at his desk, two-day-stubbled, sipping cold coffee, reading something else while he checks in with me.

I pause, letting out a long, slow breath. I could disclose my relationship with Alec. I *should*, probably. But I know what would happen: Billy'd pull me from the story, pass it to someone else. I'm too close to give this up, and it's not like Alec told me anything, anyway.

"His source backed out," I say. "He didn't have permission to discuss it once I got there."

"Shit." Billy growls. "What happened? Did you push?"

I close my eyes. Guilt twists through my gut. "Yeah, of course I pushed."

"Maybe we'll go with what you have. Let's go through it real quick."

I sit up, adjusting my laptop screen. "Okay, well, we start with women being assaulted in the VIP rooms at an exclusive club and powerful men using their influence to cover it up. Then we'll give the backstory. No one in the US has probably heard about any of this, so I have some background on the club. Jupiter opened nine months ago, yadda yadda, jointly held by a pop star and a group of successful businessmen who have owned several popular clubs in London. Established in the heart of Brixton, it boasts a guest capacity of over eight hundred, with several VIP lounges. And, it turned out, private rooms equipped with video cameras." I stare at the article on my screen, wondering what level of detail Billy wants included. "You want me to withhold the bouncer's name, right? Even though his Twitter account was public before he deleted?"

"Right," he says. "Just to be careful. Keep everything top-level, something like: a few weeks ago, a bouncer told his boss women were being harassed in the club. The bouncer was beat up, claims it was in retaliation. He complained to his boss's boss—got fired."

"Then his Twitter account vanished," I say, nodding.

"Right. Bouncer fired, he shares his story on Twitter, and then posts screen caps he says someone sent him of these private chat rooms where it's clear the club owners are sharing sexually explicit content being recorded in the private VIP lounges."

He takes a bite of something and continues talking around it. "Then what."

"Then his account vanishes. By the time I found him in London, the bouncer—Jamil Allen—wouldn't talk to us. Dead ends everywhere. We don't know who is hosting the online chat rooms, or who sent him the screen caps. Then a couple days later, Ian and I were in a pub, going through our notes, and he got a call from a woman who got his contact information through Jamil. She had been approached by execs from Jupiter who asked out of the blue if she would take a financial settlement."

I wait for Billy to react to this. It takes a second and then, "Wait. For what?"

"Exactly, *for what*," I say. "Turns out, she had been ID'd by police in one of the videos linked in the chat forums, but no one had notified her. She'd been assaulted—*on video*—but had no recollection of it."

"Holy *shit*. So, the cops were looking into it after all but then giving information back to the club?"

"It sounds like it. Hers is the only face that's visible. It's possible all of these videos are like that. I mean, what are the odds that out of all these videos the police have she's the only one who was drugged? Slim, right? And I swear it goes down to the owners, Billy. Four of them—their names kept popping up in every conversation we had. Gabriel McMaster. Josef Anders. David Suno. Charles Woo. With waiters, hostesses—everything off the record—everyone saw them all the time in the VIP areas, with different women all the time. Even a few construction guys told me that Anders and McMaster were both super hands-on during construction. They had the rooms built with cameras. And not just one for surveillance, but several pretty high-tech ones. Suno's dad owns the company that does the club security. I'm not sure how exactly Woo fits in yet but I wouldn't be surprised if his name starts popping up more, too."

Billy shouts, and I hear the sound of his fist slamming down on a table.

"We'll push with this," he says. "Club background, bouncer's story, screen caps of the videos being shared on the online forum, cameras in VIP rooms. Anonymous source's story about being offered a settlement for an assault she didn't even remember. Keep digging about these four owners. We don't want to report high-profile names until we're absolutely sure and we get the info on the record. And whatever else you can get while this new source is in town, we'll include in a follow-up. This shit is going to blow up."

I push aside my unease about the complication of using Alec as a source because inside, scrappy Gigi is beaming. My first big story, and the possibility of a follow-up only a few days later? I work to control my excitement. "Sounds great."

Billy laughs, reading me like a book. "One thing at a time, kiddo."

We ring off, and I dive back into edits for a few hours before reading the story through one final time. Holding my breath, I hit send. I think it's good.

No, I think it's great.

And then I tumble into bed, burrito myself—clothes and all—into my blanket, and fall asleep within minutes.


I wake up at 3 a.m., feeling woozy and starving, and kick my covers away. Out of deranged hope, I check my new Batphone.

I have four text notifications from Alec. My heart takes off in a dust cloud.

Some things got moved and I have an unexpected free day tomorrow.

I was wondering if you wanted to go down to the beach?

I just realized you're either working or sleeping.

I hope you're sleeping.

The last text was sent at midnight, and if he was up then, there is no way he's awake now.

Right?

Then again, if his body is still on London time, it thinks it's noon.

Finally, at 3:17 a.m., I can't help it. I make myself a cup of coffee and text him.

I'm free all day if the offer still stands.

Three dots appear to tell me he's replying, and my blood turns to static.

You're up?

I grin, typing, I sent my story and crashed around eight.

Send me your address. I'll pick you up at seven so we can get out before it's busy.

My smile feels too big for my face. Did you get any sleep?

A few hours, he responds.

You should rest today.

No way. I'll exist on California sun, caffeine, and Gigi.


Because he's picking me up and I haven't seen him in anything less than full luxury, I'm obviously expecting a fancy car. So when a bright-red economy-size Ford pulls up at the curb, Alec has to honk for me to realize it's him. The car's horn sounds like a high-pitched laugh.

I climb into the car beside him, delighted. "Wow. Sweet ride."

"I picked this baby up near LAX this morning." He pulls away from the curb and smiles over at me. "We are going for incognito."

"I could have picked *you* up, you know. What kind of Angeleno would I be without a car?"

Alec shakes his head. "I like driving and I never do it in London." He turns onto Washington and deftly gets into the correct lane to merge onto the freeway.

Music on, windows down, Alec by my side . . . I let the story, the worries, the entire world slip away for a little bit. I just want to soak up the feeling I have being near him.

He finds my hand, weaves our fingers together, and sets it on his thigh.

"Where are we going?" I ask.

"I'm taking you to my favorite beach."

I take a long look at him in a black T-shirt and baseball hat. Even incognito, he isn't very incognito. "Is a public beach a great idea, Dr. Minjoon Song?"

"No one will recognize me at this one."

I laugh. "Yeah, tell that to the mob at the airport."

He grins at the road ahead of us. "I didn't expect that, either."

"You know, that was the first time it occurred to me to google you."

He glances briefly at me before following signs for the 405 South. "Really? Because I had Yael google you while we were in line waiting for rooms."

Oh, I'm absolutely sure he did. I bet he had a full background report before he ever offered me use of his shower. "Well, once I have an assistant on 24/7 call, I'll be better about googling my one-night stands before we hook up."

He frowns. "We aren't a one-night stand."

"Fine," I relent, grinning at him. "Two-night stand."

Alec smiles out at the road. "Two-*week* stand." He glances at me. "I want to see you as much as I can while I'm here."

Nodding, I bite my lips to keep my words in: *That sounds like just enough time to get attached.*

I turn and look out the passenger window at the freeway flying past, the cloudless blue sky above, the concrete jungle dotted sweetly with jacarandas and palms, bougainvillea and pink oleander climbing over the freeway barriers. And then I realize we are driving south.

"Okay, but where are we actually going?" I ask, grinning. "All the nice beaches are north of my place."

"We're going to Laguna."

I gape at him. That's an hour away.

He does a quick double take. "You said you sent your story in and have the day off."

"I do, but Santa Monica is *right there*."

He laughs. "I want to take you to my favorite place, and I haven't done this—gotten in a car and driven myself here—in probably ten years." He looks around, and I wonder what it must feel like to have spent his entire life here until he was almost twenty.

"Do you miss California?"

"Yes and no. I mean, it's nostalgic, and there are things I love. But I've been away almost a decade and a half. I can't really imagine living here again."

I don't know what to say to that, but a weird darkness settles in my chest—for only a second—realizing that we're fifteen minutes into what is our true first date, and I'm already having the best time. But he'll fly back to England in a couple weeks, and I might never see him again.

A few minutes of easy silence pass, with music quietly filtering into the car and LA growing smaller and smaller in the rearview mirror.

"You got quiet," he says finally, taking his attention from the road in a couple of small flashes. "Everything okay?"

I veer away from any heaviness, nodding. "I like your accent now."

"Do you?" It's growly, the way he says this, and sends a

shiver of electricity through me. Alec catches my sharp look and grins. "What?"

"I'm not sure how I'm going to be able to be on a beach with you using that voice and not be able to touch you."

"We'll do our best. I know we're capable of exerting some self-control."

"You have zero evidence for this," I say, laughing.

He laughs, too. "Yael knows about us, of course—"

"I feel like the underwear purchase was a big clue."

"It was, indeed, but if my manager, Melissa, knew that I was on a date, and that I was skipping out on a free day and going to the beach?" He whistles. "I would be in a lot of trouble."

"You're a grown man!"

He nods. "Sure, but there are some freedoms those of us in the public eye have to give up, and anything like this should be cleared. Especially if I am out with a woman—I wouldn't be alone with a woman in public at home. Melissa doesn't like to be surprised."

"Does she know about Seattle?"

"Yes."

"Wow, she knows *everything*? Even when you have sex with someone?"

"I mean, we don't discuss it in such explicit terms," he says, laughing, "but I let her know I spent time with someone there and it was just overnight, so I'm sure she read between the lines." He pauses, sobering a little. "She doesn't know that we saw each other again in the hotel in LA, though."

My brows go up. "I'm a secret lover."

"You're a *friend*," he adds, winking. "Right? My sister's best friend from childhood. Of course we'd reconnect."

"We'll be good," I promise. "I won't even treat you like a celebrity. If you get hot, you can fan yourself—"

"Fan *myself*?" He pretends to start to turn the car around.

"—carry your own towel," I roll on. "I won't grope you out in the open."

Alec laughs, changing lanes to exit in Long Beach.

I gape at him. "Are you really turning around?"

"We need supplies."

Off the freeway, we park in front of a Walgreens, and I stare blankly up at the entrance. "Okay, I realize you're a celebrity but you're taking me to a drugstore? This date might be too fancy for me, Alec."

He laughs. "Give me one," he says. "Before we get out."

I'm about to ask him one what, but he leans over the console, cups my face, and sweetly settles his mouth over mine. At first it's just a peck, a drag of his lips, and then another that's even softer, but then he's tilting his head, coming at me deeper and longer, pulling my bottom lip into his mouth. When he grasps the back of my neck and holds me still so he can have his way with me, he is only one soft groan away from being dragged into the back seat.

Thankfully, he seems to swallow the groan but lets out a happy, breathy laugh into my mouth when I scrape my teeth over his lip. I remember this kissing; I remember thinking what a relief it was to find someone for the first time in my life who kisses the exact same way I do.

My brain shrieks in alarm at this thought. I'm taking a mental stroll across hot coals. This, whatever it is, is starting to defy an easy label. In reality, it's a fling, and we both know it has a very clear expiration date. He gave me a secret iPhone, for fuck's sake!

But flings don't spend every free second together; they don't sneak kisses every chance they get. They certainly don't think how great it is to have found the kissing equivalent of a soulmate.

My heart fills with stars, expanding.

Alec pulls away, focusing on my mouth. "Ready?"

"Yes." I pause, dazed. "Ready for what?"

He laughs, thinking I'm joking, kissing me lightly again. "Let's go."

Inside the store, we get bottles of water, granola bars, the sunscreen that we both forgot, cheap beach chairs, and various dorky floaty toys. He buys me an ugly Post Malone hat; I buy him some aviator sunglasses with iridescent pink lenses.

Back in the car, each of us wearing our gifts, he turns the music up; we roll the windows down and drive in contented quiet with his hand resting lightly on my thigh.

At least, it rests lightly at first. But soon his thumb strokes the fabric of my cutoffs to the rhythm of the song. Tiny circles widen and narrow, widen and narrow. Finally, he gives me a moment to breathe, moving his hand to adjust the volume, but then he returns and now it's worse, because his fingertips toy with the frayed hem of the denim. Gradually, they sneak under, touching me featherlight, dancing aimlessly along the skin of my inner thigh, almost as if he's doing it without knowing, but inside I am an inferno, with crackling campfire heat snapping beneath my skin. Does he know what he's doing to me? Touching skin that he's kissed, skin that has slid up around his hips, pressed against his face. Skin that feels bruised from the ache he's building.

I reach for his hand, taking it in mine and bringing it to my lips, kissing his thumb knuckle. When I chance a look at his face, he's biting back a grin. The little shit. He knew.

"Are you going to tease me all day?" I ask. "You realize you were, like, two inches away from making me launch myself into your lap."

He bursts out laughing, looking at me and then away. "You're so soft. I didn't realize what I was doing until you moved my hand." He pauses and blows out a slow breath. "I'm thinking the beach was a terrible idea."

"Like I said earlier?"

He laughs again and squeezes my hand. Given that we're exiting the freeway toward the beach cities, his realization—one I voiced almost as soon as we got in the car—comes too late. At least I have the weather to distract me from my lusty brain. It's one of those ridiculously gorgeous Southern California days in April: breezy, hazy morning skies, temperature hovering around sixty-five, but when the marine layer burns off, it will be perfect for a day at the beach.

We fly down the Pacific Coast Highway, practically alone on the long stretch of coastline, and then Alec turns us down a winding street into a neighborhood of beautiful houses perched precariously on a cliff. Cars pack the curbs, parked bumper to bumper, and I imagine us walking a mile loaded down with all the stupid gear we bought at Walgreens. But then we see it in unison, a spot directly next to the stairs leading down to Crescent Bay Beach.

"Well," he says smugly, "that was easy."

*But,* I think, *that's exactly the problem.* Everything about this feels *too* easy. Like the way he stroked my leg without thinking. Like climbing out of the car and handing over my purse without thinking, him taking it and stowing it in his backpack also without thinking. Like unloading the car, wordlessly packing things up in easy silence like we've done this a thousand times. But in reality, today is our first time together out in daylight.

"When was the last time you were here?" I ask.

He leads us to the narrow, steep steps. "Probably a week or two before we moved."

"Moved to London?"

He nods, carefully navigating the wooden slats, still damp from morning dew. "Do you ever come down here?"

"You know how it is," I say. "It's an hour drive, but Orange County might as well be New York."

This makes him laugh, and I watch his toned legs descend, muscles bunching and relaxing beneath the length of his black swim trunks. I tear my attention away, looking up to the sky, out to the endless stretch of the blue Pacific. It seems to go on forever.

*Get in a boat,* I think. *Live with this man, out there, forever. We could exist solely on granola bars.*

At the bottom of the steps, he hangs a left, walking toward a stretch of smooth white sand bordering the rocky, craggy southern boundary of the beach. He walks with purpose, heading, I presume, to a favorite spot. But frankly, we have our pick of spots. It's only eight thirty; the beach is busy, but not with people looking to set up for the day on the sand;

instead, it's surfers catching the choppy morning waves, couples strolling together, people walking their dogs, joggers. The surf is high, water crashing down with showy bravado, painting staggered half-moons on the wet sand.

We unload against the cliff, in an area that will be shady at midday. After he sets up our chairs, our towels, and the flimsy beach umbrella he bought, he turns to survey our new plot, and I pull my T-shirt off, squirting some sunscreen into my hand to put on my chest and stomach.

It feels quiet, like heavily quiet, and when I look up, Alec's eyes are on my body. I start to crack a joke about him and my boobs, but his expression is so focused the words evaporate on my tongue. He reaches forward to adjust my necklace where the clasp has slid to the front, but once he's fixed it, his fingers slow and it feels like everything grows blurry around us as his gaze grows unfocused on my neck.

"What?" I look down, trying to see what he sees. Nothing there but the vague sheen of sunscreen.

"Just thinking," he says, dragging his touch down over my breastbone, between my breasts.

"Thinking what?"

He exhales slowly. "That I've felt you here. That I fucked you here."

These words light a fire beneath my skin I'm sure he can feel under his fingertips. He angles his fingers down, like he might simply slip his entire hand into the cup of my bikini top, but then makes a fist around the strap instead.

"Okay." I press my hand to his chest, and he lifts his head. "I think we need some ground rules today. Like . . ."

He swallows as he waits for me to finish my sentence, and now it's my turn to be distracted by the long line of his throat. Finally, he prompts, "Like?"

"Well, to start, you can't say things like that."

He grins. "I can't?"

"At least not if we can't be alone somewhere later."

He exhales, dropping his chin to his chest before straightening and stepping forward. Alec cages me in the shadows, against the side of the cliff. His body heat warms me all down my front, and I glance to the side. No one is paying any attention to us, but even so, I feel like we're in a fishbowl.

"What are you doing?" I whisper.

"Thinking."

"You're thinking very deep into my personal space."

"Should I move?"

I lift my hand and rest it on his abdomen. "No. I like when you invade my personal space."

He tilts his face up, looking me in the eye. "I'm going to be honest."

"Good. I like honest."

"Very blunt, in fact."

"Even better." A bluff; my heart is halfway up my throat and out of my body right now.

He licks his lips, studying me. "I'm not a very casual person," he admits quietly. "I've actually never slept with anyone outside of a long-term relationship before. I don't think I'm very good at it."

"Okay." His admission is devastating. This would be so much easier if one of us knew how to navigate something light and temporary.

"I'm afraid I'm going to get attached if we spend another night together."

He drags his focus from my mouth back up to my eyes.

*This,* I think. *This is what it feels like to fall.*

"Well," I say carefully, "I'm okay with not spending the night together, if that's what you need." I reach up, tracing the line of his T-shirt along his collarbone. "But I'm pretty sure at this point it's going to be hard for me when you go home no matter what we do. And I think it would be harder to know you're here and not be able to see you than it would be to see you and have to remind myself what it means."

"What it means, as in we agree it's only this? Just these two weeks?"

"What else can it be?"

At this, he mumbles, "Right," and bends, resting his lips on mine. My first instinct is to gently urge him away, to remind him where we are. But my stronger instinct is to lean forward, softening against him. He sends one arm around my waist, pulling me close. Even when he ends the kiss—we are in public, after all, and the beach is slowly filling—he holds me against his body, lifting my feet onto his in a chest-to-chest hug.

I drape my arms around his shoulders. "I thought we weren't going to kiss outside today."

"We're hidden."

"We aren't at all hidden, you goober."

He growls as he bends and pretends like he'll take an enormous bite out of my neck. It turns into a tiny kiss, and then he whispers, "Maybe I could stay at your place tonight."

"Really?" I pull back and grin at him.

"Really."

# Eight

With that sorted, I feel a certain amount of tension evaporate from the air around us. We leave our things and wander over to the rock shelf only a handful of yards away, watching the tide ebb, exposing the famous local tide pools. For the next hour, we clamber around the rocks, sharing every discovery: fluttery anemones, tiny rocklike barnacles, silvery fish, and coral. When the sun is high, we head back to our spot, spreading our towels out beneath the umbrella and staring at the unending cycle of waves.

He reaches over, pulling my hand into his lap, spinning the one ring I wear around my ring finger on my right hand. It's a simple band of sapphires.

"Who's this from?"

"My parents."

"Pretty." He touches my fingers, then turns my hand over, running the pad of his thumb over my wrist. "Birthstone?"

I nod. "September sixth. You?"

"April eighteenth."

I do a double take. "It was your birthday the day we flew to LA?"

He nods, laughing. "I don't usually make a big deal out of it. Sunny always goes overboard no matter what."

"Well, then it's a good thing you have a sister to make you celebrate yourself."

He kisses my wrist before releasing my hand. "Do you ever wish you had siblings?"

I nod. "I used to a lot. Now I have Eden, and she's like an irritating younger sister, even though she's a couple years older than I am."

"Will I get to meet her tonight?"

Squinting out at the water, I calculate whether she'll be home later. Today is Wednesday; she usually works, and unless we're back by four, we'll miss her. "I don't think so."

"I'll leave her a note."

I lean over, bumping his shoulder with mine. "She'll die. I'm serious."

He grins down at my hand.

"What's your favorite project you've ever done?"

Alec quirks an eyebrow over at me. "I thought you googled?"

"It was only a panic-google. I skimmed just enough to feel sufficiently mortified for asking whether you still skate-board."

He laughs the open-mouthed laugh I love. "That was possibly my favorite part at the bar."

I reach over, smacking his arm.

"I mean it when I say I've loved everything I've done," he says, "but I really love *West Midlands*. It's fun to do something where we develop relationships with our costars over time, and this cast is amazing." He reaches for my hand again, weaving our fingers together, resting them on his thigh. "The early stuff all feels a little blurry. It was so exciting but so crazy. I got the role in *Saviors,* and I know people say this all the time, but it felt like everything changed overnight."

"Do you like it, though? I bet it's cool to be recognized."

"Yes and no," he admits, releasing my hand to dig into the backpack for our waters and granola bars. He passes me mine and then takes a long drink. "At first it was exciting, but it can be draining, too. And the press in London are unrelenting."

"Oh. I hadn't really thought of that."

He lifts a wry eyebrow. "It makes it hard to be in a relationship, for example."

I carefully steer away from the personal aspect of this minefield. "You dated your one costar, though, right?"

"Park Jin-ae? Yeah. For a couple years." He grins at me. "I see you read that Google result carefully."

"I probably don't need to tell you that when you type 'Alexander Kim' on Google, 'Alexander Kim girlfriend' is the first option that autofills."

This makes him groan. "That relationship—we actually had to do a press release," he tells me. "Every interview, someone would bring it up. They even asked our current and past costars so much about it. Finally, we acknowledged we were together. It's a big deal to do that, and as a rule I don't share personal things publicly."

"I'm sure it's hard to trust." He goes quiet at this, and I can feel him staring at me, trying to figure me out.

"I can see you looking at me, thinking that I must be talking about myself right now."

He laughs, and I know I'm right. "You said you only broke up with your ex a few months ago?"

"Yeah. Six months now."

"How long were you together?" he asks.

I wince because I already know how this answer will land. "About six and a half years."

As expected, Alec goes still next to me. "*Wow*."

Nodding, I say, "I hate how much time I gave him. I think I was over him a long time before everything fell apart." I take another sip of water, clearing the heat in my throat. "I'm not mad at him as much as I'm mad at me."

"Why?"

"For being lied to for so long."

He leans in to catch my eye. "*You* didn't do the lying, though."

"True," I say, and finally look over at him, "but it would be the same for you. To be with someone who was lying to you for a year. Acting a part for a year and somehow you didn't pick up on it. You're an actor. It's your job to know when someone is acting. I'm a journalist. It's my job to see the story underneath. I didn't."

His mouth forms a little *ah* of comprehension. "I get it."

"And it's hard to imagine that none of our friends knew. I wonder if some of them did and were trying to help Spence get back on his feet without telling me."

"Ouch."

Nodding, I say, "So it's hard to trust my instincts."

We stare out at the water for a couple quiet moments.

"Well," he says, "my instincts tell me it's time for us to go play in those waves."

I want to kiss him for this easy redirect. We grab a couple of pool noodles and slowly inch our way into the freezing Pacific, carefully dodging the huge crashing waves, diving under them and pushing past where they break, out to where the water is clear and calm. From out here, the people on the beach look like tiny dots.

Tucking the long foam cylinders under our arms, we float facing each other, catching our breath. I want to bottle this feeling so I can sip from it in the days and weeks and years to come. I keep pushing it down, but the awareness that Alec is genuinely perfect rises up in unexpected moments, shooting a spear of pain through my chest.

And then he meets my eyes, and my lungs do a tender wilt at the piercing realization that he brought me out here specifically to talk. I liked our Laguna Beach bubble.

"I have permission to tell you everything now," he says quietly.

"Wait—why? What changed?"

"I told my source that I was talking to you specifically, and they told me it was okay to share."

"Me *specifically*?"

He nods.

I don't understand. But— "As much as it kills me to say this, you'll have to tell me only as your two-week stand." I try to smile. "Conflict of interest, you know?"

"Well, it would be off the record anyway." He dips his fingertips in the water and lifts his hand, letting the drops catch sunlight as they fall. "But I think it would feel good to tell someone who understands. And maybe the information can help you find something else, even if you can't write up this specific account."

Gray area. The life of a journalist. "Tell me anything you're comfortable sharing."

"I'm not sure of the best place to start." He stares up at the sky for a beat before taking a deep breath. "Okay." Alec blows his cheeks out as he exhales. "An old uni friend of mine from the UK is a man named Josef Anders."

He glances at me, logging the reaction I know I can't hide. My stomach positively bottoms out and I feel shocked blankness take over my expression.

He smiles sadly. "I take from your reaction that you've heard the name."

"I have. A lot. He's one of the owners. His name is all over this."

Alec places a hand over his brow, squinting over at me. "I suspect it is."

Thunder. My heartbeat feels like thunder beneath my breastbone.

"During college I had a group of friends with whom I was very close," he says. "And then when I returned to London after my time in South Korea, a few of us reconnected. I mean, we were all busy, so we weren't as close as we had been, but we would see each other once a month or so."

"I swear I've looked at every photo of Anders online, and haven't seen any of the two of you together," I say, confused. "I never came across this connection."

"Because our friendship is older than either of our careers," he says. "We didn't go out together for photo ops. The group spent time together at each other's homes." He swallows, blinking past me. "In the way that my family isn't photographed at home, we all protected our old friends."

A ball of black tar settles in my stomach. I am dying to know everything Alec knows but am also preemptively devastated over whatever it is that he might share about a once-close friend.

"Also around the time I moved back to England, Sunny began modeling. She was making a small name for herself in the industry. My friends would spend time at my family's home." He swallows. "And at some point, Josef and Sunny began dating."

"Oh wow." I mentally scroll through my file on Anders. "I had no idea."

"You wouldn't. Sunny's private life is even more locked down than mine." He nods, dipping his chin beneath the water's surface. "But this would be maybe two years ago? Of course they'd known each other since Josef and I were at uni together, but he met her when she was thirteen, so that was a little weird." Alec looks briefly at me, and then away again. "At first they kept it from everyone. Not even the other guys knew. We would all get together for dinner or to watch a match, and he never said anything about it. *She* was the one who told me, after they'd been together several months."

"Were you mad?" I ask.

He thinks on this for a few quiet moments, and the water laps up over his chin, touching his lips. He slips beneath the surface of the water, emerging after a moment and swiping the glimmering droplets out of his eyes. "Honestly, I think I was more worried than mad. I'd known him to be a mostly decent person, but he'd had a lot of girlfriends over the years, and he knew that I wouldn't want for my sister to get wrapped up in someone who might not be careful with his lovers' feelings."

"I get that."

"But whatever, she was an adult," he says. "Wasn't really up to me, yeah?" Alec squints behind me, to the waves crashing on the beach. "You probably know that Josef was in a band, the Tilts, that had a hit song before they dissolved." He trails his fingers in the water and we float in tight silence for a minute, bobbing gently in the ocean. Alec continues to draw shapes in the water, and I wonder if he's spelling something out. Somehow, even being an actor, he seems like the kind of person who first writes longhand what he wants to say in difficult moments like this.

"But he was the primary songwriter, and 'Turn It Up' is still played at nearly every major sporting event in the UK. It's made him a good deal of money, and Josef invested very well. He channeled some of this income into Jupiter."

It's information I already have, but it still feels like a gut punch. "Right."

He looks at me and reaches forward to absently stroke a hand along the goose bumps erupting on my arm. "When it really grew in popularity, he was there all the time."

My stomach has burned away by now. I want to hear this—morbid curiosity and professional investment keep me riveted—but I also want Alec to rush through it just to be done, just to wipe the expression of bleak dread from his face.

"He and Sunny were together maybe a year and a bit before she ended things, and most of it was during the building and launch of Jupiter. There's a lot Sunny won't tell me, especially now. But I think the split had to do with how much time he was devoting to the club. That said, I got the sense that he didn't want things to end with her. We all noticed that he was distraught."

He adjusts his position on the float and angles his face up to the sky. I stare at his profile, at the carved hollow of his cheekbones contrasted with the plush fullness of his mouth. I feel his face imprinting in my brain.

"Around four months ago, Sunny got her first real blockbuster modeling contract—with Dior," he says. "It seemed like she went from scraping to book every runway she could to being an absolute supermodel. She was in tube stations and billboards and in magazines. It's been a huge deal." For a moment his expression softens, and he looks over at me, grinning. "It's really cool."

"I bet," I say. "That's *huge*."

"Yeah." Alec moves again, restlessly slinging his arms over the floating pool noodle, leaning his chin on it. "Even though she'd broken things off, she still considered him a family friend, you know." He swallows and then swallows again, clenching his jaw. Turning his eyes up to me, he says quietly, "This is really off the record?"

"Entirely." I force my voice past the lump in my throat. "I promise."

He looks back down at the water. "A couple months ago, another one of my mates from this group, Lukas, was staying with me. He'd moved to Berlin, but while he was in town, he wanted to check out Jupiter to see what Josef was up to. I didn't much feel like going, but he and a couple of our friends went. A couple hours later, Lukas calls and tells me that Sunny had come in, but he hadn't seen her in a couple hours, and when he had seen her, she looked already pretty drunk. He thought I might want to come get her."

I feel like I've been punched. "No."

"Sunny doesn't drink much because she can't handle liquor very well." He goes quiet for a long minute, and I reach over, setting my hand on his back and rubbing lightly.

"We can do this later."

"No. This is good. I need to do it." He wipes a hand over his mouth, and the rest comes out robotically. "At first, I wasn't worried. Like I said, it would be strange for her to drink a lot, but again—she was doing really well professionally. Maybe she just wanted to celebrate with Josef—they were still friends, after all. I went down there anyway, to check on her. Called Josef. No answer. Called Sunny. Her phone was turned off, so I couldn't even locate her." He rubs his face again. "I called Lukas, who came to find me, and together we started searching all of the VIP rooms."

I exhale a quiet "Oh shit."

"Yeah. We found her. It was a huge party, but it was like my eyes just immediately zeroed in on Sunny passed out on a couch. She was—" He cuts off, shaking his head. "Everyone scattered like roaches when I walked in. I picked her up, found her clothes. Took her to the restroom. She was completely unconscious. I put her . . ." He swallows, squinting unseeing into the surf, unable to finish the sentence, but I understand that he's telling me he had to help get her clothes back on. "And I splashed water on her face. We sat there for a long time. I don't know how long, but people knocked on the door. I turned off my phone. I just talked to her. Told her she was safe and had to wake up. Finally, she woke up enough to walk, but barely. I put my coat over her, walked her out a back entrance, and took her to hospital."

Again he goes quiet, jaw working.

"She didn't remember anything about the night. I'm thankful for that, but unless there is video footage, we may never know exactly what happened. Do I even wish for that?" He passes a shaking hand down his face. "She had an exam, of course," he says. He pauses for a pained beat, and then nods.

This feels like another punch to my solar plexus. "Alec, oh my God."

I understand why he wanted to do this out here, where he can say it out loud and let it be swallowed by the ocean.

"She was really sick the whole next day," he says. "They found a cocktail of things in her system—certainly nothing she could have ordered at the bar. Josef called in the morning." Alec looks at me, and the hollow pain in his eyes is gutting. "He was so worried. Said he didn't know where Sunny had disappeared to. Naively, I told him what I'd seen in that room, and he was shocked. He was really quite convincing."

I feel sick.

"To be honest, I wasn't able to process anything or anyone else once I saw Sunny on that couch. It never occurred to me that he'd seen her in that state. Because if he had, of course he would have helped her, right? His ex? My sister?"

"Alec . . ."

Alec shakes his head and blinks past me. "Later that day

Lukas called me to check in. Needed to talk it out—he was traumatized by it all, too. When I told him about my conversation with Josef, he was furious. He said, 'Alec, mate, Josef was right there. He bolted the second you walked in.' He'd *been* there, Gigi."

I knew it was coming. I knew it. But it doesn't make it any easier to hear. "So, when Josef called you, he was trying to find out what you'd seen? What Sunny knew?"

"That's my assumption, yes."

We let this horrible truth dissolve between us. "Does Sunny want them to bring charges?"

Alec shakes his head. "It's been two months. But because she doesn't remember, because she doesn't want to be dragged through the tabloids, because she's justifiably worried about how this would affect her public reputation, and because she went there willingly—she's very hesitant."

"I bet you want to kick his ass."

He laughs once, a sharp sound. "You have no idea." There is violence in those words; the sounds scrape out from between his teeth. He turns his face away and pulls in a deep, steadying breath. "What kind of a monster can do this—at the minimum witness what happened to Sunny and very likely be the one behind it—and call me the next day playing innocent like that? I felt so incredibly stupid."

"You gave your friend the benefit of the doubt. That's not stupid. That's what good people do."

"I suppose."

"No one from the club has said anything to authorities about him?"

He shakes his head. "Gigi, there are probably a hundred

people who've seen women come in and leave drugged every week who don't say anything."

It's the one thing I haven't been able to figure out—how this could be happening at the club on such a scale without someone getting caught.

"I've felt hopeless. Not wanting to push Sunny to come forward but worrying that this story will continually get buried if she doesn't. I felt rather cynical about it all until I heard the fire in your voice at the hotel the other night." Alec catches my gaze and holds it. "I assume you know where I'm going with this: the only thing I need you to do on the record is to keep pushing, keep looking into Josef Anders's activity."

My heart breaks for him. "I promise I will."

He closes his eyes, and when he opens them again, he tries to smile. "That's all I know."

"That's a lot." I reach forward, carefully sweeping his hair off his forehead. "You okay?"

Alec leans into my hand. "I won't pretend that this hasn't been the hardest thing I've ever had to deal with."

"Oh, I'm sure."

"Worrying about her, knowing what happened to her that night—all I want is to support her the way she needs. Are there videos out there? Who else was in the room? I'm glad she doesn't remember what happened, but I also wonder if eventually she will."

I gnaw my lip while I decide whether or not to tell him this next bit. Not because it's a secret—it'll be out in my story tomorrow anyway—but because I know it will hit him hard.

Alec reads it in my face. "Just say it."

"Okay, well, one of the women who apparently was captured on video was approached with a financial offer to settle, and before that, she didn't even know she'd been assaulted." I wait while he processes this, eyes squeezed closed. "So even though the police confiscated all of the video footage from the club, someone on the inside is feeding information to these guys. Even if charges are eventually brought, the perpetrators are getting their hands on all the evidence first."

"Shit." He blows out a breath into the water. "So there probably is video out there with Sunny in it?"

"I honestly don't know. But it's possible."

"These past several weeks I've worried about everything," he says. "It's one of the reasons I left a few days later on the trip than the rest of the cast. I wasn't even sure I could leave her right now."

"Is someone with her?" I ask.

"She's with our parents, yes."

"How is she doing?"

He tilts his head from side to side. "She's okay. Obviously, she knows that I'm talking about it, off the record. That's a huge step for her, letting me do this."

Watching him struggle with all of this, I dog-paddle closer so that I can come right up against him. "I'm so sorry."

He nods, adjusting the noodles so that he can pull me into his arms. Alec presses his face to my neck, and even when my legs wrap around his waist, it isn't sexual. We hug, floating aimlessly in silence.

But then his lips move against my neck as he speaks.

"Thank you for listening to all of that. I'm so glad we haven't been eaten by sharks."

I laugh. "Thank you for planting that thought in my head, but really, thank you for sharing this story with me. I hurt for you and Sunny."

"I haven't talked to anyone about it yet."

I pull back to look at him. "No one?"

He shakes his head.

"Honey," I say, cupping his face, "you can't take this on by yourself."

Alec pauses, and then a grin slowly breaks over his expression.

"What?" I ask.

"You called me 'honey.'"

"I call everyone 'honey,'" I lie.

He frowns, skeptical. "You absolutely don't strike me as the kind of person to call everyone 'honey.'"

I kiss his chin. "Well, don't read too much into it. Remember, two weeks only."

Lifting his hand, he presses it to my neck, threading his fingers into my hair. Against the sun-warmed skin of my cheek, his palm is cool. He leans forward, salty and wet, and brings his mouth to mine.

Minutes later—many, many minutes later—when we are wrinkled from water and tight with need, we swim back to shore and fall asleep on our towels under the umbrella, beneath the bright, clear blue sky, scores of miles away from stress or responsibility or the eyes of anybody who might want to find us.

# Nine

It's clear Eden has no idea what to do with her face when I walk into the apartment with Alexander Kim only two steps behind me. Her brown eyes go wide and then squeeze shut, and then she does the very last thing I would ever expect brassy, battle-ready Eden Enger to do. She turns and just . . . walks away.

I burst out laughing. "Eden!"

"I can't," she calls out over her shoulder.

"Get back here!" I look at Alec, grinning in amused apology, and pull him inside before chasing her down the hall.

Hooking a hand around her forearm, I turn her to face me. Her cheeks are flushed, eyes wild. "George," she whisper-hisses. "You should have called to tell me that you were bringing—" She points helplessly down the hall. "That!"

"It's Wednesday! I assumed you were working! I'm sorry!"

"People get life in prison for lesser offenses."

I bend, bringing her knuckles to my lips and half laughing against them, half kissing them. "I'm sorry. If I'm being honest, I expected him to realize he couldn't come over and bail. I didn't want to tell you and send you into a cleaning frenzy."

"Alexander Kim is in our apartment," she says, "and I'm unshowered, wearing a Lakers T-shirt and old jeans. The state of our perpetually tidy living room is the least of my worries."

"You look adorable." She really does. Thick black hair in a messy bun, dark eyes glimmering. Everyone who meets Eden loves her because she is so unapologetically herself. "Come on. We're sweaty and tired and sandy anyway." I make puppy eyes at her. "And he's so sweet. Don't be uncomfortable. Think of him as Alec and maybe that will help?"

She presses her fingertips to her lips like it's hitting her all over again who's in her living room. "I swear there was still a part of me that thought you were making shit up and it wasn't him."

"I know you did."

Pointing down the hall, she whispers, "But he's *right there*, Gigi."

"He's gonna hang out, if that's okay?" I tilt my head and smile winningly at her. "Come on. Hang out with us?"

I return to the living room with Eden trailing behind me. Alec stands there in the black jeans he put on before we drove home, with his hands placidly tucked in his pockets, looking around. I am grateful that Eden and I are both relative neat freaks and keep the apartment clean, but even so, it's hard to not see the space through his eyes.

It's small, furnished with a random assortment of furniture we've both collected over the years. A yellow sofa. Big comfy blue chair. Low coffee table we decorated with tiles ourselves a few weeks before my UK trip. The walls are dotted with a hodgepodge collection of paintings by local artists and framed photos of our families and ourselves. I'm sure Alec's place in London could eat our little apartment for a snack. I wonder what he thinks while looking at this space, if he senses what's missing, feels the ghosts of the beloved art and framed photos from college and after, ones we put away in boxes and agreed didn't deserve to grace these walls.

"Eden, this is Alec."

He turns and smiles his real smile—the one that triggers the instinctive smile in response, even through a television screen. I watch her try to keep her composure together when his dimples make a prominent cameo.

She essentially has to frown to keep her face from cracking wide open. Eden narrows her eyes, humming vaguely. "Alex, is it?"

"Stop it." I smack her arm, and beside me, Alec bursts out laughing. "Alec, this is my roommate, Eden."

"It's great to meet you." He reaches out to shake her hand. "Gigi has said wonderful things."

"He's lying," I say, grinning at the two of them. "I told him you're a hell beast."

She shakes his hand and I know her well enough to guess that every molecule of blood has risen to the surface of her skin and is banging at the door. I bet her hand feels like a piece of burning coal in his palm right now.

"I have to say this," she says, voice tight. "I'll do my best to be cool, but I've seen everything you've ever done, and it won't be easy for me to not lose it a little that you're standing in my apartment."

He smiles sweetly. "I get that. I still get nervous around actors I like, too."

She makes a hilarious sound—half moan, half yelp—as she covers her face.

"What can I do to make you feel more comfortable?" he asks.

She laughs from behind her hands. "Probably nothing." She turns jerkily in place, unsure what to do with her body. "Actually, I might drink."

"Well," he says, "I'll drink, too. And if it makes you feel better, I have done incredibly stupid and embarrassing things in front of Gigi."

A laugh rips out of me. "Oh, please. When?"

"You once walked in on me dancing to Eminem in my underwear."

I gape at him. "When was this?"

"I think you were . . . seven? I was thirteen. It was terrible."

"I have zero recollection of this," I tell him, awed. "I'm deeply disappointed in my subpar brain."

Alec laughs. "I really thought I traumatized you."

"Clearly not."

"And the hip-hop at the Larchmont talent show?" he says, wincing.

An image floods my memory and I clap a hand over my mouth. "How did I forget this?"

"Hip-hop?" Eden echoes, finally.

Alec nods, looking at her. "A few of my friends and I were pretty sure we were going to be the next big thing on the LA hip-hop scene when we were . . ." He looks up. "God, maybe sixteen? Gigi and Sunny would watch us practice after school for months."

"They were so bad," I confirm, remembering the routine they'd worked up, with lots of aggressive hip thrusting, empty space being filled with mumbled "yo, yo, yos," and dubious attempts at break dancing. "Wow, keep going, this is great."

"I think that's enough for now."

"This did help a lot." Eden takes a steadying breath. "I can remain conscious for whatever happens next, but I don't think I can call you Alec."

"Okay." He squashes down a charmed smile, and it does nothing to help the dimple situation. "What will you call me?"

She studies him. "Frank."

He lifts one eyebrow. "I look like a Frank?"

She nods. Already I can see her unwinding. "You are my roommate's friend, Frank."

"Sounds good," he says with a decisive nod. "Can Frank order some pizza for Gigi's roommate, Lucy?"

"Does Gigi get a new name, too?" I ask.

"No," Eden says.

Alec agrees easily. "Too many new names to remember."

I turn, walking into the kitchen. "You two seem to have it figured out. Who wants a beer?"

Eden calls out to me, "Just bring the entire six-pack out here. I think we're going to go through them pretty fast."

She's not wrong. We go through the six-pack in only the time it takes us to play four hands of poker, all of which I lose. We're knocking them back not only because beer pairs great with pizza but because the two jokers with me are apparently long-lost fraternity siblings and have turned the entire evening into one big drinking game.

No elbows on the table.

Drink beer in single swallows only.

Last one to touch their nose when the word *love* is used in any song on the Spotify playlist has to drink.

I find out there's a drinking penalty for innocently questioning whether we're freshmen in college again.

And, of course, there are drinking penalties for using the names Alec or Eden. Given that they've never spent time together and therefore have no habit at all of calling each other by their real names, I am the one drinking a lot more than anybody else.

Even so, I realize at some point that Alec is brilliantly dissolving Eden's fangirl tension, and she is unknowingly distracting him from the weight of everything we discussed at the beach today. I adore them both for it.

He sets his third empty bottle down on the table and groans. "I don't think I've had this much beer in years."

"How could you," Eden asks, "and maintain that six-pack?" She squints and I realize she's mentally counting. "Or is it a twelve-pack?"

"Okay, Lucy: drink." I close one eye to focus across the table at her. "New rule, every time Lucy's a creep, she has to take a sip."

Eden laughs, tilting her bottle to her mouth. "Now you're getting the hang of this."

"What if *I'm* a creep?" Alec asks.

"Frank," I say, pointing at him, "is allowed to be a creep, but only with me."

He pauses and then leans over to kiss me before going still with his mouth against mine. His eyes open and he slowly pulls away in realization of what he's done. Across the table, Eden's jaw hangs open.

"You just—" she says, and then tilts her bottle to her lips, taking a single, preemptive Creep Drink again.

With his cheeks flushed from either the beer or the kiss— or both—Alec picks up the cards, shuffling.

He turns his hat around, and the movement catches my eye. Alec Kim, right now, is deadly. Black T-shirt, black jeans, hat on backward. Dimples to die for and they're making a constant show because he's tipsy and Alec is, apparently, a delightful drunk. I keep seeing the realization pass through Eden's expression: *Alexander Kim. Right there.* But the way he teasingly laughs at her from behind his cards, the way he sings badly with the music, the way the professional actor in our house drinks some beer and then has no actual poker face . . . there's just something so perfectly ordinary about him, too.

"We're going to play Trash now," he says, dealing us each ten cards.

"I don't know how to play Trash," I admit.

"Then you'll lose a lot." He grins at me and Eden laughs, delighted. "And this is speed Trash. Here are the rules: If you take longer than two seconds to start your turn, you drink. Winner each round is exempt from rules the following round. Any swear words result in a penalty that is chosen by the previous hand's winner. Got it?"

I can't stop smiling at them. "Not at all," I admit, but Eden is nodding, so we move on. These two are two peas in a pod.

Alec drums his fingers on the edge of the table. Eden cracks her knuckles. They stare each other down and clink bottles, and we begin. I have no idea what the rules are or what we're supposed to be doing but it doesn't matter. Even as the game speeds up, for me time slows, and the music seems to grow louder, and I'm watching my best friend and this part stranger, part lover solve a disagreement over cards with Rock, Paper, Scissors. I'm watching his open-mouthed laugh when she beats him and launches herself to her feet for a victory dance. I'm watching him slap a pile down faster than she does and fall backward laughing. I'm watching her forget for longer and longer bites of time who she thinks he is while she's in the company of who he really is.

I think, *This is a moment I will remember for the entire rest of my life. No matter what happens after this, I will file tonight under Happiness.*

We go hunting for more beverages in the kitchen. Eden digs cookie dough out of the fridge and Alec leans back against the counter, pulling my back to his chest before reaching over and stealing a mound of cookie dough from her spoon. He takes a bite and feeds me some and then presses his cookie lips to my neck.

"Still weird," Eden says as she spoons more out onto a baking sheet. But she doesn't seem to be standing on shaky ground anymore. In fact, she says this teasingly, like it's settled and sorted: Alec-and-Gigi is no longer weird.

But aren't we? Isn't this? We are count-on-one-hand days into this whatever-it-is-we're-doing and not once have I felt like I've had to put on an act to impress him. Maybe that's because I expect it to end, because we stated clearly today that it would—and cleanly. So why pretend? If he doesn't like what he sees, then the worst thing that happens is it ends a little sooner than it would have otherwise. It's not like I won't be devastated either way—I will. I know that now.

We return to the living room with a plate of warm cookies and tea, and Eden turns on John Oliver. I sit on the couch, and before I can pull my legs up crisscrossed on the cushion, Alec sweetly invades my space, lying down with his head in my lap. He takes a bite from his cookie, chewing as he studies where he might take his next one, and on instinct my hand goes to his hair, combing it off his forehead. It feels like silk between my fingers, and I remember touching it when he made love to me in Seattle, when he kissed me between my legs only yesterday, when I swept it off his forehead today in the water.

He hums quietly, taking that second bite, and our eyes meet. "Want one?" he asks, even though I am perfectly capable of reaching the plate myself.

I shake my head. It's a struggle to push away the world outside of this apartment, where the reality of him and our circumstances and the impossibility of an Us feels like a weight on my chest. Instead, I try to remember what it is that he wants, why he's *here*. He's here to just be a guy with his head in a girl's lap.

Eden's voice rises from where she's lying on the floor. "Frank, how does someone like you get an entire day off on a trip like this? If something's canceled, don't they have a million other things waiting to take up your time?"

I can feel his nod on my lap. "I asked them not to reschedule me," he says. "I really needed a day off. I haven't had one in . . ." He pauses, thinking. "I don't even remember the last time I didn't have something scheduled."

His first day off in who knows how long and he spent it with me. My heart feels too big for my body.

"Do your people know you're with her?" she asks, tilting her head to me.

"No," he says. "But they know I grew up around here. So they probably assume I'm seeing old friends."

"Which you are," I say.

He stares up at me, and another vine grows up inside me, wrapping around my wildly beating heart. "Which I am."

# Ten

I dig under the sink for a toothbrush for him, coming up to find him standing directly behind me. His smiling eyes meet mine in the mirror, and like this we brush our teeth, mouths foamy and grinning. Does he feel it, too? This anticipatory giddiness? It's a little like being ten and handed a crisp twenty-dollar bill outside a candy store. There's something delicious in my future and I don't even know where to sink my teeth first.

When I bend to spit and rinse, his hand comes over my waist, beneath my shirt, fingers seeking skin. When we switch positions and he bends, spits, rinses, I wrap my arms around his middle and let myself go blank inside, just holding him and feeling the hard planes of his back pressed flat against my cheek.

In the bedroom, he peels away my clothes without hurry. A gift teasingly unwrapped. It isn't the first time we're touching and looking, but it's the first time there's no ticking clock in my ear.

Though there may be one in his.

I pull his shirt up his torso. "What time do you have to leave in the morning?"

He pauses his exploration of my chest to look at his watch. "Around six."

I glance at the clock on the nightstand. It's a few minutes before eleven. I can work with this.

He moves to taste my neck, hands sliding up over my breasts.

"What are you doing tomorrow?" I ask.

"Some promo shoots." His thumb and finger close over my nipple in a soft pinch. "A fan meet-and-greet and signing at around one thirty, I think." He straightens, looking at me, and finally lets me get his shirt off. "Do you have an office you have to go to?"

I shake my head. "I have a desk, but I'm rarely there."

"Are you working tomorrow?"

"I'll probably make calls," I say. "Follow up on a few things." I don't say Josef Anders's name but it penetrates the space between us like a dark spot in a photograph anyway. My heart begins to thrum in anxiety. The pressure to do this right is intense.

He unbuttons his jeans, distracting me from my impending panic by kicking them off, and then pulls me back onto the bed, guiding me over him.

I look down at him, tracing his jawline with a fingertip. His eyes fall closed, he hums, and from this vantage point, I register how much I like being on top of him because I get to witness how he gives in to pleasure so absolutely. Alec's eyes drift open and he watches me watching him, and the silent moment of understanding makes me ache. Reaching down, he shifts under me to get his boxers off.

I feel like I've been hungry for this since he grew hard

against me underwater, arching in futile weightlessness as we bobbed in the deep ocean surf. The hunger grew with him sleeping silently next to me on the hot sand and on the quiet drive home where he resumed his wandering exploration of my thighs—occasionally pressing a firm hand between my legs and then sliding away, teasing—and somehow reached a frantic peak as I saw how easily he integrated into my life with Eden.

I come over him now, trapping him between us, sliding over his length. Not taking him in, just rocking. "I've been worked up like this all day."

Eyes closed again, he smiles at this, mumbling a soft "Me too" as his hands come up over my breasts. I want to capture this view on film, burn it into my long-term memory: Alec on my bed, Alec underneath me. The long line of his neck, the sharp point of his Adam's apple, the masculine curve of his collarbones. He has a small bruise on his chest that looks like a bite mark, from yesterday or the time before. I don't even know. It would easily be hidden beneath a shirt, but it's there in front of me like our perfect little secret, and the knowledge of it lights me up like sunrise inside.

"Gigi," he says, eyes drifting open. "Take me in."

He licks and sucks at my chest when I lean over him to dig in my nightstand. I feel him go still for a fraction of a second when he hears me open a new box of condoms. And I see the smile in his eyes when I look at his face as I tear the foil. He's still looking at me as I turn my attention down, as I put the condom on him with less grace and speed than when he put one on himself our first time.

"Why are you smiling?"

"You know why," he whispers.

I can't help it. I love the weight of him in my hand. If I didn't feel the gravity of my own need, I would play and tease and touch with fingers and tongue, but I'm impatient and he is, too, arching his hips, hands urging me forward and over him.

It's only the second time he's been inside me, and the moment I sink down I have to cup my hand over his groaning mouth, bite down on my own lip so I don't cry out.

He presses his head back into the pillow, neck corded with restraint, and it feels like every part of my brain turns on. My body becomes a precision machine, working the hard length of him into me again and again, moving against him, finding what feels good. After we find a rhythm together, he stares up at me, eyes black, mouth moving in silent speech. His mouth forms a silent, *Like that?*; a soundless *Fuck* spoken through a smile. I stare at his lips as I move, watching him lick them. Watching them make quiet sounds of pleasure. Watching as he pulls them back in a dirty little growl.

This focus means pleasure comes at me sideways, rising like a ship out of darkness until it's there in the deepest part of me, climbing up my spine and filling my chest with a cry I trap there, lips sealed and head thrown back. For a second I lose track of what he's doing while I'm falling; all I can do or feel is my own relief and what seems like a streak of wild silver tearing through me.

Just as I start to come down, he sits up, almost like he can't take it anymore, digging a hand into my hair and coming for my mouth. Alec rolls us over, taking charge again, and I have a thought that feels almost like a brag, a betrayal, that if anyone ever saw him like this, they might fall into madness knowing he's exactly what the world wants him to be behind closed doors.

I love his breathless laugh—the sound I've come to recognize as his elated disbelief.

"Shh," he whispers down at me, and then I get it, what made him laugh, what made him happy—my melting down beneath him, the way I'd started to let out these tiny rhythmic cries, forgetting where we are, and the roommate only two walls away. His hand comes firmly over my mouth, and he presses a kiss to my cheek, reducing his movements into tiny, teasing snaps of his hips. "Are you trying to wake up the neighborhood?"

Turning my face into his neck, I press my mouth there, whispering an apology I don't mean, an apology he doesn't want. "I like watching you struggle to be quiet as much as I like making you loud," he says, and then, testing me, he pushes up onto his hands, staring with playful warning before he starts to move in long, hard strokes.

But at some point, we transition from frenzied to slow. With him over me, holding me, his mouth open against my neck, I fall into a pleasure trance. This is making love without a goal, just moving together, lost in the same thing. I've never in my life felt so connected to someone before, like we're sharing the same high. I wrap my arms all the way around him and try to focus on every tiny sensation: the smooth glide of his chest over mine, the quiet sounds carried on his breath against my neck, the warm, gentle friction of his hips against my thighs, and the thick drag of him in and out and in and deeper in.

Afterward, a long time later, when he's come to a gasping stop over me—sweat-slick and worn-out—he collapses at my side, turns on the light, and runs his fingertips along my hairline, down over my jaw, looking at me. Touching my ribs, tracing the mark his teeth left on my breast. Sliding his hand down my stomach, he comes to a gentle stop between my legs.

"You're so warm. Are you sore?"

"No." Sleepily, I drag my finger along his collarbone. "Maybe I will be tomorrow."

He turns his gaze away from my face and down to where his fingers rest over me. My fevered pulse still beats there. "I can't stop touching you."

"I know." I close my eyes. I don't feel like I'm living in the same world I do during daylight. If this is what contentment is, I never want to leave this bed. "I like it."

His fingertip runs over my clit, slowly circling. "I like this tiny, soft part of you. I like what happens to your expression when I touch you here."

My voice is slow and drowsy. "What happens?"

"I'll have to make up a word for it. It's like relieved begging." I laugh as he pushes up onto an elbow to get a better look at my face. I'd be self-conscious if I were more awake. Or if it wasn't Alec. "You're so beautiful it makes me feel this sweet sort of anguish. I'm desperate for you, Gigi."

"Desperate for me? Please. I'm a sure thing."

A distracted smile is there and gone. "Before I return to London, I'd like to state for the record that I claim this bottom lip." He shifts his touch. "But also this single freckle on your shoulder. I've gone hunting and it's your only one."

He gives me a thoughtful once-over. "Your eyes when you laugh—they're also mine. The curve of your spine when you're coming. The soft skin of your thighs against my neck." His hand returns, cupping me between my legs. "And this, right here. I'm greedy for these things."

"My turn." I reach up, tracing his mouth. "I claim *your* bottom lip."

He blows out a breath against my touch. "You have to pick something new."

"Shh. You don't make the rules." Moving my fingertips down over his chin, I stroke lower. "Your throat. I have a thing for throats and yours is perfect. The back of your neck." I trace down. "Collarbones. This muscle right here," I stroke just inside his hipbone, and he shifts away, ticklish. I pull his hand up, kissing his palm. "And your hands."

He laughs. "Of course my hands."

I squint at him. "I'd say your dimples, too, but everyone says that."

"Do they?" he asks, already knowing.

"There is a Twitter account called AKDimples that has, like, three hundred thousand followers and it's almost entirely just pictures of your dimples when you're smiling in various photos."

He laughs again. "You're making that up."

"You know I'm not."

"How do you possibly know about it?" he asks. "You won't even watch my show."

"Eden showed me." I take a deep breath, pressing my hand to his chest. "She follows it. Asked me if they really do taste like candy."

He takes a second to process this.

"Asked you whether my *dimples* taste like candy?" His next laugh comes out as a quiet puff of air, and he looks mildly horrified. "People wonder this?"

"That's probably the most innocent thing they imagine tasting, Alec."

He frowns, and I kiss his sweet pout. "Well, do they?" he asks, finally, grinning.

"Do they what?"

"Taste like sugar."

"No."

"What do they taste like?"

"Happiness."

Beside me, he goes still. I think I've made it weird; we were being silly and playful until I got sincere. I'll have to do a better job at tucking away these new spring-green feelings, because they're too exuberant. They want to burst out into the sky.

Finally he says, "I'll start the account Gigi's Bottom Lip."

A relieved laugh erupts from my throat. "You'll get one follower."

"No way. Wait till you see my profile pic."

"Do you even know how to use Twitter?"

His *Shhh* is as good as a no, but he waves me off. "I'll have more followers than that guy on your new hat."

"You only need one follower: AKDimples. They're already well acquainted."

"They are," he says, kissing my chin. "Best friends, even."

Something foreign clutches my heart, twisting the organ in its grip.

"Have you ever really been in love?" I ask, out of absolutely nowhere.

But the question doesn't seem to surprise him at all. "I don't know." He looks down at his hand as it roams up my waist, coming to a gentle landing over my breast. "Have you?"

I close my eyes and coax his head to my neck, answering just before sleep pulls me under. "I don't know, either."

Alec's alarm goes off at five, and we drag our eyes open, doing everything from the night before in reverse. We touch and cuddle for a few drowsy minutes, wordlessly, with slow, sleep-heavy hands. We stand at my bathroom sink, brushing teeth, making foamy-toothpaste faces in the mirror. And then we pad out to the kitchen, where I insist on making him some coffee before he goes.

"You could still be in bed," he whispers, careful to not wake up Eden only two doors down the hall. "You don't have to get up, too."

"Then I wouldn't get more time with you," I say, "and you wouldn't get to taste my coffee."

"It's good then?"

I reconsider while filling up the kettle. "Maybe I shouldn't brag. I bet you have a robot that handpicks your beans and roasts them to order before brewing."

"I usually drink whatever Yael brings me or whatever's on set. I'm not that picky, actually."

I point to a stool at the kitchen counter, set the kettle to heat, and reach for my canister of beans. "Do you have to return the car today? I can do it for you."

He shakes his head. "I think Yael picked it up last night."

"What?"

Alec clearly doesn't understand my astonishment. "What what?"

"She came over while you were hanging out here last night and stealthily returned the rental car?"

"What else did she have to do yesterday?" he asks, laughing. "She was more annoyed that I took off than she was to be given something to do at, what? Seven at night? It isn't like I called her at three in the morning to drive to San Diego and back."

"I guess." I measure out some beans, pouring them into the grinder. "Plug your ears."

He does, cutely, bringing his shoulders up like the sound of the beans grinding might actually be earsplitting. The sharp cracking and metallic whir cut through the quiet, and then I pour the grounds into the filter and glance over my shoulder at him. "Yael," I begin, treading carefully. "What's she like?"

Alec hums, pulling a pen from a mug on the counter and doodling on the back of some junk mail. "She's incredible," he says carefully. "She's quite reserved. Shy. But although it takes a while to get to know her, she's deeply loyal. She just isn't going to bend over backward to please someone she doesn't know."

Well, that certainly explains the silent elevator ride the other day. "How long has she worked for you?"

"About five years," he says and, at my look, clarifies, "She moved to Korea after I finished my military service. But I've known her since she was about fourteen."

"Wow."

He nods. "Her mother was my parents' housekeeper. She was at our house a lot."

"She is around my and Sunny's age, then?"

"They're close." He pauses, chewing on the next bit of information. "Yael modeled for a bit when she and Sunny were eighteen and nineteen, but she didn't enjoy it. She's organized and bossy but shy." Drawing a series of concentric circles around the border of a Trader Joe's mailer, he says, "I guess that's a better fit behind the scenes than in front of a camera."

"Does she know that I know you from before?"

He nods.

My next question feels sticky in my throat, but I have to ask it. "Have you two ever . . ."

He meets my eyes, and when understanding hits, Alec lets out a short, easy laugh. "No. It hasn't ever been like that with us." Smiling, he adds, "Yael is a lesbian."

The kettle whistles and I turn to get it, pouring the water carefully over the ground coffee and watching it percolate into the carafe. The quiet feels full, like he's swallowing his next words down.

"This looks very fancy," he says.

"It is. Be impressed and grateful."

Alec laughs. "Oh, I am." When I hand him a steaming mug he takes it but then sets it down on the counter and reaches for me, pulling me between his legs. "Thank you, Georgia Ross, impressive barista."

"You're welcome." I kiss him, fighting the urge to sink further into the contact. "How do you take it?"

Alec's hand comes up under my T-shirt. "However you'd like it."

I lightly flick his forehead. "I mean your coffee."

"Cream, sugar. The more it tastes like ice cream, the better."

I groan, turning to the fridge. "This coffee is wasted on you."

"It's not," he protests, laughing as he takes the offered cream and tilts it generously over his mug, "I promise to enjoy it."

"If you don't have your car, how are you getting to your hotel?"

Alec lifts his arm. "Pickup in about ten."

"Yael?"

He nods.

"And then busy all day?"

He nods again. "You should come to the cast signing."

"I don't watch the show," I say, quickly adding, "*Yet!* I promise to start. But I'd feel bad taking a ticket from a fan."

For some reason, this makes him laugh. "You wouldn't need a ticket, Gigi. I'm not suggesting you go stand in line for an autograph. You'd come as my guest. Bring Eden."

I cover his mouth. "Careful what you offer. She kept it surprisingly bottled up last night. If you invite her today, she might show up wearing a shirt with your face on it. Or even worse: a shirt with your torso on it."

"It's all fine," he says, "as long as she's aware the dimples are taken."

I cup his face, kissing each cheek. "Gigi's bottom lip approves."

# Eleven

I get a brief text from an unknown number about an hour after Alec leaves and identify Yael from the brevity: Meet at the side entrance to the Ace Hotel off Blackstone at one sharp. Text this number when you arrive.

With this information in hand, I dance my way into Eden's room, where she's lying on her back in bed, her laptop balanced on her knee. I hear Alec's voice through the tinny speakers, and it's shockingly surreal.

"What are you watching?"

"*West Midlands*." She glances briefly at me and smirks. "Your boy's just about to get in a car accident."

I scoot over beside her. "Will this traumatize me?"

"The crash?" She glances at me. "No, but the kissing will."

"Oh." I wave this off. "I watched all those gifs in the Lyft home."

"I knew it, you little shit."

I steal one of her pillows and tuck it under my head. "Okay," I relent. "Catch me up."

"You want to watch it *now*?"

"Well," I say, and grin over at her, "we're going to a cast signing today as Alec's guests, so I should know at least a little about the rest of this show."

She stares at me, unblinking. "What."

"It's at the Ace Hotel. Oh," I say, realizing, "you need to call in sick to work. Alec's cyborg assistant sent me directions to get in the side door." I point to my chest. "I'm Hollywood connected now, you know."

Eden lets out an earsplitting scream and tackles me. Somewhere in the distance, her laptop knocks against a wall. "Do I get to meet them all?"

"I assume so."

She screams again, and I wrap my arms around her wiry body.

It's the last moment she's pleased with me for a while, though, because I am hopeless otherwise. I need a full summary of the show, can only point to faces and say, "He looks familiar," or, "Oh, he was in that one movie where we saw a flash of dick, right?"

But by the end of this very cursory overview, I can say three things with absolute confidence: (1) This show looks dramatic and addicting; (2) I can absolutely understand why the entire world wants to believe he's sleeping with his co-star, Elodie Fabrón—as in, their chemistry is genuinely fever-inducing; and, relatedly, (3) without question, I need to find a way to make sure Alec Kim ends up in my bed tonight.


We get to the event early—parking down the street just after noon and hovering outside the side door. It's hot as hell, and

Eden pesters me to text Yael early. I don't know Yael but I know her enough to be able to tell Eden to shut it; we will text at exactly one o'clock and not a moment sooner.

But from where we stand, we're able to see the line that snakes around the block and loops back on itself. I know many of the fans lined up are here to see the famous *Doctor Who* actor who plays *West Midlands*'s first heartthrob, or the bombshell from the blockbuster DC superhero franchise, but some of them—many of them, probably—are here specifically to see Alec.

I have a handful of copyeditor questions to address for the article before it goes to press and a call to take with Ian about what he's digging up back in London, so I am grateful for some downtime. Even so, it is a surreal experience to do my job surrounded by hundreds—maybe thousands—of people who have likely taken a day off work to come see a group of famous people in person. Once I send my last email, Eden and I fall quiet in mild awe at the scale of this event, eavesdropping on scattered breathless conversations. I love my best friend's fangirling side, love how fully and unself-consciously Eden loves the things she loves. But I've never had that bone, even in moments when I watched her and it looked like she was having a blast. Unless it's for work, I don't have the ability to dive headlong into something and spend hours thinking of nothing else.

But people-watching here—listening in on the conversations of the people who stand idly in the line that stretches down Blackstone and past us—makes me realize these fans easily know more about Alec's life than I do. Some women near us talk about the pens they brought in his favorite color (red) and wonder whether he'll sign their shirts (Alec is, apparently, the only member of the cast to never sign an item on someone's body). They talk about his smile, how it takes him a few minutes to look comfortable, how he is always the slowest in the signing line because he talks to everyone. They argue over whether he's scheduled to be at Comic-Con, and say inside-joke lines to each other that I can only assume are dialogue from one of his shows.

I have to tune them out once they pull out their phones and start opening their favorite photos and gifs. I'm sure he's shirtless in more than half of them. I have a weird dark shadow in my mind thinking about them looking at his naked body.

"Is this weird for you?" Eden asks quietly, reading my mind.

I laugh at her timing. "Very."

"Fangirls are intense."

"I don't mind that," I tell her, honestly. "I love seeing you get excited about things. I just feel like a fish out of water. I'm aware these women probably know more about him than I do."

I feel her watching me, agreeing silently, and my mood sinks further into discomfort. I want to see Alec in his element, but there's a part of me—even though I know he doesn't operate this way—that worries that I'll disappear in this crowd. That he'll see me here and realize I'm nothing special. I never felt that way, never worried about it for a second until I was surrounded by hundreds of his fans. Why are we mixing our lives like this?

But it's too late to bail: Eden is vibrating next to me.

I would never dream of dragging her away from this. I think, *Just get through it.*

At one, I finally text Yael, We're here.

There's no response, but a few minutes later a door opens and she pops her head out, meeting my eyes for only a second before she's gesturing for us to come in. I catch the grumbling of some women behind us, the loud cries of some farther down in the line—"Take us, too!"—and then the heavy steel door seals us up in a long, bare hallway.

Yael and her mile-long legs march us quickly down the hall, and she stops at a blank door. "Just hang out, okay?" she says, her words clipped. "Alexander will come say hello when he can."

I think that's code for *Don't pester the talent*, but she doesn't have to worry, regardless. As soon as we step into what I realize is the cast greenroom, I immediately regret coming. There are maybe forty people milling around, talking, and they all look like they've been professionally groomed since birth. Eden is unironically wearing a *My Lucky Year* T-shirt with Alec's face on it, and I am dressed for obscurity in black jeans and a black tank top. My hair is twisted up on top of my head; I went for minimal makeup, figuring no one would be looking at me anyway.

I couldn't be more wrong. Everyone looks up as we enter, gawping in silence for a second at the entrance of two women who are clearly Just Fans. Conversation hiccups awkwardly until they decide we are uninteresting, and we are immediately forgotten. Somehow this makes me infinitely more self-conscious. Any movement we make could bring attention back to us. I recognize a few faces from film and TV, including Alec's on-screen girlfriend, Elodie Fabrón. Finally, I spot Alec near the far wall, engaged in conversation with someone I don't recognize. Alec is so engrossed, in fact, that he and the other man are maybe the only people who didn't look up when we entered.

Skirting around the edge of the room, Eden and I try to find a space to occupy where we aren't in anyone's way. My best friend is clearly in fangirl heaven and looks like she hasn't lived a minute before today, but I am so uncomfortable I might as well be naked in the middle of a foreign city. I am aware that everyone in this room is somehow connected to the show—everyone but us. We hover at the edge near a snack table, but then someone wants to grab something, so we shift to the far wall, but it's where the cast have left their personal items and we're asked to move. Alec is still busy talking with the man who looks vaguely director-y and hasn't even seen us yet.

*Why are we here?* I want to text him from the Batphone, which, coincidentally, felt like a fun secret-agent gadget before but now makes me feel vaguely sleazy. I'd be so much more comfortable hearing about this event from him later, in the privacy of his room or my apartment, but I know if I tried to tug Eden's Alec shirt and coax her to the door, she would burst into flames and burn me alive.

Suddenly there is a commotion near the door, and a woman stands on a chair, clapping her hands.

"Hey, everyone," she calls. "Give me your eyes for just a second." The room slowly settles into a rumbling quiet. "They've started letting people into the venue. We'll head in there in about ten minutes. The order is: Dan, Alexander, Elodie, Ben, Gal, Becca, then Dev. The format is a moderated

Q&A and your host is"—she points to the side and grins— "this guy right here."

I can't see The Guy Right There, but everyone breaks out in loud applause, whistling and catcalling, so I have to assume he's someone interesting. Only when Eden leans over and whispers, "Trevor Noah," do I actually start to feel the impact of how much celebrity is in this room with us.

When the woman is done with her spiel, she gets off the chair and everyone returns to the conversations from before, but there's a new energy in the room. I can hear vague sounds coming from down the hall: applause, screams, the vibrating cacophony of a lot of bodies in a small space. I look around, and just as my eyes pass over the corner where Alec had been, his scanning gaze catches mine.

I watch his mouth form a surprised *There you are*, and he immediately excuses himself to push through the room toward us. He's wearing a slim-fitting black button-down shirt and dark jeans, but his best accessory is his face-splitting, eye-crinkling smile. My heart drops to my feet.

A few people notice us again, and my skin itches at their attention. I resist the urge to hide behind Eden. Alec comes up to us, shaking our hands—this, too, is very weird—and smiling warmly at us. "You two made it!"

Eden utters something high-pitched and unintelligible in response, and Alec whisks her away to introduce her to a few people nearby. Great. And now I'm alone.

But only a minute later, she is enthusiastically engaged in conversation with a hugely famous American actress, and I am watching Alec return to me, wearing a different smile now. One that feels like a private gift just for me.

I ignore the eyes on him as he approaches, wanting his expression and this secret between us to be the only thing I see and feel. He stops a foot away and, with his back to the room, has the luxury of giving my body a long, seductive once-over.

"Hey."

I try to plaster a polite smile on my mouth. "Hi."

"Why didn't you text me that you were here?"

"You're . . ." I flounder. "You're in famous-person mode."

He pulls his lower lip into his mouth and narrows his eyes, studying me. "You hate this, don't you?"

"A normal amount."

Alec laughs. "I wanted you here, but you look uncomfortable. It was selfish."

I glance to the room behind him. "I'm okay, I promise. I just—" I look back at him and laugh. "You'll get maybe one minute with me before you go."

"I just like knowing you're here," he says. "Does that make sense?"

I nod. It does make sense. Everything about him just *makes sense*.

He looks like he wants to kiss me. His cheeks are flushed, eyes bright. In my peripheral vision, I see the woman from the chair lead Trevor Noah out of the greenroom, and only seconds later, sound reaches us. I can hear people screaming. *Women* screaming. It sounds like a cloud of bees, a roaring swarm.

I don't think I'm ready to be truly faced with the reality of his celebrity yet. All of our moments up to now—except for the airport in LA—have been just us. Him as a man, me as a woman. The two of us falling forward into something neither of us can really label. I'm not a person who ever wanted something like this. Being with a celebrity isn't in my fantasy spank bank. I want the Seattle hotel, the LA hotel. I want our beach day; I want last night, goofing off with Eden. I want later, in my bed, with him telling me again how he needs to find a new word to describe my expression when he touches me. I want to hear him say again that he's desperate for me.

Alec captures my chin with his thumb and finger, redirecting my attention so that I meet his eyes. "Don't."

"How can I not?" I shake my head, laughing. "I knew, but I didn't *realize*."

"Look at my face." He stares at me, and his focus is so intense that slowly, the sound of screaming ebbs away. The periphery turns milky white. "I need to ask you something important."

I bite back a smile at his earnest sincerity. "Okay."

"You don't have to answer right now, but I probably won't get another chance today."

"Okay."

He leans in, and his lips are so close I feel them moving against the shell of my ear. "I think you should move into my suite for the remainder of my stay." I feel a pop in my ears as my brain equilibrates. Alec pulls back, wide-eyed, gauging my reaction before leaning back in, moving on. "You can work from there. We won't have to worry about press or moving back and forth. We can maximize the time we have left."

"So that it can be even harder when you go?" I say unintentionally—the words just fly out of me, unattended.

Frowning, he looks back and forth between my eyes before dropping his focus to my lips. He licks his, like he's thinking about how it would feel to press his mouth to mine, and instinctively, I lick mine, too.

"Well," he says finally. "That's why you don't have to answer now. Just send me a text. If the answer is yes, I can give you a key."

The cast is led out and the rest of us follow in a long, disorganized mob of hangers-on. Eden and I have no instruction as to where to stand or what we're expected to do, but once we emerge out to the event space, I forget to be at all concerned with that. Because all I can focus on is the wall of sound, the sea of people.

The room is massive, filled with rows and rows and rows of seats, and there must be no fire marshal within shouting distance, because standing bodies line the side and back walls. At the front of the room is a long table with chairs for each of the invited guests, with name placards crisply propped on the white tablecloth. As the group files in and the *West Midlands* team find their seats, the room shakes with noise. It takes Trevor a good minute to get everyone to settle down so that he can make introductions. And after that, there is a short Q&A session before the signing.

None of the questions mean much to me; they are about previous seasons, or teaser tidbits for what's coming up. One or two are personal in nature, even though fans were requested not to ask those. Is Ben dating that singer? He reminds the audience he's married. Are Alexander and Elodie together in real life? They both give vaguely unconvincing answers, but I get it: the rumor keeps viewers locked in.

I focus less on listening to his answers than I do on noticing Alec's easy manner in front of a crowd this size. I would be a fidgety, stammering mess; even when he's answering something that seems impossibly intimate, he seems to slow down, settle into his spine. His deep, quiet voice takes on a sparkling, flirtatious edge.

He wants me to stay in his hotel room with him. Would that be insane? I'm already hungry for every second I can get with him, but watching him like this makes me feel like a greedy monster, plotting how I can sneak behind the table and drag his chair behind the BBC-Netflix curtain to put my hands all over him.

Just as I have this thought, a voice rises up from beside me. "This trip is a novelty for him."

I look over, surprised to find Yael standing not two feet away. "I'm sorry?"

"Alexander." She lifts her chin, indicating the man himself now welcoming the first group of fans at the signing table. "This trip isn't how things usually are," she says. "The time he has with you?" She looks at me, brows raised as if I might not know what she means. "He doesn't generally have time for relationships."

I rarely go mentally blank, but right now I have no idea what I'm supposed to say to this. "I'm sure he's really busy."

"He is." She pauses and then delivers her thesis: "I don't want you to have expectations, Georgia."

Still at a loss for words, I can only give her a little nod so that she knows I've heard her. Expectations? I don't know what that means. He just invited me to stay in his hotel with him for the rest of his trip. Maybe her first conversation should be with him, not me.

Yael walks away, leaving me staring at Alec as he leans in to hear a teenage fan better. He ducks down to her level, making eye contact. I know exactly what she feels right now with those warm brown eyes fixed right on hers: that teenager feels like the only person in this entire room. But for me, the room spins. Alec invited me here. Asked me to stay with him in his suite, and his assistant is telling me I should leave him alone. Of course I want to be near him, but I also want to do what's best for him.

"Am I supposed to pretend I didn't hear that?" Eden asks from my other side.

"No."

She sucks in a breath through her teeth. "Ouch."

"I don't think I've done anything to indicate that I think this is going anywhere."

"I think," Eden says, "that she's trying to tell you she's worried Alexander Kim *wants* it to go somewhere."

Digesting this, I watch him accept a handmade gift from a fan. A handler tries to take it, to put it in a box, but Alec shakes his head, wanting it with him on the table. "He asked me to come stay at the hotel with him."

"Seriously?"

I nod.

"Are you going to?"

"I want to, but I think that's the equivalent of sticking a hot skewer in my own heart in nine days."

"God, you are dramatic."

I look at her. "You'd do it?"

"You know the answer to that. But I'd probably also take the job of Alexander Kim Belt Polisher if it was offered."

I chew my lip, staring at the view of his long neck as he leans over the table to shake the hand of a fan in a wheelchair. I can so easily imagine his sweet, attentive expression, the deep pull of his dimples when he smiles and thanks her for coming.

But also I can imagine the sound he'll make when he kicks off his shoes later. When he falls into satisfied exhaustion onto the sofa in his suite. I can imagine how he would pull me onto his lap and unleash a happy little growl into my neck.

Maybe we'd order room service for dinner. He'd offer me a bite of his food, nodding happily when he sees I like it. He would ask what I want to watch on TV. He would distract me anyway, with his hands and mouth. We'd give up and make love instead.

My brain shorts out at the phrase. *Make love*.

That isn't what we're doing, but even if it were . . . I want it. Even for just a handful of days, I want it.

OK, I text him from the Batphone, and try to ignore the way my stomach tightens when I imagine Yael's reaction to the rest of it. I'll stay in your suite.

# Twelve

I knew it was coming today, but when Billy texts me at three thirty that my story is going up online in advance of the print edition in the morning, I am consumed with the jittery nausea I've only felt a handful of times before. I'm in an Uber, headed to the Waldorf Astoria in Beverly Hills, with a key to room 1001 burning like a lit match in my pocket, and my first big story at the *LA Times* is going live in a half hour.

Alec will probably be at the signing for at least two more hours. I couldn't follow all of the specifics—blue, green, and red wristbands, VIP fan packages—but when they took a break while switching wristband groups, he found me, pressed a key into my palm, and told me to head over whenever I wanted and he would meet me here later. For a handful of seconds, I thought about telling him that Yael wouldn't be thrilled, that in Yael-speak she'd asked me to chill the fuck out, and that essentially moving in together is the opposite of chill. But he's known her for nearly fifteen years. Without question, he'd already have to know where Yael landed with all of this.

The entire walk through the gleaming hotel lobby to the

elevator, I expect to be stopped and asked if I need directions or help. I grew up in Santa Monica; I went to school with the children of celebrities. I don't feel out of place in the fancier LA spaces, but I was also raised by parents who help me when needed but don't support me anymore. I carry myself, and that means I support myself in LA each month on what many people in this hotel are paying for a weekend getaway in California. My suitcase is probably worth less than a box of the straws they use in the bar, and I'm still wearing what I had on for the signing. After a sweaty, muggy day, the straps of my black tank top are—predictably—much less robust than the straps of my bra and seem to take turns sliding off my shoulders.

But stepping into the air-conditioned calm of Alec's suite feels like stepping out of the LA I've known my whole life. I mean, at no point in my adult existence would I ever experience a hotel this way unless I was here for an interview. A villa suite, it said on the gold-plated placard outside the door. A hallway leads to a wide circular living room with seafoam-green furniture, gold and white accent pillows, and lamps and a coffee table that probably each cost more than my monthly rent. A dining room is separated from the space by an open bookshelf dotted with tasteful curios: a black-and-white Art Deco vase, a brushed-brass statue of a horse, art books, framed black-and-white prints.

Dragging my hand along the dining table, I take in the Asian-inspired sideboard, the delicate gold prints on the walls, the plush white chairs—six of them, like we might host a dinner party. The windows span the back wall of the dining room and living room, curving along the path of the building and revealing an unreal view of the enormous terrace and the Hollywood Hills beyond. This is the view people imagine when they think of Los Angeles. Not the traffic-clogged, billboard-dense stretches of Sepulveda north of LAX or the wire tangle of freeways smack in the middle of the city but this: wide-open sky, lush green hills, palm trees lining wide streets.

I pull out my phone, texting Eden. Having a Pretty Woman moment.

Be more specific, she answers. Were you shunned from stores or are you in a bubble bath?

Neither. But this suite is unreal.

It had better be.

I grin down at her Alexander Kim adoration and drop my phone in my purse, leaving it slung over a dining room chair as I explore the rest of the suite.

I've had this man inside me, have kissed nearly every inch of his body, and yet I still break out into a cold sweat when I see the enormous, neatly made four-poster bed stacked with plush white pillows. It's such a picturesque bedroom it's almost absurd, and all I can think about is how it's a bed for honeymooners. For consummating something, and we're going to sleep here. Out of four nights, we've already spent two together, and now *this* is our bed. I think about my bed at home—a comparatively tiny full-size mattress; it wasn't nearly long enough for him, but it didn't matter. I know now that if Alec could have his way, he would curl up, be my big spoon all night. Better yet, he would sleep on top of me.

Just as I walk into the bathroom and catch sight of the truly mammoth tub overlooking the Hills, my phone starts to explode with texts, with emails. For a few minutes I'd forgotten that this room wasn't the only way my life was changing today.

The story is live.

I hear the sound of the key, the door unlocking, and then Alec is making his way down the short hallway.

"Gigi?" he calls out.

Relief and excitement hit with laser precision right at the center of my chest. I've been reading a book—getting my mind off the comments flowing in online, the reactions from the community and the *LA Times* staff—but I drop it onto the coffee table just as he emerges into the suite's living room. His face erupts in a relieved smile.

"You're here."

I bite my lips, attempting to tamp down my urge to scream in happiness. He's wearing what he had on at the signing, but it feels like he's changed; everything about his posture is somehow more relaxed. Relieved, maybe. "Hey."

His gaze tracks around the room as he clocks my shoes at the end of the hallway, my suitcase tucked against the wall, my book facedown on the table. "Good," he murmurs. "You brought things."

What a weird feeling this is. We're going to be staying together. *Living* together, in this suite. Meals and sleep and showers and work. We can't commit to anything beyond this, but we've committed to this much, at least. Temporary cohabitation but indefinite infatuation.

He comes over, bracing his hands on the back of the

couch as he bends to kiss me. "I'll be right back." Disappearing, he heads into the bathroom and I hear the water running. Alec Kim would never dream of touching me with dirty hands.

But when he returns, we don't immediately strip down. Instead of being rushed and heated, the vibe in the air is wide-open, full of oxygen and space and time. He crosses the room to the minibar, bending to retrieve two bottles of water. "How was your afternoon?"

"My story went up."

He turns, eyes wide. "Wait—today?"

I nod, beaming.

Alec pulls his phone from his pocket. "Drop me the link." When I do, I watch as his eyes scan the story before jumping back to the top to start all over. "This is good."

Pride is a warm hit of sunshine. "Thank you."

"I mean," he says, and comes to stand closer, "this is a really well-written story on the subject. Informative but not rubbernecking."

I fight the urge to deflect the compliment, saying only, "Good."

"How's the response?"

"Great so far. My phone was blowing up, and I started to feel restless in my own skin, so I put it down to read for a while out on the terrace." *But then I came inside*, I don't say, *knowing you'd be here soon.*

Alec looks up. "It's nice, isn't it?"

"The terrace?" I laugh. "'Nice.' Yes, it's nice."

He collapses beside me on the couch, unscrewing the cap on his water and tossing it onto the table. "On a scale from it-was-perfect to you-almost-never-called-me-again," he says, "how much did you hate the signing today?"

Reaching over, I pull a tiny piece of paper confetti from his collar. "I didn't hate it."

"Liar."

"I didn't," I insist. "I'm used to being around important people, but in a professional capacity. There I felt a little bit . . ." I try to find the right word. "I felt a little dismissed because I was 'just' there as a fan. It was a weird experience."

Alec takes a long drink and nods as he swallows. "I get that. It's the thing I probably like least about the culture."

"Let's just say your celebrity status is *not* why I'm with you."

His dark eyes shine when he looks over at me, smiling. "Why are you with me?"

I poke a finger in his dimple, drag it over his lips and down his throat.

"Of course." His laugh vibrates against my fingertip, and he sits up, reaching for my book on the table. "What's this?" I don't answer because he's already looking for himself. "Is it good?"

I shrug. "I'm only about fifty pages in, but I like it so far."

As he reads the cover flap, I reach over, finger-brushing the hair at his temple. "How was the rest of the event?"

"Good. Photo ops." He sets the book down and reaches up, massaging his cheeks.

"Lots of smiling?"

He laughs, nodding, and shifts so that he's lying with his head in my lap. Alec stares up at me. "I'm so glad you agreed," he says finally. I watch as he takes a deep breath and gives it ten beats to fully exit his body.

"Me too." Seeing my presence as a relief to him is a bit like drinking champagne. I tingle all over.

"I don't think I realized how badly I wanted you here until I saw you."

"Well," I say, bending to kiss his forehead, "I'm glad."

"Will you be able to work here?"

I nod. "It'll be quieter here than it would be at my place. This week is going to be nuts, so I can work while you're out being England's heartthrob."

"Oh." This piques his interest. "What's going on?"

"Billy is all in," I say. "He anticipated this blowing up and brought in our London correspondent to do the heavy lifting on the follow-ups, which means a shared byline, but I honestly couldn't do it from here anyway. This guy, Ian, usually covers the politics desk, so he's great. He went back and looked into guest logs and video footage and discovered what I actually knew already, which is that there is no record of who came into or left the club on the nights we know the chat-room videos were recorded. Or the night you went to get Sunny."

Alec frowns. "Really?"

"Those records have been 'misplaced,' " I say with implied air quotes. "However"—I hold up my index finger, and grin proudly—"there is a hotel next door to the club, the Hotel Maxson. Well, the parking lot where nonhotel guests tend to park to access the club is not attached to the hotel. It's a separate structure that is closer to the outdoor entrance of Jupiter. And the company that manages security there is independent of the club security, which you probably re-member is run by the father of one of the owners. Turns out this other security outfit keeps footage for six months, and no one has bothered asking them for it."

Sitting up, Alec turns to face me. His voice is quiet, but every letter is enunciated: "What does that mean, specifically?"

"It means that although we don't have a guest log for Ju-piter for the dates corresponding to the videos, Ian was able to get the footage from the parking lot that most club guests use to park their personal vehicles. It isn't ideal—obviously, video of everyone entering or leaving the club itself would be better for time-stamp purposes, but if Josef—or any of the other owners or affiliated VIPs—parked in this structure, we'll get a record of the dates and times they could feasibly have been inside the club."

"This is great," he breathes.

"And," I add, beaming, "although things are sketchy with the club surveillance, the Hotel Maxson is cooperating so we can cross-reference their lobby footage with the parking structure surveillance footage so, for example, if we see Josef parking in the lot but do not see him in the Maxson, he can't simply say he was visiting the hotel bar."

"How many hours of footage is there to go through?"

I laugh. "*So* many hours." Finger-combing his hair again, I say, "Welcome to journalism. But it helps that we have a number of dates to start with, and Ian has a few interns work-ing on those. They'll send us possible segments to review to-morrow and cross-check against names. I'm only going to be support from here on out so I can more quietly focus on the Josef Anders of it all."

He looks up at me and nods. I know without having to ask what this means to him, that I can help like this. "So you're done working for the night?"

"I am done working for the night."

He sits up and reaches for me, coaxing me over into his lap so I'm straddling him. "Are you hungry?"

"Well, now I am."

"Food hunger," he says, laughing. "Since the coffee at your place this morning I've only had half a muffin. I could eat everything in the minibar right now."

"Room service?"

"Read my mind." Alec reaches past me to feel for the menu on the coffee table. Bringing it between us, he turns it to the side so that we can read it together, but I go in for his neck.

"Pick something salad-y for me," I say.

"Like a Caesar or like . . . a grilled veggie platter with brown rice?"

"Yes. That."

He hums and the sound vibrates against my lips as I kiss across his throat. "That does sound good. If I got the margherita pizza and gave you a slice would you give me some veggies?"

"Yes."

"Done." He shifts me back onto the cushion, walks over to the phone, and orders. "Okay if I shower?" When I nod, he tosses me the remote. "Pick a movie for us to watch."


A movie. Dinner on the coffee table, sitting cross-legged on the floor, side by side and laughing at the same stupid parts of *Office Space*. With his eyes forward, mouth open in a laugh, Alec takes bites of food off my plate without asking and I love it. He refills my wineglass and distractedly kisses my shoulder when he's done eating, like if it's in kissing distance, it's his damn job to do it.

And when that movie ends, we put on *Spotlight*—I can't believe he's never seen it—and scramble up onto the couch. Alec stretches out and pulls me over him, aligning our torsos, our legs, and wrapping his arms around my midsection.

"You're the comfiest mattress," I mumble against his chest.

He laughs. "Is that a compliment?"

"I like a firm bed."

He kisses me, sweet and chaste, and I rest my head back on his chest, hearing the movie out of one ear and his heartbeat out of the other. Like this, I fall asleep.

I wake up in bed, with the remnants of a dream caught in my thoughts like a photo negative. I ran into Spence somewhere—a café, I was enjoying a scone and iced tea—and he was astonished that I wasn't happy to see him. He had no idea what I was talking about; hurt, shock, and eventually anger bled into his voice until I started to feel like maybe I'd made it all up. Like I'd fabricated all the pain and isolation and betrayal.

The film of hurt lingers, and it takes me a few cloudy seconds to register that I'm not in my bed, that Alec is curled behind me, his arm slung heavily over my side, his front pressed all along my back.

He seems to be in nothing but briefs, but I'm still wearing my lounge pants and tank top and have no recollection of being carried here. Alec breathes slow and deep, fast asleep, and when I glance at the clock, I'm amazed to see that it's only midnight. I can't have been asleep all that long. I fell hard, fast, and in my dream, I was being blatantly gaslighted by my ex—and my sleeping brain had prepared to weather it stoically—but it wasn't real.

I'm safe in the tight circle of Alec's arms.

Something tears sharply right down my midsection, as though I'm paper being ripped in two. The middle of the night is always a tender zone for me, but this is something else entirely. It's one thing to have a night of room service and movies but this, between us, is about sex. At least, it's the lie I have to tell myself if I'm going to keep my head on my shoulders and my emotions sealed tightly in my veins.

But if we do this, live together and move around the space like two people who enjoy each other's company for things beyond the physical, then what? Why am I inviting pain back in?

Carefully, I slide out from under his arm and shuffle quietly into the bathroom.

I brush my teeth, splash water on my face, and then crouch on the floor, head in my hands and mind spinning as I try to still the wild thumping of my heart inside my body. It's already a broken organ; what am I doing bringing it out like this? I swear I've barely stitched it back together. I rarely think about that final day anymore, the day I tore it into pieces, when I decided to let Spence know I was there, at the park, and stepped out from behind a tree in the middle of the workday. I'd texted him, asking about his day, and had watched him reply right there, on the bench, with a made-up story about an interminable meeting and irritating coworker. I stood in front of him for ten full seconds before he registered my presence, before I saw understanding land in his expression.

We had so much to dig out after that. Extricating our lives felt like carrying an ocean's worth of water uphill in leaky buckets. Bills together and all our belongings intermingled. Packing up the apartment in alternating blocks of time, leaving notes about what needed to be taken care of. I didn't hear his voice again after that day in the park. Still haven't. I could barely stand to be near him after that. Touching all his things when I had to move them aside to reach mine—I hated it. Every point of contact with a plate, a pillow, a pair of his jeans felt like a stab, someone shouting in my ear, *How did you not know?*

I don't know how I missed it. Spencer didn't only lie once; he lied every single time he spoke to me. *I'm fine* was a lie, and *Good night* was a lie, and *I love you* was the biggest lie of all. I said to Eden in the pit of my heartache—and maintain it to this day—that it would have been easier if he'd gone home with another woman one night. Even if he'd done it once and never returned afterward, deciding immediately that I was the lesser of two options, that would have hurt less than the ability he had to lie directly to my face day in and day out.

But we don't get to choose our heartbreaks, and we never truly know the paths that could have been even more terrible. All we can ever say for sure is that we'll never know what's coming around the bend. So what am I doing here? Pulling my heart outside of my body and laying it cleanly on the chopping block? Alec won't devastate me with lies—I know in my bones that he isn't going to hurt me with that kind of betrayal—but that's the problem. This heartache is an unknown and already the magnitude of it is terrifying. Yes, this is new, but pain is pain.

I am so stupid.

It's only a split second after I register a shadow passing over the light before a warm body crouches behind me. His legs come up alongside mine and he bends over my back, wrapping his arms around me, sweetly caging me in. "Hey."

I swallow back a thick sob. "Hey."

"Are you okay?"

It's dark in here; the middle of the night swims blurry and thick all around us. Daytime is for deflection and denial. I don't have it in me right now. "Just quietly freaking out."

He presses his mouth to my neck, asking against my skin: "About what?"

"You know what."

Alec is quiet for a long stretch. "I do know." He takes a long, deep breath. "I actually thought you left."

"I'm not sure I can do this," I admit.

"Why?"

"Because it was supposed to be just sex."

"Gigi . . ." he says quietly. "I mean—I don't think it was ever just sex."

I feel the dual blast of relief and embarrassment at this obvious truth. "I don't think it hit me until tonight that we aren't even pretending."

"I understand."

"It's only been," I say, thinking, "four days since Seattle. Feelings don't happen like that."

He's quiet in response.

"Four days is nothing," I say. "It doesn't even make sense. This is . . . I mean, it feels too good to be true."

Behind me, he stands, cupping my shoulders. "Come back to bed."

He helps me up and we find our way back in the darkness. I climb between the sheets and watch the shadow of him follow me in. He reaches for me, coaxing me into the warm solidity of his body, tucking my head beneath his chin and sliding his hand beneath the hem of my top. Just resting it there low on my back.

"It's probably the worst time for either of us to get involved with anyone," he admits, and the vibration of his voice dances across my scalp. "You're just out of something that ended badly. I've been completely wrapped up in what's happening with Sunny. Yael and I almost didn't make this trip."

Her words from earlier slither between us. *He doesn't have time for relationships. I don't want you to have expectations.*

"There's that, too," I admit, not wanting to say too much but needing to at least voice her concerns between us. "She doesn't . . ." I don't know how to finish the thought. I don't want him to think I'm bad-mouthing her, or tattling. "Yael doesn't seem to think this is a good idea."

"Well," he says, and kisses the top of my head, "it isn't really up to her."

"I know, but she's important to you."

"She is, but in this case—Yael, I mean—it's complicated." He breathes in and out and we both fall silent for a handful of seconds. Finally, Alec admits, "She is, and has been, in love with Sunny for a very long time."

My eyes fall closed under the weight of understanding. "Oh."

He swallows. "I don't know whether Sunny has ever—" He stops, choosing his words carefully. "I don't know if they have a more intimate history or not. I sometimes think they do, but I'm not sure and it really isn't my business. Regardless, Yael wanted me to stay back in London. To take care of Sunny, to figure out what really happened with Josef that night. I couldn't miss this trip, but the plan was that we would come, take care of the promotion responsibilities, and go home." He pauses. "Did she say something to you?"

"She did, but it's okay. This all makes a lot of sense now."

I'm grateful that he doesn't ask me to tell him the specifics. He says only, "To Yael, you're probably an emotional complication we don't have time for."

I swallow past a tangled ball of feelings in my throat. "I get that."

"But I see it differently," he says. "It's only been a few days, and it's true that there is a lot more we don't know about each other than we do, but my bone-deep sense of you hasn't changed since Seattle. And I'm not sure what to make of that." Slowly, he strokes circles on my back. "I usually have a pretty good sense of people, but I also don't fall into things the way I've fallen into you." He exhales a quiet laugh. "That combination is a little bewildering."

"Yeah," I agree, and smile into his neck.

"I guess my instinct is to keep putting one foot in front of the other until a decision is forced on us, but then what do we do if we reach the end of my trip only feeling more than we do now?"

I shake my head, pressing my face right up against him. That possibility is the best- and worst-case scenario. "I feel compelled to tell you that I do not think I am capable of handling a long-distance relationship very well," I say. "Even though you are *nothing* like Spence, and I consider myself to be a pretty levelheaded person, I think the distance wouldn't work for me right now. I would be an anxious mess."

This truth settles like another body between us.

"I get that." Alec pulls away slightly to look down at me in the darkness. "And if you want to go home tonight, I understand. It's been an emotionally intense day for you. My preference is you stay. I'm—I mean, I am obviously deeply attracted to you, but beyond that I *like* you. I want to be around you as much as I can until I leave." He pulls his hand free of my shirt and cups my face. "I also understand why you panicked tonight. It does feel too soon for this kind of conversation, but given how we are together—how natural this is—I'm not sure whether it is. It's probably good that we're having it."

I nod, looking at his dark, glimmering eyes in the weak light sneaking in between the heavy curtains. I think about climbing in a cab, going home, sleeping alone in my bed knowing he's here alone, too. My blood sours at the thought. "I'll stay tonight."

He kisses my forehead. "Good."

Inside me is a whole vocabulary of feelings and thoughts,

scattered in loose piles of mismatched words. It sends a chaotic shiver through me; a mess of emotions press up against my ribs, tap at the underside of my skin.

"I'm sorry I woke you up. I know your day tomorrow is crazy."

"Don't be." He rests a hand on my hip, squeezing. His finger lands on the stretch of skin where my shirt has risen from the waistband of my pants, and he traces long, slow ovals there.

His neck is so close to my mouth. Inviting and warm. I press my lips to his pulse point and hear the sharp intake of his breath; his hand flexes against me, instinctively grabbing. Low in my belly, the familiar hunger flares, pushing aside everything else. "Do you want to?" I ask.

"I always do." Alec's voice is so low it shakes my blood. "But would you feel better or worse?"

I hadn't considered that.

I press my hand to his chest and he shifts his hips away. Beneath my palm, his heart is a steady *bum-bum-bum*.

Not just his heart; *all* of him is steady. He doesn't leave things left unsaid, and he wants to know me, and he came to find me in the bathroom, and he knew why I was in there. He knew, because it occurred to him that I could have left.

"Come here," he says, and shifts me so that I'm lying on top of him. But it isn't for sex. It's the way we were on the couch, with his body as my firm mattress, his shoulder as my pillow, and him groaning quietly at the relief of a full-body cuddle. "Let's sleep."

"I had a bad dream," I admit after a few seconds of silence.

His deep voice vibrates against my temple. "About what?"

"Doesn't matter."

He strokes my back and says very quietly, "I'm never going to lie to you, you know."

Squeezing my eyes closed, I press my face into his neck. I don't know where to put everything I feel but I'm going to have to figure it out. I don't think I'll have anywhere left to hide my excuses and these bright, urgent feelings once his gentle light illuminates each of my dark corners.

# Thirteen

Without Alec, the hotel room feels enormous and eerily quiet. Daylight streams in, painting a band of gold across the bottom half of the bed. I straighten my legs, inching my toes into the stripe of warmth.

The windows are such good quality that they block out all the street noise outside. The sheets beneath me still smell like Alec's soap from his shower last night. I roll into his pillow, placing myself in an Alec isolation chamber.

I tried to read for a while; I tried to write. But I'm unfocused, antsy. Why didn't I pull him over me last night? Why did we bother to sleep? I need to start working on a new story between the bursts of new information from Ian, need to fill my days better. Being in this suite without Alec all day long is going to leave me itchy and impatient.

I run my hand down my stomach, wishing it was his.

The Batphone buzzes on the mattress next to me.

My heart pushes against my ribs, and I bring it to my ear, answering. "You're not supposed to be done until late."

He hums. "What're you doing? You sound drowsy."

"You just busted me relaxing in this huge bed."

He laughs and then groans.

"I'm sorry," I mumble. "I'm a dick."

"Why on earth are you sorry?"

"Because you're running all over Los Angeles," I say, "and I'm lounging in your hotel room in the middle of the day." If memory serves, Alec got up at three for a satellite interview for *Good Morning America*, drove to Burbank for a taping of *James Corden*, and then had a full-cast *Vanity Fair* photo shoot before some gala dinner.

"It's your room, too," he says, "and I would lounge in bed in a heartbeat if I could."

"Exactly." I laugh. "That's why I'm sorry."

"Come on. With everything you've had going on the past few weeks, you must be exhausted."

I stretch, limbs shaking with euphoria. "You aren't wrong."

The line falls quiet and still. *I miss you*, I think.

"You're doing okay today?" he asks. "I'm sorry I couldn't check in until now."

Rolling over onto my side, I stare out the expansive window. As expected, every big feeling is so much more manageable in daylight. I'd be embarrassed about my meltdown last night but maybe that's Alec's superpower. He doesn't make *emotions* feel like a dirty word. "I'm good." I adjust the pillow under my head. "I'm glad you called. I was just missing you."

"Yeah?"

"Wishing I hadn't just gone back to sleep last night. Feels like a wasted opportunity."

The line falls into a tiny pool of silence. "You're in bed thinking about me," he says, half question, half realization.

His tone has changed, dropped, quieted. And in an instant my body is awake. "I am. Where are you?"

"Walking to a car," he says. "One place to the next." Another pause and then a playful, "Are you wearing anything?"

I look down at the terry cloth twisted around my midsection. "I finished up work and then showered, thinking I'd climb into bed for ten minutes. So," I say, "I'm half wearing a towel."

"And nothing underneath?"

My hand slides up over my stomach. Tight anticipation builds under my palm. "No."

I can just hear his quiet groan over the sound of him walking, the clatter of a cart.

"Are you alone?" I ask.

"For now. Walking out to the back of the building to meet my driver."

"Ah." I bite my bottom lip, imagining his long, purposeful strides as he moves down a hallway, along a back alley to a private car. I remember what he put on this morning: black trousers, a simple white button-down shirt. Three-quarters asleep, I'd watched him check his reflection in the mirror, hands in pockets, hands out.

"When you're alone," he begins, breaking into my thoughts, "alone and . . . turned on . . . what do you think about?"

I grin, and my cheeks heat. "Really?"

"Really."

I close my eyes, thinking. "I haven't really done that in a while."

"Then think about me," he prompts quietly. And then adds, "Tell me about the time you liked the most."

"That is an impossible request."

"Pick one. Don't think."

His full mouth flashes in my mind. "The first hotel room in LA."

"Why that one?" I can hear his smile, like he already knows the answer.

My hand slips over my breast. I was still a little mad at him, full of heat and sharp edges. I remember his kiss on the swell of my breast, the way he groaned. The wet, placating circle of his tongue on the peak. And then the obliterating heat of his lips trailing down my body. "You put your mouth on me."

I hear another man's voice greeting him and then a car door closes. "In the car now," he says quietly. Formally. "You'll need to walk me through this from here on out."

My hand stills on my breast. "I—" I open my eyes, blink up at the ceiling. "You want me to get myself off while you just listen?"

"Yes."

Heat floods my cheeks. "I don't usually talk."

"I honestly can't tell you how thrilled I am about this collaboration," he says with a laugh in his voice.

"Shit." I laugh into the phone. "You're serious?"

"Very much so."

I swallow audibly. "I feel a little self-conscious."

"That's fine," he says. "Take your time."

Am I doing this? I close my eyes, letting the calm resonance of his voice bring me to a place where I can begin to pretend my hand is him, that he's not in a car somewhere, listening to my every sound.

"Do you remember how I sat on your lap that day?" I ask.

"Yes."

"I made you stay still so I could kiss you all over your face." He hums in acknowledgment. "I think I wanted to convince myself you were real."

"Yeah?"

"Yeah. And you let me. But you slid your hands up under my shirt."

He pauses. "I recall."

"I love the way your big hands hold me."

"Hold what part, specifically."

"My breasts."

"That's right." His voice is so measured and professional and somehow it makes my skin heat.

"You rolled over onto me," I say, teasing the peak. "You love my chest."

"I do."

"Why?"

He clears his throat. *Right.*

But then he answers anyway. "It's the ideal proportion."

I laugh into the phone. "That sounded porny. I bet the driver is listening now."

"I doubt it." Alec laughs quietly. "Go ahead."

"You like the taste of my skin?"

A deceptively even: "Very much."

My hand moves lower. "I wish you were here kissing me."

"Where are you in the script right now," he says, "if I may ask?"

"Your mouth is kissing down my stomach."

"Okay. Continue."

I reach lower, and suck in a breath. "I'm wet."

He can't stifle a quiet groan.

"I haven't done this in—" I pull in more air, imagining him feeling this. "Since before London. Before you."

"That's right."

"I imagine what you feel when you touch me here."

He's quiet on the other end.

"How soft it must feel."

"Very."

"If you touch me here, do you immediately want to push into me?"

"Yes," he says with an edge, repeating more quietly, "Yes."

I arch my neck, stroking. "It feels good."

"Explain, if you don't mind?"

"I'm imagining you kissing me here," I say, and my skin grows warm, humming. "And how you started with just kissing but then licked me."

"That sounds like a good progression."

I love the deep rumble of his voice. "You were so sweet," I say. "But when you put your fingers in . . ."

He's quiet, but I can almost hear how he strains to hear every word.

"You just," I say, pleasure climbing, "you *fucked* me."

"Georgia." A sharp, breathless reprimand, but it only makes me moan.

"So hard," I whisper. "You were wild."

"I know. I was."

"Oh God, you liked it, didn't you? How many fingers?"

"You tell me."

"Three." My fingers circle; tension builds in my spine. "I couldn't spread my legs any wider."

"I know."

"Are you hard?"

"Without question." A car door slams, I hear his short, broken gusts as he walks. Very quietly he manages, "Use your other hand to touch your breasts."

I do, and my eyes roll back, another sound escapes. "I'm close."

"Not yet." He's moving through a building. I hear him murmur a quiet thanks to someone.

"It feels so good," I whisper.

"Continue."

"But not as good as you feel."

A quiet laugh. "I'm very glad to hear that."

I'm reduced to this pinpoint of focus, breathing in, and out, imagining his head between my legs, his silken dark hair sliding through my fingers. "I want to grab your hair."

"I would agree to those terms."

"I want to move against you. Fuck your mouth."

He laughs again, breathlessly. "I wish you would."

"I'm so close."

A quiet beep and then, "Not yet, Gigi."

But I realize the beep echoed; I'm hearing it two places. Through the phone . . . and here.

Awareness sinks just as the door slams, and a second later he appears, rounding the corner into the bedroom. Alec is already tugging the button of his shirt open, finding me on the bed, legs bent and open.

Doing exactly what I've been describing.

"Holy—" He yanks his shirt off and comes over me, kissing me, mouth open and groaning. Pulling back, he stares down our bodies, reaching to keep my hand from moving away. "Show me."

He watches me touch myself, reaching to unbuckle his pants. The belt slaps my thigh as he struggles to get his button undone, his zipper down, before pulling himself free. With my free hand, I pull his head to mine, wanting his tongue in my mouth, his sounds vibrating down my throat. The movement brings our bodies closer, and his fist bumps against my hand as he strokes himself faster—

Alec breaks away to kiss in a frenzy down my body, pulling my hand away and guiding it to his hair. Before I can even get his name out, his mouth is there, open and urgent, sucking my soul out of me. When I rock my hips up into him, he lets out a desperate, encouraging groan. For a few perfect seconds, I make good on my fantasy, fucking that sweet, plump mouth, and at the feel of his kiss, the view of his face between my legs, my back arches away and an orgasm slams into me, twisting me so sharply Alec has to press a firm hand down on my hips to keep me planted on the bed.

I let my legs fall loosely to the side, spent, and he presses his forehead to my hip as his free palm slides up my side to my breast. It's only a couple of dizzy seconds before I realize what he's doing, and I push up onto my elbow to watch his hand move, faster and faster. I sink a hand into his hair and his fist stills as he comes with a quiet groan.

For a few still seconds, we catch our breath. "I wanted to," I manage, finally, figuring he knows what I mean.

"I know." His hair slips through my fingers, silky, and he

turns his face, kissing my thigh before reaching for the shirt he dropped on the floor, cleaning us both up. "I don't have a ton of time and knew if I let you, I would want it to take longer."

After helping me to my feet, he kicks his clothes all the way off, bending to remove his socks, and then leads me into the bathroom. Alec leans in, turning on the shower. "Come in with me."

He steps in, guiding me in after him, and the water is luke-warm and perfect for my overheated skin. But when he tilts his chin up, letting the stream of water soak his hair, I pretend to pout. "I liked the idea of you going to your thing tonight with your hair all messed up."

Laughing, he cups my hand and squeezes shampoo into it before guiding it to the top of his head. "I would have smelled like sex."

"And?" I scrub as he lathers me up with body wash.

"*And* I'm supposed to be getting a quick bite and change before meeting up with Yael at six."

He really is in a hurry.

"You think she doesn't know you came back here for this?" He's quiet in response, and I realize my mistake. "Yael doesn't know I'm staying here, does she?"

"I'm sure she suspects, but it's one of those things with us. A don't-ask-if-you-don't-want-to-know sort of thing."

"Mmm." I tilt his head back into the water again, rinsing the shampoo, and then reach for the conditioner. "That reminds me, actually."

His attention seems to be on getting my breasts as clean as possible, thumbs circling and circling . . .

I lean in, whispering, "You are doing a very good job at that, but I did shower only about an hour ago."

Busted, he relents with a laugh, leaning back to rinse his hair again. "What were you going to say? Reminds you of what?"

"Does Sunny know I'm the one you're talking to?"

"Yes," he says, and turns me so that the water rinses the suds from my skin. "I mentioned I ran into you. I mentioned you were working on the story. And I'm sure even if I hadn't, Yael would."

"True." I chew my lip. "What did Sunny say?"

"I mean, we didn't talk about our run-in at length because—"

"That would be an awkward conversation."

"Right." He begins quickly lathering up his skin and I help, only in the sense that I basically slide my hands around and around the muscular bunching of his shoulders. "But she thought it was weird and great."

"'Weird and great'?"

"Those were her words," he says, laughing. "She says hello. Wanted the full Gigi update. I told her to call you sometime."

"I like that plan."

I stare at the way he quickly rubs soapy hands down his chest, his abs, his cock. Legs and shoulders. When washing me, he was slow, nearly reverent. He catches me watching. "You're looking at me like you're going to eat me."

Very serious, I nod. "I feel I should return the favor."

Laughing again, he reaches behind me to shut off the water. Steam rises around us, and water drips like crystals from his eyelashes. Alec licks his wet lips. "I promise you can eat me later." He kisses me then, warm and sliding, and when he moans quietly, it sucks me into a spiral of want. But too soon he pulls away and glances at the watch I am genuinely hoping is waterproof. "Shit. I have forty-five minutes to get to Santa Monica in a tux."

I sit cross-legged on the bed, watching him as he gets ready. Alec pulls a suit bag out of the closet and drapes it over a chair, unzipping it.

"I'm excited," I sing.

He leans down, pulling the suit free. "Why?"

"I get to see you in a tuxedo."

He slants an amused look my way. "That's exciting?"

"Don't play dumb with me. You're gonna look like the world's hottest cake topper."

Alec laughs at this. "I only brought one, so Elodie had better not spill wine on me." He steps into the trousers, then shrugs on the shirt. "It started out as a joke," he says, buttoning. "But she's spilled her drink on me on three separate occasions."

"Is this woman trying to get you to take off your clothes?"

"She's notoriously clumsy."

I laugh, picking a thread from the duvet. "That's cute."

"You're not bothered by that, are you?"

I look up at him, wide-eyed. He's turned to face me. "By what?"

"Elodie," he clarifies. "And our . . ."

"Your flirty public dynamic?" I guess. He nods, returning his attention to his buttons. "No—I mean, I know it's part of the promo. Also, I assume if you wanted her, she would be in this hotel room, not me."

He grins. "Very true."

"Whoever you end up with," I say, watching him carefully tuck his shirt in, "is going to have to be very chill about those things."

He hums in agreement, reaching for his cuff links on the bedside table.

"Need help?" I ask, feeling naked and lazy watching him get ready for a night of nonstop schmoozing after a long day of work.

He grunts out a no and then lifts his chin, indicating the flat bow tie on the hanger. "I can't do those, though."

"A tie?"

Alec responds to my sarcasm with a playfully flat look. "A *bow* tie."

Standing, I pull a discarded dress shirt from where it's draped over a chair, tugging it on and buttoning it haphazardly. "Let me make myself useful."

When I look up, Alec is staring at me. "Are you trying to make it harder for me to leave?"

The obvious *yes* is perched right on the front of my tongue, but in fact I have no idea what he's talking about. "What?"

"Wearing my clothes when I need to leave?"

Ah. Even Alec is predictable in such delightful man ways. "It would be easier for you to leave if I was naked?"

He smirks down at me. "No."

"Okay, then." I pull up YouTube and type "tying a bow tie" into the search bar.

"What are you doing?"

"Tying that." I lift my chin to his neck. "I just need to look up how to do it on YouTube."

"Yael can do it when I get there."

"But then you'll deprive me of the chance to stare at your throat for a few minutes." I'm not looking at his face, but I know he's smiling. Threading the tie through his collar, I look down at where I've propped my phone on the bed and carefully follow the steps.

My first attempt is . . . not great. I try again.

Alec puts his palms on my waist, bunching his shirt up over my hips until he finds bare skin. "I wish I could bring you with me."

I frown at my hands, thinking this would be significantly easier if I had four of them. "I love that sentiment, but I promise you, I am fine with missing it."

"I know." Patiently, Alec stands in front of me, smelling like soap and toothpaste and emanating warmth like the sun. "What are you going to do tonight?"

"I was thinking of being deeply lazy, but my parents got back from their trip this morning," I say. "I'll probably go over there for a bit."

He stills, and I look up when I feel his attention on my face. "What?"

"Your parents are back in town?"

I stretch, kissing his chin. "Alec, you don't need to meet my parents."

He doesn't seem so sure. "Shouldn't I say hello?" He bends to grab his phone and opens his calendar. "We could do dinner with them on . . . hmm . . . lunch on Monday?"

I step back, inspecting my handiwork and needing a second to push down this weird ball of anguish. I let myself be distracted from the mess inside me with the simpler mess in front of me. Without question, Yael is going to retie the bow tie when she sees it, but I'm not sure I can do better than this.

"Seriously, you don't need to make time for that," I say, and pat his chest. "I'll tell them you said hi."

When he leaves, I know he's reading something else into my answer—that I don't want him to come over, that I'm hiding him. But the fact is that my parents are hilarious and welcoming and warm, and Alec is charming and adoring and funny; they would love everything about him. But I'd like to have at least two people left in Los Angeles who aren't mourning his absence when he leaves.

# Fourteen

With his inconsistent, scattered schedule, we tumble through the next several days. I barely see Alec on Saturday and spend the day hiking with Eden before meeting my mom for dinner at her favorite Ethiopian place. She can finally vent to someone who understands all the ways that my dad was an uptight, overscheduling menace on their trip, and her need to unload lets me avoid the Alec conversation entirely. Being with Mom is like recharging my battery; she's the version of adult-me I hope to meet someday: responsible, loving, but not so responsible and loving that she won't fuck shit up if the situation warrants.

I drop her off at home, kiss my dad, and then drive myself back to the Waldorf, greeting my new favorite valet, Julie, on my way in. Back in the suite, and long after midnight, I feel Alec's long, warm body slide into bed behind me.

"I'm back." He scoots up close against me, sliding a cool hand under my tank top. I try to drag my brain out of deep sleep. His hand is still slightly wet from having been washed, and his breath smells like toothpaste when he speaks into my shoulder. "You awake?"

I mumble a sleepy no into my pillow, rolling into the heat of his bare chest. He kisses my hairline, my forehead, my mouth. We talk in broken fragments about our days until he falls asleep midsentence. He's gone again before sunrise.

Sunday I catch up on work, and get a surprise hour with Alec when he crashes into the room to quickly change for a dinner with some industry people. I follow him around the suite while he undresses and throws his clothes everywhere while ranting in a hilarious stream of anecdotes about a music video cameo he filmed that sounded like a textbook example of bratty Hollywood shenanigans.

I don't see Alec again until Monday, when he wakes to me straddling him with a toothbrush jammed in my cheek. "Why are you here?" I ask. "Are you late? Were you supposed to set an alarm?"

He rubs his face, squinting up at me. "I'm off until tonight."

He tugs a pillow out from under his head and presses it to my face to muffle my happy scream.

Yes, we make love, but instead of spending the entire rest of the day in bed or having sex on every flat surface of the suite like I would have guessed, we sneak out in hats and sunglasses for doughnuts, and on our way back he impulsively stops in a local gaming store and buys a full Nintendo console. We invite Eden (who accepts) and Yael (who flatly declines), and the three of us spend a solid block of the day in the suite, shit-talking and going cutthroat in *Mario Kart* with a bag of chips blown open on the table and bottles of beer scattered all over. Around five, Alec drags his day-drunk body into the shower and then finds me out on the terrace, where Eden and I had moved to gossip and soak up some late-afternoon sun.

"I'm headed out now." He bends, kissing my forehead.

"Don't go." Eden groans in protest. "Gigi sucks at video games."

"Believe me," he says, "I'd rather stay here on the terrace."

When he straightens, I squint up at him, shading a hand over my eyes. He steps into the sun, shadowing me. "What is it tonight again?"

"Dinner with the cast and local Netflix team." Backlit, he looks like a marble statue radiating sunlight.

"What time will you be back?"

I very intentionally did not say *home*, but the word rings out between the three of us anyway.

"Late," he says. "You don't have to wait up."

"Wake me up?" I say quietly, and he nods, kissing me one more time.

Alec says goodbye to Eden and then disappears inside, and I hear the heavy click of the suite's door a few seconds later.

Tilting my face to the sky, I keep my eyes closed but can feel my best friend's attention on me in the following silence. "It's been a *week*," she says.

"I know."

The *but* swings like a pendulum in the air, but thankfully she doesn't say any of the rest of her thought aloud. I know all of the permutations already.

*But watching the two of you, it seems like it's been longer.*

*But he's still going to leave next Sunday.*

*But this is all just pretend, Gigi. Get yourself together.*

Instead, we lazily shuffle back inside, order room service, and talk about the sweet and banal non-Alec details of our lives. When she leaves, the room falls oddly silent.

I clean up the detritus from our gaming and junk-food binge. I shower, make the bed, pack a bag of our clothes for laundry services. I check my work email, but Ian took the day off, too, and there's nothing new to read. I'm not tired, but nothing draws my attention on social media, and there's nothing I can think to watch on TV. But I turn it on anyway and find myself on autopilot, navigating to Netflix, to *The West Midlands,* and pushing play on episode one.

By the time Alec walks into the suite, well after one in the morning, I'm six episodes in and already deeply invested in Dr. Minjoon Song's first romance arc—one that clearly does not stick, because this woman is not played by Elodie. Google tells me that this character—Eleanor DiMari—dies in a plane crash at the end of season one and I immediately resent my inability to live without spoilers because I am *devastated.*

"She *dies?*" I whine.

He drops his jacket over the back of the couch and braces his hands there, bending to kiss my temple. "What are you—oh. Yeah."

I am delighted that he returned in the middle of a make-out scene where his costar—a woman Google also told me is named Mariana Rebollini—is topless.

"This is some real strategic filming," I say. "Do *you* actually see boob when you're filming this?"

"She has stickers," he says, and when I look over my shoulder, he gestures to his chest and then glances at his watch. "God, what are you doing up?"

"Couldn't sleep."

He walks over to the fridge in the small kitchen area and pulls out a bottle of sparkling water. "Wow, we killed a lot of beer today." He cracks open the top and joins me on the couch. "No wonder I'm dragging."

"On a scale of one to let-us-never-speak-of-this-off-set," I say, lifting my chin to the TV, "how awkward are these sexy scenes to film?"

Alec slides his arm behind my neck, coaxing my head onto his shoulder. "Depends." He tilts his water to his lips, takes a sip. "Sometimes they're awkward if someone is new or very uncomfortable—"

"Are you ever uncomfortable?"

"Not really," he says, amending, "not outwardly, I think. If it's a body double you haven't met until that day, then it can be. But usually love scenes are perfunctory. There's minimal staff on set and there's an unspoken agreement that everyone is a professional and it's just part of the job. The scenes are all so carefully blocked it's almost anti-romantic for the actors." He leans his head against mine. "I'm always surprised how sexy they look when they're edited."

"But this one." I point to the screen. "Great or terrible?"

"This one was fine." He drinks another sip. "I was bummed when her character was written off the show. Mariana was funny."

"You say that like someone else is *not* funny." He gives me a wry look and I lean over, kissing his cheek. "Did Elodie spill her drink on my man tonight?"

He turns and looks at me, eyes unguarded and surprised. *My man*.

I'd try to take it back or soften it into something meaningless, but it's late and I'm feeling sparky. Alec sets his water bottle down and then coaxes me back so I'm lying along the length of the sofa and settles his hips between my legs. "No, she didn't." He rests his mouth on mine, humming.

"Good," I say against his lips.

"I'm too tired to talk about it now. . . ." He drops individual words into my jaw, my neck, the hollow of my throat. "But tomorrow or Wednesday or whenever we have time . . . we should talk about what we're going to do."

"Do?"

"After Sunday."

*After Sunday*.

These two words land like a slab of marble.

"You mean," I say, as he sucks on my collarbone, "me and you?"

"Me and you." He comes back up to my face and nods, staring down at me. "Okay?"

I nod and stretch to kiss him. "Okay."

But we don't get time to talk Tuesday—I have an early call with Ian, and Alec is gone before I'm done. Wednesday he's up before sunrise—this time for a livestream in Korea that he does from the living room of the suite and we have discussed that I am not even allowed to roll over in bed for fear of making a sound. Yael picks him up barely five minutes after he finishes, so all I get is a quick peck goodbye.

Still, I remind myself, it's more than I would get if I was staying at my place. At least here I see him. I imagine going this entire week without Alec and something vital inside seems to desiccate. I do everything I can to not think about life After Sunday.

It's a lot of time alone in the suite, but I'm used to it now; it allows me to get a massive amount of work done with Ian on the follow-up story. And in the end, Wednesday is the jackpot for investigative journalism. After Alec leaves with Yael I learn that Ian managed to obtain a full transcript of the chat forum spanning the two months when the explicit videos were shared, giving us the usernames of everyone sharing and engaging with the videos. These scumbags call the women in the videos "Bambis," for fuck's sake, and I have never in my life wanted to take someone down more than this. Even Spence.

Perhaps unsurprisingly, our first story initiated an investigation into police payoffs, and London's Metropolitan Police Service, otherwise known as the Met, is all in. By cross-referencing the parking garage video footage with the Hotel Maxson's footage, we're able to confirm that at least three of the owners—Gabriel McMaster, David Suno, and Charles Woo—were present in the club on the dates of each of the videos. Unfortunately, Josef Anders continues to be hard to pin down. He moves like a ghost.

But Thursday morning, an absolute bombshell hits.

Alec's call finds me sitting on the bed, staring intently at my computer screen. My hands are shaking—they've been shaking for nearly an hour. "Hi."

"Hi, I—" Alec pauses, I assume, at the tight strain in the single word. "You okay?"

"That depends on what 'okay' means." I stand and pace the suite, feeling the adrenaline spike hit my bloodstream in earnest. Holy shit, we did it.

"Tell me."

"Are you sure you have time?"

"Yeah. I have about fifteen minutes. Was just calling to check in."

"Okay, well," I say, and then take a huge steadying breath. "About a half hour ago, the *Times* received an email from an anonymous source. It was blank except for an attachment: a four-second but good-quality iPhone video of a couple having sex on a long bench seat."

"Okay," Alec says slowly, interested but cautious.

I tell him how it appears to have been taken covertly by someone in the room. The woman does not react at all in the short clip; her head is turned at a sharp awkward angle; her arms are passively bent near her head. Pulsing music covers most of the sound, but audio stripping indicates that no one in the room speaks during the brief recording. Someone with black polished shoes steps in at 0:02:53 on the far right of the frame, and a tumbler with clear liquid appears in the lower-left corner at 0:03:12; it seems this is in the free hand of the person recording the scene. Details that are consistent with Jupiter's interiors can easily be made out in the background.

"But Alec—okay, are you ready for this?"

"Should I sit down?"

"It's not about Sunny," I reassure him quickly, and squeeze my eyes closed, pulse thundering. "But we have a face."

"What? Who?"

"Josef Anders is clearly identifiable as the man engaging in the sex act."

"Oh my God."

"And a tattoo on his hip has been seen in a number of screen caps from videos in the chat forum. This is the first time it's conclusively linked to a face." I pause. "Do you get what I'm telling you? We've got him. We don't know who she is, and don't have proof that she's been drugged, or whether this is consensual, but we now have proof that it's Josef in all of these videos." I pull the phone away to make sure I haven't dropped the call. "Alec?"

"Write it up."

"Oh, we will as soon as we get—"

"Sunny's story, I mean," he cuts in. "Include it."

I freeze. "What? I thought she wanted it all off the record?"

"She let me know the other day that she's okay with it coming out as long as we remain anonymous. I didn't know if or how it would be helpful but this . . . Just—keep any identifying details out," he says. "No names. Nothing about my friendship with Josef. Nothing about him and Sunny. Nothing about Lukas. Just write that a man was warned by a friend to come pick a mutual friend up. That she'd been drugged and assaulted. Write what I saw. Can you do that?"

"I'm not sure I'm comfortable including information I got from a source I'm sleeping with."

"It's not illegal, though, is it?"

It isn't, he's right. But especially for something this big, it's discouraged.

But maybe that's the point: This *is* big. And with our new evidence that it's Anders, Sunny's story—even included without attribution—locks it down as potential assault in every video.

We ring off, and my heart scales up into my windpipe at the enormity of what we have in our hands. Ian and I send a copy of the video to the Met in London. I add Alec's anonymous details to the article. It's only maybe a hundred more words, but he's right—it does lock it down. Ian and I Face-Time briefly to read the entire thing through.

It's a terrible scandal—all centered around horrifying cruelty, really. As proud as I am to be the one unearthing it, it still doesn't feel good at all to spend so much time thinking about what these women have gone through. So there is a tiny moment of relief at the end when Ian's eyes meet mine and he nods, just slightly. This story is going to break wide open, and we did that.

Out of professional courtesy we send the article to Alec— it's unusual but in this case I feel strongly that he should be allowed to give his okay on the wording before it goes to print. But even though it still needs to go through production, the piece is done, and it's good.

I fall back on the bed, letting my laptop slide to the side and stare up at the ceiling. For the first time, I feel like a bad-ass at my job; I feel like I'm finally getting my life moving in the right direction; and despite my anxiety about a long-distance romance, I am hopeful that Alec and I might be able to make something of this.

My regular phone rings, and I pull it up to see Billy's face on the screen. "Are you calling to tell me I'm amazing?"

"No, I'm calling to ask what you're doing tonight."

I frown, thinking. I don't remember Alec mentioning what

he's doing later, but I assume he's gone because he didn't specifically tell me to be here. "Probably either hanging out with my parents or going for a run. Or both."

"Meredith isn't feeling well, and she was my plus-one to the AP gala. Want to come?"

An Associated Press gala? With my boss? That is a hell and a yes. I bolt up. "Wait, seriously?"

"Do you have a formal dress?"

I stare blankly at the wall. The nicest thing I own is the red jersey dress Alec and I have dubbed The Naked Dress. "What time is the event?"

"I'll swing by your place at six."

I pull my phone away to look at the time. It's almost two. "I will have a formal dress on my body by six."

"You are having one hell of a day, kid." He laughs. "Someday you might even achieve amazing. See you tonight."

I roll into the pillow and scream.

Alec returns to the suite just as I'm packing up my purse to leave. Already speaking, he calls out to me, "I saw your email with the story and can read it this evening on my way—" He drops his wallet and room key in the dish by the door and freezes when he sees me about to head out. "Where are you going?"

"Billy invited me to a thing," I say, still breathless and elated, "and he's picking me up at my place, and I have to go get a nice dress first."

Alec's face falls. "I have a few hours until I need to be at the AP gala. I was hoping we—"

I burst out laughing. "No way."

Alec frowns. "Yes . . . way?"

"That's where I'm going with Billy."

"We'll be at the same event?" His shoulders slump, and I immediately understand.

"Without the ability to talk to each other," I say, nodding. "Or make out in the corner."

"Get a really ugly dress," he commands.

"No way, I'm going to get something slutty."

"Wool turtleneck."

"Short enough to find religion." I grin at him. "Imagine the sex we can have later after intensely ignoring each other all night."

He walks to me, pulling me into a hug. "You're a horrible tease."

"It's why you like me." I tilt my face up for a kiss, and he delivers a loud smooch.

"It is one of many reasons." Another kiss and then, "Go. I'll read your story now."

# Fifteen

In the end, I compromise on the slutty-modest battle. Eden and I find a dress at Neiman Marcus that is floor-length black chiffon but with a deep plunging V neckline that ends just at my solar plexus. The dress is so revealing, in fact, that I'm grateful the lining is very grippy. Without question, 100 percent of the reason I chose this is because of Alec Kim's appreciation for all things related to my cleavage. Eden and I decide on dangly earrings, hair down, no necklace. I practice walking in Eden's three-inch heels. Not too bad, but I am not headed for the runway, either.

"Is this what it always feels like to be five-foot-seven?" I ask Eden. "I am drunk with power. The air is thinner up here."

She laughs. "Let me grab you a purse. You can't take your enormous hobo."

"Excuse me," I call after her, "that hobo is a very convincing Burberry knockoff."

Eden returns a few seconds later with a sleek—and also very convincing—fake YSL clutch and opens the clasp for me to deposit my phones, keys, hotel room key, and lipstick inside. "Don't forget the rules."

I nod dutifully. "Find good lighting. Don't drink too much. And if I see Chris Evans, I will slip him your number."

"Try not to stare at Alec all night."

"No promises."

She pecks my cheek and steers me to the door when a horn honks at the curb.

Billy makes a valiant effort to not notice my boobs when I climb into the passenger seat. "Good," is all he says—I assume he's letting me know my gown is sufficiently formal—and then pulls away from the curb.

While we drive, I update him on the basics of the piece, and his excitement shows in the white of his knuckles as he grips the steering wheel tighter and tighter. "When can we push it?"

"I'd like to get the okay from Mr. Kim for the portion related to his tip."

He nods. "I'm fine with that."

My stomach gnaws at itself. This thing with me and Alec . . . every passing day it feels less like a fling. It's one thing to explain away a temporary conflict of interest, easy to justify that Alec came forward as a source only after we'd already slept together. But at this point, I should tell Billy about it.

He glances over at me, and at the eye contact, the car shrinks down to a thimble. His gaze is notoriously sharp, stonily intimidating. Doubt drips into my blood like ice water and my confession dies in my throat.

"And actually, he'll be there tonight," he continues unaware, looking ahead. "If he gives a thumbs-up, we can run it tomorrow. Send it to me."

It's a few seconds before I find enough courage to push back on this. The pit in my stomach is the instinct I need to follow, and this isn't only about Alec being my secret lover. It's about social grace. "I don't think I can approach Mr. Kim like that at a gala. Not about a story related to his sister's assault."

Billy blinks at me again and then turns back to the road. "Ah, you're not cutthroat." I can't tell from his tone whether that's a simple observation or a criticism. "Send it over to me as is, George."

I can tell he's not going to ask nicely again, so I open my email and forward it. "Don't pass it until I say." These words are out before I think better of them.

Billy lets my demand sit for a few seconds and then he glances at me slowly, like I'm very stupid. He could chew me out for being a jerk insubordinate, but he doesn't, thankfully. He says only a dryly amused, "I won't."

"Sorry," I mumble.

Without question, Billy will be reading this on his phone and mulling it over most of the night, and I will be at his side, trying to very slowly sip my wine and find the best moment to casually mention that I've slept with my source. But at least I'll also get a chance to people-watch and covertly spy on Alec being hot in his element.

Once we park, we bypass the red-carpet photograph area and sign in. The party itself is as sparkling and upscale as one would expect a gala held at the Beverly Hilton to be. Pulsing, upbeat music that doesn't drown out conversation. A cash bar with proceeds going to Human Rights Watch. Clusters of seating dot the perimeter of the room. Billy and I grab drinks and then he points us to a side of the room that gives us a good view of the entrance and the bar, where most people will congregate early on. I approve of his choice, too, because the lighting is great. Imaginary Eden high-fives me.

He sips his drink and pulls his phone out just as I expected.

"I knew it."

Billy doesn't look up. "Knew what?"

"That you wouldn't be able to resist reading it as soon as we were situated inside."

"You wouldn't have, either." He scans the words and lets out a low whistle. "Unreal. Unreal." He pauses, taking a sip of his beer. "Who wrote the part about the tech guy—Sano?"

"Me."

He nods, gesturing to me with his bottle. "It's great. Sharp breakdown of his timeline. These guys are fucked."

I open my mouth to reply, to thank my boss for this rare praise, but my gaze trips over Alec walking in with Yael at his side. For the duration it takes to inspect him head to toe, I stop breathing. He must have bought a new tux today. This one is modern—slim lines, jet-black. His shirt is black, too, and open just at the collar, exposing the smooth skin of his throat. No tie. Long, lean legs. Hair combed off his forehead. He looks like he was designed by scientists to make females spontaneously ovulate.

"What're you—?" Billy pauses and follows my attention. Alec moves deeper into the room, and heads turn. "Oh." I feel my boss look back at me—I register that I'm being weird levels of quiet—and struggle to get my face back under conscious control.

I point out the obvious: "Mr. Kim is here."

Billy gives a low *mm-hmm* in his throat, adding, "I see that."

Why didn't I tell Billy in the car? It's a blatant omission now, an intentional one.

A board member for the AP approaches Alec, whose smile is bright, but I recognize the formality at the edges, the way he keeps his physical distance, shakes hands, doesn't hug. My brain pulls an image forward, pointing to it with gloating urgency: Alec bringing me into his arms in our suite. Telling me I'm a tease. Kissing me in a loud, playful smooch.

I drag my eyes away.

"Is there a conflict of interest happening in that brain of yours?" Billy asks, and the question injects a bolus of adrenaline into my bloodstream, immediately cooling my lust.

I feel the hot flush of anxiety crawl down my arms. It's not like I haven't thought about that exact issue every time the subject of Alexander Kim comes up between Billy and me, but until today we weren't using Alec's information in the story.

And if Alec and I do make a go of this, Billy will eventually find out. He wouldn't fire me over it, but sleeping with a source on a story this big—especially since I'm withholding it now—could change the dynamic between us, could affect the stories he's willing to let me tackle from now on.

I swallow heavily, deciding it's now or never. "Billy," I begin, but he lightly punches my arm, laughing.

"Come on, George. I'm teasing you."

"No, but actually—"

"You're not the only person in here with a crush on him." With an exasperated eye roll, Billy reminds me that we do not do personal backstory. "Lighten up, kid."

The opportunity is slammed closed. I blink back over to Alec as my heart stutters with nerves and realize Billy's not wrong: there are at least five different people standing near Alec, waiting for that opening to approach, pretending to be absorbed in something nearby but really watching him like a hawk. An unfamiliar brand of adrenaline swarms my blood, a jealous one. I want to crash through the crowd like a possessive Kool-Aid man and drape his long arm around my shoulders. *Isn't he gorgeous? He likes me. We have sex.*

As if he can sense the weight of my gaze on him, Alec looks up, and our eyes meet across the room. I can't help my smile from cracking open; in response, he fights his. I watch him take in my dress, see his eyes do the full circuit of my body before his attention slowly passes to my right, to where Billy stands just a little too close. Close so I can hear him over the cacophonous, bustling room, but still. Too close.

At that moment, my boss grips my shoulder and playfully turns me so that my back is to the room—teasingly suggesting that I need help redirecting my focus. It means that I'll never know if I imagined the bright flare of heat that passed over Alec's face.

Billy immediately breaks into storyteller mode, and when a few of our colleagues join us, I am soon laughing so hard that I let myself forget that Alec is across the room, being plied with drinks, being flirted with.

But then a cool hand comes around my arm, gently turning me.

It's Yael, and up close I see how stunning she looks tonight. Statuesque; hair that's normally in a tight bun is down and wild. A slash of crimson lipstick. "Alexander Kim has asked for a moment of your time."

Immediately, my heart is beating in my mouth. "Uh—sure."

Billy practically shoves me away, murmuring, "Get his permission."

I follow Yael as she leads me across the room, out into the lobby, and down a hall, wondering if permission is all I'm going to get.

We walk in silence away from the murmuring crowd and around a corner.

"Is everything okay?" I ask.

"I presume so."

I have to hand it to Yael. She really is most likely to win Least Amount of Fucks Given at the end of this trip, and it's hard to not respect a woman who won't kill herself to make friends in LA. She leads me to a private powder room that seems like it's used for bridal parties but is otherwise empty. Two walls are lined with vanities and mirrors, and at the back of the room standing facing the door is Alec.

Yael sweeps her arm, gesturing me in, and shuts the door once I cross into the room.

I walk slowly forward, enjoying the view. This close to him, in that suit—I might need smelling salts. "Are you requesting an official *LA Times* interview?"

"I read the story."

Drumbeats fill my chest. "And?"

"It's brutal." His dark eyes flash with pride. "I forwarded

it to Sunny, but I should be able to get you an answer early tomorrow."

I know that won't be the news Billy wants, but no one else has Alec's part of the story, and given that he only decided today to go on the record with it, I can't exactly rush him. I have to hope Billy can allow the Kim family this courtesy for another twelve hours. "Okay."

Alec reaches an arm out, pulling me close, spreading his hand over my bare back. I am immediately uncorked. I didn't realize how carefully I'd been holding myself together until he puts his hands on me.

"You look amazing," he says.

"So do you."

He drags his nose along my neck. "This dress."

"You like?"

"Mm-hmm." He kisses my jaw. "I'll let the lack of turtleneck slide this time."

Something in his voice feels different. Quieter, stiffer. "You okay?" I ask.

Alec pulls away, adjusting his collar. "Who was that man you were with?"

*Ah*.

"Out there?" I hook a thumb over my shoulder. "That's Billy. I should introduce you."

"Sure." He drags his fingertips possessively along my collarbone. Over my shoulder. His touch teases down the low front of my gown. He directs his question to my cleavage. "He's your boss?"

"Yes." I stretch, kissing his chin. "He's a grouch and a perfectionist and doesn't need sleep, but he's great." I feel the presence of words he's not saying like an elastic band pulled tighter and tighter. "Alec?"

"Hmm?"

"Am I here because you're jealous?"

He meets my eyes squarely. "A little bit, I think."

I can't help it; I laugh. "Seriously? I'm surprised you even noticed me in the room."

"I noticed you within about thirty seconds but it took a while for you to look over at me."

"Not true," I say. "I saw you the second you walked in with Yael."

He draws a finger over my bottom lip. "I realized this story is going to get you a lot of attention, and there is a roomful of men out there you might date when I leave."

Reaching up, I cup his face. Is he serious? I cannot imagine how any other man could measure up now. Before Alec, this kind of connection would have sounded made up, preposterously fictional. Now I worry every morning that this will be the last great romance of my life—extra devastating if it ends in a matter of days. I try to shape these thoughts into words, but I can't. I am a thin glass vessel, carrying too many volatile emotions inside.

So instead, I fall back on teasing. "How dare you be jealous. Have you seen yourself?"

But Alec doesn't play along. "Have you?" He grips my shoulders, turning me so I face a mirror.

And my breath feels suctioned from my chest.

We've stood side by side at the sink, brushing teeth. We've passed the mirror together on our way out of the hotel room, headed in separate directions. Out on the terrace, we are surrounded by gleaming windows; clearly, I know what we look like in a reflection. But here, with both of us dressed completely in black, and with mirrors in front of us and behind us, reflecting a thousand versions of the black-tie couple in smaller and smaller boxes, we're . . . *so* good together. I come up to his shoulder, and his big hand curves possessively around my waist. He's golden; I'm olive-skinned. His hair is neatly combed off his forehead; mine falls straight and glossy down my back. His eyes are dark and soulful, mine hazel and dancing. Together we are perfect. And for a flash, maybe only a handful of seconds, I know we experience the same thing: we can see ourselves standing side by side in a reeling collection of future moments. Welcoming friends at our front door. Walking through LA with fingers interlinked. Standing at the bedside of a loved one. Standing at the altar.

I blink, and it's gone. It's just the two of us in front of a thousand reflections, in a mirror ringed with golden lights, but I know by the look on his face that it happened to him, too.

He pushes my hair aside, bending to suck my neck, and I can't take my eyes off our reflection. I watch his hand slide up my side, up over my chest, spreading over the deep V of the bodice, cupping my breast.

"I promise I'm not possessive," he says quietly. "Not usually." We both stare at the reflection of his fingertips drawing slow circles over my nipple, above the gown. "So why do I feel this way?"

"I don't know. Why do you?"

"Is it crazy? Feeling this after only eleven days?"

"I mean it," I say. "Why *do* you feel this way?"

He meets my eyes. "Are you not looking?"

"Come on." I still his fingers on my breast. "I'm confident about how I look, but there are beautiful women everywhere. That isn't why you feel this way about me specifically." It's weird how the question swells in my mind until it feels like a hot-air balloon, carrying every other thought away. Why me? Why now? And God, why is it *like* this?

He closes his eyes, bending to kiss my shoulder. "Okay." Nodding, he seems to consider this. "Aside from the chemistry between us? I'm aware that you're genuinely amazing. You went to London to chase down a story you saw on a random Twitter feed and are fearlessly pursuing it, no matter how sinister it's become." He looks up, meets my eyes. "Your long-term boyfriend lied to you for an entire year about something enormous, and you had the strength to cut him out so completely that not only have you not spoken to him since the day you told him you knew about his lie, but you let go of your entire friend group who encouraged you to forgive him. You tore into me for not telling you who I was, and you don't let Yael bully you into doing what she wants. You're funny and vulnerable and honest. You don't stare at your reflection in the mirror unless I point it out to you. You're reasonable and confident. You know where I come from, who I was before I became Alexander Kim. You're passionate in bed to a degree I've never experienced, and every time I find out something new about you, I seem to f—" He stops, adjusting his mouth around a word. "I seem to feel more."

I chew my lip, bite-strangling the smile.

His eyes shine as he watches me. "I take it that answer is acceptable?"

I laugh, turning to hug him. "That answer is acceptable."

"I can bring you to London at least once a month," he says, and his gaze moves back and forth between my eyes. "I want to be with you."

"I want to be with you, too."

And just that simply, it's settled.

# Sixteen

Several hours, and a respectable number of drinks later, I leave Billy inside talking to colleagues and head out. There's a line of cars about a block long outside the event, all idling at the curb. My goal is the string of Ubers waiting across the street, but a tall figure in a black suit catches my eye. She's got a shock of wild red hair spilling around her shoulders. This still-surprising version of Yael leans against the front passenger door, reading something on her phone. As if sensing me in the crowd, she looks up, flicks a graceful hand for me to peel away and walk down the block toward her.

In front of her, I stop, smiling. "I didn't tell you earlier, but your hair is awesome."

She nods but predictably doesn't say anything. I expect a lecture, an update, maybe some instruction for how to get back to the room without running into Alec along the way, or even how I should go home tonight. But to my surprise, she reaches out, opening the back door and gesturing for me to climb in. "He insisted."

Alec is in the back, his face partially hidden in shadow. I want to ask what on earth he's thinking, inviting me into his car right out in front of an Associated Press event. I'm not really a somebody, but we're in a place where people who want to find out who I am can do it quickly and connect the dots to the *LA Times* story. Even if his part of it hasn't gone public yet, Alec's privacy is critical and there are at least forty people still here who would recognize Yael for who she is.

Yael climbs into the front seat and quietly tells the driver we're ready to go. Silence seals up inside the car with us.

Alec's hand comes over mine, but this is the only contact we risk. We're otherwise upright, facing forward. We don't speak. I think if I looked at him in that tux again, I'd immediately forget that Yael's disapproving presence is right there, that the poor driver doesn't want to watch me straddle Alec in the back seat. He bends his neck, looking down at his phone, typing with one hand, and I pull my Batphone out of my clutch when it vibrates.

I didn't want to sleep without you.

I grin down at my screen, replying. I would have been really bummed to be alone knowing you're so close.

Three nights left. I wouldn't let one pass.

I squeeze his hand in reply, shoving down the tide of sadness that rises. Slowly, he pulls our joined hands onto his thigh.

His voice surprises me, rising out of the blank silence: "Did you have a nice time after I saw you?"

I glance at him and then Yael. She is undoubtedly the strict teacher and I am the unruly student, continually breaking her rules while the star student—my partner in crime—walks away clean every time. "I did, surprisingly. I usually hate those things."

It was mostly hanging out with other press people, trading stories, digging for information. Fun, exhausting, and the usual—just in fancier clothes.

He slides my hand higher and leaves it at his upper thigh. In the darkness of the car, it's an invitation.

I glance at him and he stares forward, offering only an amused eyebrow flick. So I arch only my pinkie, dragging it along the shape of his cock, half-hard beneath his zipper. Out of the corner of my eye, I catch the jerk of his chest, his sharp intake of air.

I'm still worked up from seeing him across the room with celebrities and nobodies, everyone wanting a bite of his attention. I'm still worked up, too, from our stolen minutes together in the powder room.

"I did, too," he manages after a long pause. "I think because I knew you were there."

I widen my eyes at him, tilting my head: *What are you doing flirting out loud, with Yael right there?*

He grins, but it's wiped clean when I stroke my hand higher again, dragging three fingers down his length now. He's hard, and it's his turn to give me a scandalized look. But really, he put my hand there. Was he expecting me to ignore it?

Like this—my hand offering only glancing, brief contact—we carry on bland cover conversation in the back seat as the driver follows the standard route back to Alec's hotel. But instead of pulling up out front, he passes it, pulling the sleek black BMW down a tight alley, dark but for the occasional cone of yellow streetlight.

Parking in front of two heavy steel doors, the driver climbs out, opening the back door for Alec, rounding the car for me, and then proceeding to the service entry, where he swipes a keycard and opens it.

He returns to the car, but Yael follows us, sweeping inside with clear knowledge of where we're going. This view of the hotel is industrial: walls scraped from wide carts, paint dented from small, everyday collisions with cleaning equipment. She leads us to a service elevator and presses the button for the tenth floor.

Alec takes my hand as we enter, and Yael pretends not to notice. Obviously, I am more charmed by his insistence that we are an item behind closed doors than I am intimidated by her disapproval, but her judgment sits heavily. We ride in stony silence to the top, exit in the same stiff quiet, and Yael says simply, "Be careful," before she heads down the opposite direction to her own room.

Normally I might crack a joke about how much she seems to like me, about how I guess she knows I'm staying at the hotel now, about how I feel like I have to win over the surly father-in-law, but the air between us is so heated from the drive back here. All I can think about is the hard line of him against the sides of my fingers, his quiet *I'll see you later,* whispered into my neck before I left the powder room, his intense, hungry presence now.

He passes the key over the reader, pushes the door open, and our energy snaps the second we're alone. We seem to agree to deal with our own clothing as expediently as possible: With my eyes fixed on his, I'm unhooking the clasp at the back of my neck, letting my dress fall to the floor. He's jerking the top button of his shirt free at his neck, unfastening the rest of them in a blur of dexterity.

I walk backward, kicking off Eden's heels, pushing my underwear down my hips, and leaving them somewhere in the hallway. With a playful growl, he reaches for my waist as he kicks his briefs aside, laughing a sweet "Come here" into my mouth, and lifting me up. The slide of his hard chest over the soft curves of mine pulls him up short and he pivots, pressing me against the wall, pulling my legs around his waist. With a gasp he's there, sliding into me in a single, long push. Alec exhales a soft sound of relief, and whispers, "Holy shit, you feel good."

How can it only have been a matter of hours since I last felt him? It seems like an eternity. I want to take every feeling he draws out of me and translate them into touch: happiness, security, desire. I want to pour them into his body.

After only a few thrusts, I register that it's different, that it's so good I feel a paradoxical wave of desperation and euphoria. Trapped between his body and the wall, I already feel my world expanding and contracting with every breath. Alec is like velvet moving into me. And I'm wild; clutching his back with my hands, begging nonsensically because he's gliding in with such soft skin over such unbelievably solid heat. He's giving me everything already, but I'm greedy and want more. We're hard and soft, rigid and wet,

*God* so wet. Everything feels slippery and urgent—

Alec stills, his breaths broken and sharp. "Wait. *Shit*."

In that instant, I know.

It's just us. Just him inside me, no barrier. No condom. How did we forget? And how can such a small omission change every detail of the sensation of sex with him?

"Wait," he says again, gentler this time, and in the single

syllable I hear a different meaning. This *wait* doesn't mean *stop*. It's a plea for me to let him stay right here just a moment longer. He's never felt me like this, either.

Alec holds himself still, but only under what appears to be the tightest discipline. His arms are shaking. Each wild breath moves him very slightly in and very slightly out again. With him inside me, so hot and hard, I feel every tiny detail. He's so deep, pressed firmly against where I ache painfully for him. I know if I close my eyes and focus on the pressure of his body, just there, and squeeze him, I might come.

This is the madness talking, the delirium from the sensation of being so full—but with him swollen like this, a body so hungry he's nearly excessive inside me, I don't have his discipline. I dig my hands into his hair and rock up against him, slowly clenching and releasing. I drag my tongue over his Adam's apple, tasting the salt and sweetness of his skin. I love how he tastes; I think second only to his deep, quiet voice I'll miss the warmth of his skin on my lips the most.

Alec groans at the scrape of my teeth along the side of his neck, and I am on the verge of an explosion so huge I'm relieved he's holding me; otherwise, my legs would buckle.

So close. I feel him swell, and my own relief rises in me, filling every empty space.

His voice is a hoarse warning; he's a man barely hanging on. "Gigi."

"I'm so close," I plead, voice shaking. "I'm close."

He groans, pressing his forehead to my neck and stilling my hips. "You're going to make me come too if you keep doing that."

I turn my face, resting my lips on his temple. Do I stop us? Do I say the words that are scaling my throat?

The words win. "I'm on birth control. You know I am." He's seen the pills on the counter, watched me take them.

"I know."

He pulls his face away, staring at me for a long moment before carrying me into the bedroom. Alec sets me down and we peel back the covers, lying down side by side on the crisp, clean sheets. I pull him close with greedy, needy hands. He's warm and soft and hard all over.

Just when I get my arms around him and mumble in happy, hungry relief into his neck, he reaches over and turns on a lamp. His skin is washed in muted light, muscles shadowed in perfect angles. Alec Kim's body is the best art in Los Angeles, or anywhere.

"I've never had sex without a condom," he admits, fingers curved with devastating familiarity around my breast. He bends, kissing it.

Immediately, I feel my lusty brain cool its heels. "We can get one if you're not comfortable. I shouldn't have pressured you—"

"No," he says, palm smoothing down over my waist, along the curve of my hip. "Just trying to slow myself down."

I watch his expression shift as he follows the path of his hands with his eyes. He reaches behind my knee, lifting my leg over his hip. His mouth goes slack, lips parting as he reaches between us, guiding himself into me.

And then I can't keep my eyes open anymore. Every time we make love I think, *This, this is the most I can feel. This is the climax of longing.* But I forgot what sex without a condom can feel like—it's been so long. Everything feels so astoundingly *more*.

He comes to a stop as far into me as he can push, his hand spread in a possessive brace at my lower back. "Do that thing you were doing."

With his mouth on mine, distracted and open, wet and hungry, I rock against him, clenching in a rhythm that starts teasing but grows fevered until I'm gasping his name, begging for his help, bracing for an orgasm so intense I'm locked in a soundless scream. Alec watches my flush crawl up my chest, neck, flooding my cheeks, and he starts to move in long strokes, drawing the pleasure out and prolonging it until the cry bursts from my throat, hoarse and desperate.

He smothers it with his mouth, swallowing it down until I come to a gasping, breathless stop beside him. Rolling over fully onto me, Alec brushes my hair away from my sweaty forehead, kissing me. His eyes are dark, glimmering and wild, and with his big hands gripping my hips, he drags me along with him as he rises to his knees, settling back on his heels, and drapes my legs over his thighs. Gently, he reaches above my head and returns with a pillow to tuck beneath my lower back.

"Okay?"

I nod, still foggy, lips and toes tingling. When he reaches down, gripping himself, I wrap my hand around his forearm, wanting to feel the mesmerizing, tight bunching of muscle there.

Like this, he stares down in rapt focus as he teases me with the tight swollen tip before sliding just in and then out again. "Look at you." He bites his lip, nostrils flaring in hunger. "You're wet down to your thighs."

He tilts his face up to the ceiling, choking out an overwhelmed exhale, pulling his focus back down to watch himself do it again. "Do I need to go down there and clean you up with my tongue?" He turns his eyes up to my face and gives me a wicked smile. "You see how wet you're making me? Look, Gigi."

But I can't. I squeeze my eyes closed. Everything in my chest is tight and wild again; how does he carve me down so quickly into something primal and untamed? There's a howling beast trapped in there with my heart, throwing punches, screaming for the full length of him. *Fuck me,* the beast thinks. *Your tongue, your cock, your hand. I don't care. Shove everything into me,* it begs. *Anything.*

Instead Alec slips barely into me and out again. It's like our first night all over again, but this time there isn't anything but his skin, his unbelievable heat. This time there is emotion, too. Raw and fragile, but real.

And this time I know he's going to go longer. He's going to destroy me with teasing. Restraining himself. Edging closer and closer to his own breaking point.

I've just come. I should be drained, still turned inside out in relief, but instead I feel hollow, swollen, and heavy again. I try to watch his face, to focus on the pleasure he takes in restraint, but instead I'm desperate to feel the rough drive of him all the way into me until I'm choking. Every time he teases me with the stretch of the head just inside, he slides away, exhaling a rough grunt. Each pass, he gives me only inches, but I lose my grasp by miles.

I manage only the thinnest sound: "You're making me crazy."

"I know." He slides his thumb over my clit and then follows with the hard tip of his cock, circling. "You're like wet silk. It's all I can do to not fuck you whole."

"*Please.*"

"In a second," he rasps, "but right now I can't stop watching this. I keep thinking," he says, swallowing, "'One more time. Just one more time and I won't be able to take it anymore,' but then I want to see it again. The way it looks when I push in—"

His words cut off and he stares down again. I'm mesmerized by his face. Alec's expression as he does it over and over—pushing barely into me and then out, sliding the tip up and around my clit and then back down, barely in, back out—is hypnotic. The plump, soft curve of his mouth, the stern focus of his brow. It's almost too much. I should close my eyes—to keep myself grounded in this moment on the bed and this earth—but I can't make myself look away.

I know why he's unable to stop doing this again and again. If nothing else, I've become an expert in Alec Kim as a lover. He likes to draw it out like this; he knows how to make his body wait and then explode. But while watching him experience this in focused, careful inches, I realize there's another reason behind it, too, something more tender and sincere: this is a first. Feeling each other in this way will be earth-shaking every time, but after tonight, we never get this sensation for the first time again. That night in Seattle, we blew through so many firsts in a matter of minutes. And just like that, I'm locked into the cycle with him: just one more time I want to see that wild relief of the push forward, the beautiful devastation when he retreats, the tight anticipation when he comes back again.

"I'm so close," he whispers tightly, talking to himself. He sucks in a breath through his teeth, stroking his hand down his length then squeezing his eyes closed. "Gigi, you're wet all over me."

This visible crack in his resolve breaks me and now the greedy beast is back, louder, fists banging at my ribs. I tell him again and again that I'm close, *I'm right there.* I let a single profane plea escape, begging him to fuck me, but he teases us both again and again and again until I go quietly crazy, feeling the slide of a tear down my temple into my hair.

But I know that if he stops, that's where the real madness comes.

*I'm so close.*

He coughs out an abrupt, surprised sound, and I jerk my eyes back to his face. Sweat glistens like stardust on his brow, his lip, his neck. "Oh God," he breathes, and his voice breaks in a gasp. "I can't—"

Still—he's just barely inside me, only a few inches, and I need it all—and then he draws away, angling to tease my clit again. Alec growls in ecstatic restraint, jaw clenched tight, eyes flashing.

"Oh, shit." His voice is tighter now as he presses down and forward, breaths shallow and broken, fucking me in tiny, rocking movements. He closes his eyes as he goes just barely deeper into me. "Oh. Oh my God."

*Please,* I beg silently. *Please fall into me.*

But also: *Please, don't ever finish.*

A familiar sharp groan tells me he's about to come, but he pulls back, gasping "No," stroking the madness between my legs, tapping me with his impossibly hard cock, and I'm on the very cusp, feel my orgasm climbing inevitably, rising like the moon—

I can't help the sob that rips free and it's a tide of emotion swelling, spilling everywhere. I've tipped over: whether or not he pushes fully into me I'm coming—just from the teasing strokes, the anticipation, my body has reached the breaking point. I welcome the hard clench of it, *want it*, want it so bad, and as Alec shifts forward, giving me just enough to set me off, he watches and his own restraint snaps. He shoves in deep, letting out a sharp cry of surrender as I fall. With him thrusting with everything he has, pleasure hits me like a train, spotting everything black at the edge of my vision.

I miss the moment he tumbles after me, but I hear the force of it in his heavy gasping some unknown handful of seconds later. Collapsing to the side, Alec pulls me into his chest, kissing my wet cheeks, my neck. "Gigi." He stills, stroking my cheek again. "Are you crying?"

"Too wrecked," I manage. "Can't speak." My arms feel like concrete when I try to lift them around his shoulders. I give up. "I can't."

He laughs breathlessly. "Give me a second and I'll get us into the shower."

"Just bring the shower here." My voice comes from underwater. "Am I saying this out loud?"

He drags his hand up my stomach, between my breasts.

I'm sweaty, or he is. Realistically, we both are. "You think you don't like to be teased, but you come so hard when I make you wait."

"That was mean."

He laughs again and then wipes a hand over his face. "I almost passed out."

"I think I did pass out."

He kisses my chin. "Yeah, I think you did."

Alec stands and disappears. I hear the water running in the tub, the splash of his hand in the water. Tendrils of steam seep into the bedroom, and he comes back, carefully sliding his arms under me, picking me up.

"I can walk," I say without much conviction, and turn my face into his neck. "You're going to make me love you, aren't you?"

He doesn't even falter, in step or breath. He says only, "I'm sure going to try."

# Seventeen

It's either a miracle or a sixth sense that coaxes my eyes open just after two in the morning, because I would have assumed I'd be wrecked for at least forty-eight hours after what Alec did to me. But even though it's pitch-black in the room, I'm suddenly wide awake.

Alec is curled around me, his cheek pressed against the back of my neck. Deep, steady breaths glide over my skin. When he leaves, I want to capture this feeling and wear it in a locket around my neck. But the thought doesn't send me spiraling into sadness. I feel confident that we'll try to make this work, and that we might even succeed.

A pulse of residual adrenaline kicks to life in my bloodstream when I remember that we can publish the story today. Without a doubt, no matter what else comes in my lifetime, the hunt of this story will remain one of the most satisfying of my career. But the deeper my feelings for Alec become, the more conflicted I am about remaining involved; I am as excited about getting it out into the world as I am about passing the entire thing over to Ian and Billy to handle from here on out. Journalism is a field plagued by the increasing assumption that morality is dead. In school, we are taught a very large number of things journalists *shouldn't* do, but rarely are we told there are things we absolutely *don't* do. Sleeping with Alec always fell in that deeply gray area.

*That's it,* I think. *I'll finish this, hand it off, tell Billy about me and Alec today. I'll be free.* The conflict of interest is an ever-intensifying sour tang at the back of my throat.

I shouldn't, but I can't help it: I pull my work phone off the nightstand to peek. I'm not at all surprised to see that Billy has texted me just after 1:30 a.m. Did we get the OK to go ahead?

As soon as I read these words, it feels like a new shadow passes overhead, clearing my thoughts from the harsh glare of yesterday's excitement. Alec probably has a text from his manager, Melissa, with the answer. I could wake him up and ask. We could hit publish on this in time to get it up for the morning social media rush.

But I've worked too hard on this; I don't want to do anything to jeopardize this story, and our relationship does that. The last thing I want—the last thing any journalist wants—is to become the story that overshadows the real story. Taking Jupiter down is too important.

We have enough without Alec and Sunny's anonymous account. We have the interview with the woman who was approached with a payoff who didn't even know she's been assaulted. Screen caps of numerous videos of the same tattooed man. The chat transcripts describing these women as "Bambis"—as innocents, as *prey*. And finally, the identification of Josef Anders's face and tattoo in this damning video.

Yes, Sunny's account is the nail in the coffin that these videos are not recording consensual acts, but we don't *need* it. We don't have to drag them through this if we can take Anders down without it. There will be follow-ups to this initial report. Waiting gives Alec and Sunny time to decide what they want to include after the dust settles. Billy can assign it to another writer.

This way, the Kims are shielded, and I maintain my integrity.

I check my gut, staring up at the ceiling, waiting for confidence to cool into ambivalence. Ten, twenty, thirty heartbeats pass, and the only thing I feel is relief.

I text Billy back: Run it, but take all details from the anonymous source's story out.

Really? He said no?

I don't answer this directly. We're good without

I put my phone down and roll back into Alec's arms, pressing my face into the familiar shape of his chest.

This choice feels good.

Relief settles heavily into my body, and I easily fall back asleep.

"I don't know how else to say it," I say the next morning, and fall back onto the bed, "but it feels real, E."

Eden takes a deep, slow breath I can hear through my headphones. "Oh, honey."

Alec was already gone before I woke up, but left me an apple, some water, and a note saying,

**Excited for your big day. Melissa gave the go-ahead. Keep me posted. Last night was unbelievable. xx —A**

The story went up an hour ago. Even without Sunny's account, reception has been unreal: There are thousands of comments online; #JupiterScandal and #JosefAnders are both trending internationally. Jupiter has been shut down while an investigation is conducted; footage of Anders being brought in for questioning has been shown on nearly every network. Billy says they've been fielding calls all day and they're hoping to book me for the rounds of morning news programs this week. I want to celebrate this victory with Alec tonight, take him out to dinner. Maybe we can call Sunny together and just have a moment of quiet reunion and relief. Maybe we'll plan my first trip to visit Alec. Maybe after this I can take my first vacation in years.

The future feels like a bright glittery road stretching out forever ahead of us.

"I don't even have to finish my sentences with him," I tell Eden. "We had a big talk at the gala last night and just—" I exhale a laugh. "We must be the two biggest drama queens who just found each other. It's only been a matter of days and we're so dopey."

She lets out a tiny, happy noise.

"I didn't even tell you about my first night here. He came to find me in the middle of the night. He thought I left. But I was in the bathroom freaking out."

"Why?"

"Because we put on a movie and fell asleep. Because it felt like a relationship."

Eden laughs. "I've been with you guys. You *are* in a relationship."

"I know. I think we sort of decided that last night?"

She goes quiet for so long that I'm just about to ask if she dropped out when she says a breathless, "Holy shit."

"Right? Are we idiots for even trying?" I rest my hand over my eyes. "We only have two nights left and—"

"*George.*"

Abruptly, I sit up. When Spence and I broke up, I absorbed so much energy from Eden. I promised myself I wouldn't do that again, and look at me now, just talking about myself. "Shit. Sorry. I am being a self-absorbed monster."

Eden pushes out an abrupt "*Georgia*. Shut up."

She never uses my full name. As in, I can't remember a single time in our ten years of friendship that she has ever called me Georgia. My stomach sinks. "What?"

Her voice is shaking, her words slow. "Check Twitter."

My Batphone vibrates on the bed beside me. "Alec is calling me," I say, and then unease presses in cold at the edge of my thoughts. *He has a marathon day—why is he calling?*

"Call me right away after you talk to him," Eden says.

I frown, confused. "What?"

"Just—go." She disconnects, and I pick up the other phone. "Hey, what are y—"

"I need you to pack up." His voice is firm, tight, as if he's pushing words out between tiny, shallow breaths.

Everything inside me comes to a standstill. "What?"

"I can't talk," he says, and it sounds like he's walking. "I just need you to get all of your things and go home. Head down the back way we came in last night. Through the service elevator. Can you do that?"

My lungs squeeze in, compressing my heartbeat. I can't figure out what's happening. Is this about the article? There was nothing that Alec shared with me in the piece. The reception has been amazing, and he hasn't been exposed, so this can't be about that. I'm—I'm just frozen with confusion.

"Gigi!"

"What?" I say again, uselessly.

"Are you up? Tell me you're up and packing."

My face grows hot, my throat tight, and I stumble into the bathroom, throwing my things into my toiletry bag. Last night he washed my skin with aching sweetness. Now he's telling me unequivocally to go home?

"I don't understand. Are you okay?" All I get is the sound of feet clomping down a hall, the frantic murmur of voices. "Alec, what's going on?"

He speaks to someone else in the background, and I hear Yael say, "Stay here."

Alec returns. "Yael is going to meet you out back. She'll take you home."

"Alec, what—?"

"Why didn't you include my information in the story?"

Everything in me hits pause. "What?"

"The story. You didn't include anything I told you."

"Because I didn't need it," I say, breathless from this inexplicable panic. "I wanted to protect you. Protect us. We had enough—"

"Never mind," he says. "We don't have time. Are you packing up?"

In the empty, calm room my head is a storm of chaos. I grab my toiletry bag and return to the bedroom, staring at the landscape of his clothes and my clothes draped innocently together over the back of a chair. I collect mine, shoving them into my bag. "Are you—"

"Gigi, are you packing up?"

I stare at my open suitcase, my things spilling out of it. So many clothes I haven't worn because I live in my underwear here. I wear his T-shirts. "I *am*, but I don't underst—"

"*Gigi*," he yells, voice unrecognizable. "*Fuck*. Just—please. *Hurry*. Pack up and leave the room."

*Hurry. Pack up and leave the room.*

My phone starts shaking. My hand is trembling so hard I can barely maintain a grip. I never could have imagined how it would feel to hear him be angry with me. A physical shove would hurt less. "Okay," I manage, but the word is garbled by a confused sob. "I don't know what I did, but I'm so sorry."

"Shit." When he speaks again, his voice breaks. "I don't know—" He cuts away again, answering someone in the background again, before telling me, "I have to go."

I hear the burst of a door, wind, and a blast of voices all around him.

And in the melee, only one voice comes through clearly, the sharp sound of a woman cutting through the chaos— "Alexander! What's your connection to the Jupiter scandal?"— before the call disconnects.

# Eighteen

Yael is already waiting for me when I lug my suitcase out to the loading dock, and for once, I don't even try to make nice. With my bag thrown haphazardly in the back, I climb into the passenger seat, click into the seat belt, and wordlessly hunch over my phone to figure out what Eden saw on Twitter, what might have Alec panicking.

Immediately, in Top Trends, I find it and I feel the blood drain from my face.

A shitty British tabloid has posted seven pictures of Alec escorting a woman through the back door of a club, and the post already has thousands of retweets. In each photo, he has his arm around the woman, but it is clear she can barely walk. The angle makes it look like he's dragging her, unwilling and unconscious, into a car parked in the back alley. A coat has been tossed over her head. She could be anyone.

Fox, CNN, and BBC are all reporting the photos leaked of Alexander Kim escorting an unconscious woman from Jupiter. And because the location is so obvious—because the club name JUPITER is visible in stark black paint on the service entry just behind him, and because my enormously damning story went up only an hour ago—it was inevitable that internet sleuths would quickly discover Alec and Josef's history. The connection is made by Twitter user @AlanJ140389, who dug up and photographed an old King's College commencement program with a picture of Alec and Josef with their arms jovially hooked around each other's necks.

Whoever the hooded woman is, Twitter has decided, she's a victim. Specifically, *Alec's* victim.

> @rosestachio I am devastated. I loved AK in West Midlands but I am never watching that show again. Look at this pic and read this story. I'm gonna be sick. #AlexanderKim #JosefAnders #JupiterScandal *Link to: LA Times, Jupiter Owners Caught on Video in VIP Sex Scandal*

> @tacomyburrito This is why we can't have nice things. Literally every man is a predator. Read the LA Times story, too, it's insane. #AlexanderKim #JupiterScandal.

> @4KJules2000 These men are SCUM. #AlexanderKim #JosefAnders #TheTilts #JupiterScandal

My words are being used to bury Alec.

"He was helping Sunny, though," I say through gritted teeth.

Yael says a simple, "Yes."

"I don't understand. Can't he come forward and say that yes, he was there, but he was helping someone get out of the club?" I scroll through the hashtags #JupiterScandal and #AlexanderKim.

"No one will believe him now unless he gives a name. Of

course anyone caught like that would say they had a good reason to be there."

"Then he could explain that he's helping his *sister* out of the club on a night she was drugged." I look over at Yael. "It would take two seconds to fix this. We have it all written up; we could just give *names*. In ten minutes, he could come clean about what happened, explain what this is. He's the hero, not the villain."

I pull out my Batphone and text him, Alec you have to get out in front of this!!

I wait ten seconds while it slowly sends, burning a hole in my phone with my focus. Finally, I hit send on another: Let me help you!

Neither message sends. They turn green, hovering in the void. He's shut off his Gigi Phone.

Even so, I call, and then call again. I call our room—his room, now, I guess. With a blister forming on my lungs every time I inhale, I wonder if he'll even sleep there tonight or if he's already on a plane back to London.

I call his phone again. Each time, it goes straight to voice-mail.

I don't care that Yael is listening to every word, I am frantic; panic eats my oxygen. "Alec," I say in a final plea to his voicemail. "Call me. Let me help you get in front of this."

Hanging up, I drop my phone onto the seat and lean my head back, exhaling a quiet "Shit." Desperate now, I look over at her, willing to grovel. "Can you call him on his regular phone for me?"

Yael finally takes her attention off the road again to glance at me. Her eyes are beautiful; they're the same reddish brown as her hair. "Georgia, he could have controlled the message had you included his account in the piece. In that case, he would have simply come out as the anonymous source and said he was helping a good friend, that of course he wouldn't be cooperating with the story if he were one of the people committing the crimes. But we're behind the momentum now; *now* it's about damage control."

This speech includes more words than I've ever heard Yael use at once, and all I can think to say in response is, "We can still fix this."

"Perhaps, but Alec wouldn't possibly give Sunny's name if in the end no one believes him anyway and it tarnishes them both."

"Why wouldn't anyone believe him?"

"Revealing that Sunny was assaulted may be no big deal to the American press but it isn't like that in the UK. And I am not sure how the news would be handled elsewhere. More often than not, the victim is blamed. Given these circumstances, given how this looks, he won't force her into that position."

"But—"

"He won't force her into that position," she repeats, adamant.

"So he would rather be seen as a criminal?"

"Where Sunny is concerned, yes."

"Can you drop me at the *Times*? I need to go into the office."

She nods, changing lanes.

Two fists come around my organs, twisting. "What now?"

"For you? Hope that no one associates you with Alec."

I clench my jaw, angry and hurt. "I mean what's next for Alec, but okay."

Yael glances over, and I sense the slightest softening of her posture next to me. "For what it's worth, he's trying to protect you, too. You work for the *Times*. It will look very bad for you if anyone discovers you were staying at the hotel with him. You're beautiful and friendly. One makes you noticeable, both make you memorable. For everyone's sake, I truly hope no one remembers you."

"We cannot use his account," I say to Billy as soon as I burst into his fourth-floor office. I feel a hundred pairs of eyes on me and close the door even though everything is glass and there is no such thing as privacy here. My suitcase falls heavily over where I've left it, but I ignore it. "Do not add it."

My editor lets out a booming "Fuck!" into the air and stands, rounding his desk to stare out his office door in frustrated silence for several aggravated moments. "You can't talk him out of it? It would clear his name."

"I can't even get ahold of him anymore." I don't bother hiding the sob, and my knees buckle so that I sit gracelessly onto the couch against one wall. Out of the car, away from Yael, I feel my composure slipping. "I don't know what to do. I've been completely cut off."

Across the room, Billy goes silent. Long enough for me to count to ten, and I know now he's noticed my suitcase. "Shit, Georgia. You two?"

"I tried to tell you last night and chickened out." I cover my face. I'm too devastated to be ashamed. "I've known him since I was seven, Billy. We ran into each other in Seattle, and I didn't know he was involved until after we . . ."

"Shit. *Shit*."

"Billy, it was my call to pull his account—he didn't know," I admit, keeping my voice as steady as possible. "I was trying to protect him and also not rely on information I obtained from someone I was sleeping with. And now that he's being ripped to shreds online, his team worries that if he comes forward, it looks like he's just covering his ass unless he gives a name, and he doesn't want to come out and say that Sunny was drugged and assaulted."

Billy's seething anger ripples across the distance separating us. "You're telling me *you* decided to cut this? Without my input, and without asking your source?"

God, this is such a mess. I swallow a sob because Billy doesn't want to see me cry right now. "Yes, I did."

"This story is too big, and you are too green to make that call." The disappointment in Billy's voice is gutting. "Your relationship to a primary source in a story like this is the kind of stuff you disclose to me, George. I can help you if you tell me—I can't help you if you don't."

"I know. I'm sorry."

Billy moves back around his desk, falling into his chair and gripping his forehead.

"He's not a creep," I say. I feel sick. My insides swim.

"Doesn't matter if you and I are the only ones who know it. It doesn't look good."

"He went in there to get his sister out." Urgency, panic, heartache: they all swarm like angry bees in my chest. "You *know* this."

"It doesn't matter if we don't have it on the record!" Billy slaps a flattened palm to his desk. "His association with Anders is bad. It's *all* bad, George. He's really gonna take the hit?"

I nod, staring down at my hands. "Looks like it."

"This is fucking wild, man. Eventually he'll be cleared, but who knows what it does to his career in the meantime?"

"I know. I feel helpless." More than helpless, I feel like I want to climb out of my own skin. I want to go back to last night and talk this through with Billy. I want to go back to early this morning at the Waldorf Astoria and yank Alec into my arms. I can't imagine what he's going through right now, and I can't be with him while he goes through it. I can't even apologize, because he's not taking my calls.

*You're going to make me love you, aren't you?*

*I'm sure going to try.*

Oh my God. A sob tears up my throat as I struggle to hold it down. I want to eat my own fist and punch down the pain.

"It looks bad," he says again. It's sinking in for Billy. I can hear his conviction gathering steam. "You're going to have to stay the hell away from him."

"I know." I bite my lips until I'm sure I can get the next words out without crying. "I don't think that will be a problem."

It's mayhem at the office; everyone wants to congratulate me. No one understands the gravity of what's happening with Alec; for all they know—and because he won't come forward—he's just another trash-can human being rightfully dragged for his sins. It's painful battling my way from Billy's office, through the sea of cubicles, and back out to the street to catch a Lyft. Nearly everyone who comes up to me to say something nice, to congratulate me, to pass along their praise is my senior in some way. I'm still considered the scrappy new kid. Some of these people are writers I've admired for years. I can only hope that every single one reads my watery eyes and warbling voice as the good kind of overwhelmed exhaustion.

For the first twenty minutes after I get home, I have no idea what to do with myself. I want to leave my body through sleep but am not tired. I want to eat away this hollow ache in my gut but even the thought of food makes me nauseated. I want to distract myself with work, but I have nothing to write. Alec still hasn't read my texts. The pictures have now spread past social media and are on the news—shared with my headline.

I barely move. I stare up at my ceiling, at the fan that goes around and around and around, wishing for nothing more than the distance of time. I remember this feeling after Spence—the helpless, skin-clawing crawl of time passing after heartbreak. Wanting to skip all the pain and anguish. And on top of it, there is guilt this time, knowing that a choice I made without asking has complicated things for Alec. I snatched an easy explanation right out of his hands.

And all I can do is sit in the pain, breathing through it. Remembering the sound of his voice and the weight of his hands, the heat of him in the bath last night and his lazy, slippery kisses. I can only let this hurt and anger and sadness pass through me. I know I didn't imagine what happened between us, and I'm worried this is it for us. I'm worried about him.

I wonder whether he'll get written out of the show, whether the network will back him up, whether there is some other way to clear his name that doesn't involve Sunny. I wonder all of these things for him in a flurry, hoping that he can make it out the other side all the while knowing that if the media is unkind, the internet is a mass of bloodthirsty savages. Every minute that passes without Alec fixing this is a year off his life as an actor.

I'm in the middle of a mental tornado when Eden walks into my room. "I thought you were at work."

"I was," she says. "I came home." Dark circles carve shadows beneath her eyes; she looks like she is about to fall over. She looks worse than I feel. "Have you seen Twitter?"

"I saw his pics, yeah. It's not what it looks like."

She shakes her head and hands me her phone, and I don't even feel satisfied to have been right that we were not anonymous on the beach. That the stupid-hat-and-sunglasses trick did not hide our identities when we went out for doughnuts. And that no matter how many times Alec looked over my shoulder at the bar in Seattle, he still missed the cell phone pointed right at us.

# Nineteen

*Alec sitting across the low bar table from me, our hands are joined over the center, eyes locked.*

*Alec pinning me against the rock cliff, his hand grasping my waist, mouth sweetly pressed to mine.*

*Alec in sunglasses and a baseball hat, laughing as I feed him a bite of doughnut.*

*Me reaching to wipe a smudge of chocolate from the corner of Alec's mouth.*

All these perfect memories have been posted by TMZ for the whole world to see. Their carefully curated collection, shared in a single tweet, has nearly five thousand retweets and ten times as many likes in only two hours.

I've seen the internet dogpile before, but I've never even been a close bystander. Now, in the same tweets that contain thinly veiled rape accusations against Alec, I am accused of covering up his crimes, of using my position at the *LA Times* to shelter a criminal. With the photos of him outside Jupiter, it is a veritable bloodbath now. Eden has already had to delete all of the social media apps from my phone because I was starting to hyperventilate.

Two hours later, still numb and reeling, I'm walking to the kitchen for a glass of water when my phone rings. I've been expecting this call at some point from Billy, but adrenaline makes me light-headed anyway and I perch carefully at the edge of the couch. I can't decide whether this call took more or less time to arrive than I expected.

He's silent for a good five seconds before saying only, "Hey, George."

My voice is hoarse from yelling into the void of my bedroom. "Hey." I close my eyes and pull my brain into order. "I bet I know why you're calling. We need to craft a response plan."

A long, blown-out exhale. "Actually, kiddo, I gotta ask you to come in and drop off your credentials."

My world hits pause, and my stomach drops through the floor. He's . . . firing me? Sex with sources is frowned upon but rarely results in termination anymore. "What?"

Billy's voice comes out thinner. "We'll do a quick exit interview. I promise to keep it painless."

I stare at the wall in shock. Painless? Is he for real? I didn't think it would be possible, but this conversation with Billy is more painful than the last one we had. He sounds so defeated, telling me I'm out of a job. I've seen my boss excitedly foulmouthed, angrily foulmouthed, and joyfully foulmouthed. But I've never heard him sound resigned before. He isn't even going to fight for me?

"Billy." My voice comes out wavy with heat. I'm past devastated now and am sliding into angry. "You're *firing* me for sleeping with Alec? Are you serious? This is exactly why I didn't include his account in the story!"

"You know this isn't coming from me," he says.

I don't know what to say to that. It is absolutely him—Billy has been at the *Times* for twenty years; he has pull there. The Netflix and BBC spokespeople have already come out and stated unequivocally that Alec is not in any way involved in the alleged crimes that happened at Jupiter. Billy and the *Times* could come out with the same; they could keep me if they wanted.

"Unbelievable," I say, pacing. "You know I tried to do the right thing here."

"I hate being told what to do," he says, "but in this case, I agree the optics aren't good."

I lift a shaking hand and smother back an agitated, disbelieving laugh. It was Eden who, only an hour ago, in a brief moment of hysterical levity, suggested we revise our drinking game with some truly macabre rules:

- Take a drink every time we come across a fresh, absurd headline; the recent favorite is "Feeding Him Doughnuts While She Feeds Fellow Women to the Wolves."
- Take a drink every time a new meme is created by Alec's fangirls trashing my body in the beach photos.
- Take a drink anytime a news article says, "The optics aren't good."

"Billy," I say, with as much control as I can manage, "these tweets accusing me of helping a criminal make zero sense! I'm the one who exposed the Jupiter crimes! Firing me is absolute bullshit."

"I get it, George."

"I mean it. I was researching this story before I ran into Alec in Seattle."

"I know."

"And you know he didn't even do this!"

Billy sighs. "I know."

I make a mental note to add a rule to the game: take a drink every time Billy gives me a resigned "I know" and still does not go to bat for me.

"I'm sorry it didn't work out better, George. I don't know what else to tell you."

"I'll drop off my credentials in the lobby," I say, and hang up.


Eden understands that there is no way in hell I can sleep in my own bed tonight, not when I haven't yet washed my sheets since Alec slept here, not with his swim trunks slung over my shower door and his toothbrush in the cup next to mine, and not with him ignoring all my calls and texts. Once I'm home from dropping off my *LA Times* office keys and credentials, I give up trying to get ahold of him and toss the cursed Batphone onto my bed, focusing instead on packing a small weekend bag. My plan: head to my parents' place, crawl into my old bed, sleep for a week.

My best friend watches silently. We're now out of words. Our last exchange was a simple "This fucking sucks," repeated a few times with increasing emphasis until we fell quiet again. But as I'm zipping up my bag, Eden bolts upright when the Batphone starts to vibrate on the bed, tossing it to me.

I let out a scream, fumbling it like a hot potato.

"Alec!" I yell, answering. "Holy shit! This day! Where are—?"

"I'm headed back," he cuts in calmly, and wind whips through the line.

"Back?" I repeat, pausing my pacing between my bed and closet. "Back to the hotel?"

"To London."

Just hearing his voice triggers relief and it floods me with warmth. "Okay. That makes sense. Oh my God it's so good to hear your v—"

"I wanted to let you know," he says with quiet finality.

Confused, I carefully enunciate. "Thank you. Yeah. I— Alec, look—"

"And I want to make sure you're clear that my permission to print my account is rescinded."

"Your—?" I break off, frozen in shock. He has no way of knowing I've been fired, but I'm not going to add to his turmoil by telling him. Especially when he sounds like a fucking robot. "Of course. We wouldn't add anything without your permission."

He's quiet in response—meaningfully quiet—and I meet Eden's eyes. She's staring at me like she wants to bore a hole in my skull and read what's happening there. "Listen," I say gently, "I'm sorry I changed the story and pulled your part of it. I hope you know my intention was to protect you. You and Sunny. You and me."

"We understand."

"*We?*" I scan my mind for something better to say, some words that will pull him out of this quiet damage-control monotone and remind him that I'm here and I'm *his*, and even though this is genuinely shit, we can figure out a plan together.

But Alec speaks first. "Please take care, Gigi."

Blank inside, I stare at the wall. "I . . . wait. Alec? That's it?"

The other end of the line is oddly flat.

He fucking hung up.

Pulling the phone away from my ear, I stare at my home screen, a photo I took of him playing *Mario Kart*, his tongue sticking out, trapped between his perfect, grinning teeth. Inside I am glowing—I mean, I am positively *incandescent*—with rage. "Is he fucking serious?"

"What just happened?"

I'm trying to relax my jaw so that I can get more words out than the string of curses that want to rip free, but I can't. I just shake my head again. "Holy shit."

"Georgie, what?"

"He's going back to London," I say.

"Okay?" She's trying to keep me from blowing a fuse. "That makes sense, right? He probably wants to get his team and family together."

"He told me he was rescinding his permission to print his account and to—and I quote—'please take care,' and then he hung up."

"He just hung up?"

I look at her and nod.

Eden lets out a low, violent "No he fucking did *not*."

"He sure did."

She stands. "Be right back, I need to put all of my *West Midlands* shirts in the trash."

"That is not what we're doing here," I say to her, struggling to pull my composure together. "We are going to give him more grace than he deserves." But then I look at my Batphone one more time, turn it off, walk into my bathroom, and drop it in the trash.


My mom is beside herself with worry when I get to the house, but I promise her that I will drink an entire bottle of wine and unload everything if I can only have an hour to go pound the pavement alone.

I pull on my running shoes and bolt from the porch with angry music blasting in my ears. Eden made me a playlist titled Men Are Trash, and I admit, it's exactly what I needed to channel this confusion and hurt into something kinetic. I didn't stretch first—no doubt I'll regret it, but not nearly as much as I'll regret letting my subconscious guide me two and a half miles down the road to the Kim family's old house.

It's been repainted. No longer a pale yellow house with a soft patch of grass, it is now a rich cream with olive-green trim, a xeriscaped yard, and two Teslas parked out front. For as much as the house looks brand-new, the shape of the front window is the same, and I can imagine sitting on the soft velvet couch just inside, can hear the slapping echo of Alec's skateboard down the sun-warped street.

My brain tunnels through time. At this exact moment yesterday, I was getting ready for the gala. And less than twenty-four hours ago, Alec was cleaning my skin with body wash and his big hands, telling me about the place he wanted to take me for dinner on our first night in London next month.

I haven't cried yet, but before I can actively hold myself together, I'm bursting into tears, letting it all out on the dashed yellow line in the middle of Pearl Street.

What the fuck just happened?

I tried to do the right thing, tried to protect everyone, and ended up losing my job and my new boyfriend in a single afternoon.

My life has emptied of meaning so suddenly that it almost feels like I'm closing in on myself, collapsing inward. Sitting at the curb, I stare at a line of ants moving past the round toe of my shoe. Slowly my eyes lose focus until the ants turn into a blurred black line, waving on the concrete, doing nothing but moving forward one step at a time.

I return to my parents' place at least two hours later than I'd planned, to find my mother on the porch with her phone in her hand, Eden standing next to her. They march toward me, lectures ready, words overlapping.

I let them have this. I didn't take my phone. I was just dumped and fired. I didn't notice how much time had passed on the curb until the sun was gone and I realized my old iPod had played the playlist at least three times through.

They gather me inside, depositing me on the couch. Some food materializes. Eden is on one side of me, Mom on the other, and I hate this familiar comfort.

Even though we did this exact same thing only six months ago, this time it feels infinitely worse.

# Twenty

I spend five minutes in my car at the curb outside my apartment on Sunday morning. Just working up the energy to climb the steps, to go inside and face a laptop with a résumé that needs to be updated, face a suitcase full of things I had at the hotel, face a bed that I last slept in with Alec beside me.

The optimism and elation of Friday morning feel like they happened a decade ago. My parents wanted me to stay a few more days but I honestly could not handle the weight of their concern on top of my own terror about the future.

Under normal circumstances, I would have immediately recognized the shadow on my doorstep. If my brain wasn't full of heartbreak and insomnia, I would know the broad expanse of those shoulders, the narrow taper of the waist. I would recognize the baseball hat, the black T-shirt, black jeans. And in particular, I would see the hand carefully lowering a royal-blue shopping bag to my apartment doormat and remember that I claimed that hand as mine just over a week ago.

But it takes a beat for my conscious brain to turn on—long enough for me to instinctively say, "Um, hello?"—and as soon as the words are out, awareness hits, and my heart splinters into a thousand pieces.

I would bolt back to my car if my feet weren't cemented to the ground. I never expected to see Alec again. Thirty-six hours ago, he told me he was flying home to London and made no indication that we would ever speak again. I spent the weekend running until I had bloody blisters on my heels and strict orders from my mother to sit my ass down. But every time I did, I immediately wanted to get up and drive home to pull my Batphone out of the trash and see if he'd called, already knowing he hadn't.

Alec freezes with his back to me and then slowly turns. He fumbles to pull off his sunglasses, and the moment his eyes are visible, I feel the reaction to his appearance like a fist to my solar plexus. He looks terrible. His skin is sallow; stubble shadows his chin. His eyes are red-rimmed and glassy, perfect lips cracked.

I'm unable to easily describe what this does to my heart. The only way to blunt the instinct to move to him and hold him is to tear my eyes away from his face.

He clearly didn't expect to see me, either. "Gigi." His eyes do a quick scan of my body. I bet I look a lot like I did in the hotel lobby in Seattle, but this time I want to shove the truth of it in his face. My hair is wrapped up in a greasy, messy bun, eyes bloodshot and flat. My limbs are shaking from overuse and exhaustion.

I direct the question over his right shoulder. "What are you doing here?"

"I'm . . ." He gestures to the bag. "You left some things at the hotel."

I release a sharp, abrupt laugh. Boy, did I. My trust in men. A desire to love again. My career. Oh, maybe also some clothes. "I was instructed to pack up pretty fast."

"I know," he says immediately, but the next words take a bit longer for him to put together. "I hate—*hate*—how that happened. It was chaos. If I could do it over, I would have come directly to you."

I don't say anything to this. Having to leave the suite quickly wasn't really what hurt. I like to think he was protecting me, even if it was disorienting and painful. What hurt was how he cut me off, didn't answer my calls, and the *Please take care* he eventually gave me as a shitty parting gift.

But maybe what hurts most of all is how it feels like he's sneaking up to my front door and leaving a bag without knocking. How painful would it have been to open my door and see that there, knowing he'd been here and left without a word? It would be worse than if he'd just kept all my things.

Tears, hot and burning, threaten at the back of my throat. I've done a pretty good job since Friday of stitching myself together, but I need him to go. All weekend I convinced myself that if I ever saw his face again, it would hit me differently. I would associate it with the betrayal of not getting to explain myself, of not getting the benefit of the doubt. But standing this close to him, it isn't like that.

Even when I'm furious, his presence fills me up inside. I resent knowing that if he would only hug me, we would both be okay. The hollow space in my heart is uniquely Alec-shaped. The line of his neck, the curve of his mouth, the angle of his jaw—these are all odd comforts. So is the soft, steady gaze that held me like an anchor whether he was listening to me talk about work or pinning me on the razor-thin edge between pleasure and desperation. Those dark, searching eyes saw through me from the first moment they met mine in the airport. There wasn't one second where Alec Kim didn't look straight into the center of me, taking me in all at once. And he kept looking like what he saw there lit him up inside.

It's how he's looking at me now, too. It's *wild* to think he can still manage this façade after the way he shoved me away in our first moment of crisis. My heart squeezes painfully, closing a shutter on tender feelings.

"I meant what are you doing here, in LA," I say. "You said you were leaving on Friday."

"I couldn't." He swallows audibly. "I had to—" He stops, reaching up to scrub his face with a frustrated hand. His eyes turn a little wild. "Have you been out all night?"

I am astounded at the nerve of this question. He told me to pack up and leave, shut me out on the phone, stayed in LA after he told me he was leaving, and now he wants to know whether I've slept somewhere else?

"Yep," I say, daring him to ask where I've been.

But he doesn't. He turns his face away, jaw clenched, nostrils flared, and I realize he's struggling to not cry. "Okay," he says, finally. "Not my business."

What is he thinking? That he's catching me at the end of a walk of shame? He knows better. He knows *me* better. If we weren't currently at DEFCON-1 in our emotions, he would guess that I'd been at my parents' place. This is the insanity of our circumstances taking hold of his adrenaline and dumping it like gasoline into his bloodstream.

"I didn't want to sleep in my bed." It's all I'm willing to give him. "The last time I was there you were with me."

Alec reaches up, pinching the bridge of his nose, covertly wiping his eyes. "I get it. I changed hotels for the same reason."

*Don't break,* I tell myself when he confesses this, imagining the insanity of him even trying to leave the Waldorf Astoria, let alone check in somewhere else. He would be absolutely mobbed. What on earth would make it worth it?

Alec shifts on his feet, clearing his throat once and then again. I fix my attention on the ground between us, trying to unchain everything I'm feeling, separating anger from sadness from fear from longing, binning them into different spaces in my body so I can make room to breathe.

When he speaks, his words are hoarse. "I'll never be able to apologize enough for how I behaved on Friday."

He's probably right, and there's nothing for me to say. I wanted to talk to him, to help him fix this—help us both fix it—but he shut me out. All my words have dried up.

Silence yawns between us. "To be honest, the entire affair was a mistake," I say with careful control. "Your career is a mess. I've been fired." He barely reacts, and my anger flares. "The moment I saw you at the hotel room in LA, I should have turned around and walked back out."

I don't look at his face so I can't be sure, but I imagine Alec staring at me like he knows it would have been easier to split atoms in my fists than to walk away from him that morning.

Not that it would have mattered anyway—someone still

took photos of us in Seattle. I was screwed from the very beginning.

"I know you're angry," Alec says, "and I get it. I absolutely get it. But I was in an impossible position. I needed to figure out a plan with Sunny. I couldn't just . . ." He falters. "I couldn't just lay her story out there to save my own ass, like it was that simple."

I'm still so mad, I'm not even willing to own the fact out loud that it would have been easier to handle all of this if I'd included his account in the write-up. Because with a couple days' distance—even feeling messy and hurt—I still don't regret my instinct to try to protect the people I love. I don't regret only using information I got cleanly.

"So why did you bother staying in LA?" I ask. "Why aren't you in London, figuring it out with Sunny?"

He stares at me and then blinks away, jaw tight. I wait another few seconds for an answer before I realize one isn't coming.

*Whatever,* I think. *Say your piece. Be done.* I swallow, pushing the next words out. "Your loyalty to the people in your life is one of the things that I love most about you." He snaps his attention back to my face. "But what about *me*?" I ask, and the dam breaks. "You decided to protect your sister, and I understand, but you threw me away so quickly. When things first started with us, the story was the biggest thing that had ever happened to me. But then, all of a sudden, *you* were the biggest thing that had ever happened to me. And here I ended up with neither."

Alec sucks in a shaking breath, nostrils flared. "I know."

"You told me you were going to do your best to make me

love you," I say, "and then twelve hours later had me get my shit out of your hotel room and told me you were leaving town and to 'please take care.' I realize I've only had you for fourteen days, and Sunny is your blood, but it still tore me in half to be thrown away like that. You could have at least *talked* to me."

He opens his mouth but closes it again. I expect him to argue, but he says only, "You're right. I could have."

"I'm so glad I left the Batphone here," I tell him, and he takes this like a shove to his chest. "I would have been checking it constantly. It would have killed me to see you this morning, knowing you were in town this whole time."

"Gigi—"

I cut him off, pointing to the bag on my doorstep. "You thought I was inside, didn't you? You weren't even going to talk to me. Did you just swing by here on your way to the airport to leave my crap on my porch?"

Alec blinks away, staring at the ground. "I think you're making a lot of assumptions right now."

"You know what? I don't actually care what you think anymore."

In response to this, Alec bites his lip, nodding like I've hit my target. A horn honks at the curb, pulling his attention to the open stairwell as he says, "I wish we could just go back in time to Seattle and decide to stay there for two weeks and fuck everything else. This has been the best two weeks of my life and the worst three days of my life."

This truth hits with startling accuracy. I hate how the easiest and most passionate relationship of my life has been trashed by circumstance. I hate the way Alec is taking the hit. And I hate that the thing I admire deeply about him—his sense of duty to his family, to the public—means that he's doing exactly what everyone who knows him knew he would do. Alec never gets to belong to himself. Except with me, I realize. This thing that hurt me so acutely after our first night is now the deepest truth between us: He's been real with me from that very first minute in Seattle. He knows I can handle myself. He doesn't have to be my protector.

Suddenly my anger dissipates. I can't let it be like this if this is the last time I see him. He looks like he hasn't slept or eaten. I remember hating Spence enough to not even want to see his face but that isn't the case here. I can hate Alec and myself and this situation forever, but I don't want angry silence to be my last memory of him.

"Have you slept? Eaten anything?" I study his face, his posture, his rumpled clothes. He doesn't look like any version of Alec Kim I've ever imagined. "You look terrible."

His eyes search mine, and I remember what he asked me in the hotel that first day in LA—can see the question in his eyes right now: *How mad can you be if you're looking at me like that?*

I feel it, too, that I'm not glaring at him with anger, but watching him with carefully protected adoration. I blink and startle in surprise when tears streak down my face. I didn't even realize I'd started to cry. Alec takes a step closer, but I immediately take a step back. "Don't."

"Gigi . . ."

"I'm not going to invite you inside." I swipe at my face. "I can't."

Alec nods. "Probably a good idea. I wouldn't want to leave if I went inside with you."

Confused, I chew my lip, fighting the way a sob wants to rise up and rip out of me. Right now, he looks like he loves me.

"Okay," I say. "Have a good trip."

"Read what I wrote," he says, nodding to the bag. Alec takes a step forward and bends, pressing his lips to my cheek. When he straightens, he lifts his eyes up and over my shoulder and seems to throw an anchor there in the distance, needing something to propel himself forward. I stare at the shopping bag, listening to his footsteps as he jogs down the stairwell. I curl my toes into the soles of my shoes to keep from following after him. A minute later, an engine starts, a car pulls from the curb, and this time, Alec Kim is really on his way out of LA.

# Twenty-One

My biggest worry about being back in my bed is unfounded: there isn't any trace of Alec in here. I set the shopping bag down and pick up a pillow, pressing it to my face. The sheets are crisp and smell like fabric softener. Eden. She got rid of his things, too—the toothbrush, the swim trunks. If there was anything else he might have left here, I'll never know.

I shower until I'm loose and drowsy, dry off adequately, and pull on sweats and a tank top before falling backward onto my bed, staring at the ceiling. Pointedly ignoring the blue shopping bag. I'm not ready to see my things and remember how they looked in his hotel suite.

From beyond my closed bedroom door, I can hear Eden quietly moving around the apartment. Making coffee. Unloading the dishwasher. Taking out the trash and recycling. Her presence is sweetly reassuring. With a groan, I roll myself up in my blankets, squeezing my eyes closed.

But suddenly, I am wide awake. There is a ticking bomb in here with me. I open my eyes and stare across the room at the bag.

*Read what I wrote.*

Whatever else is in there, there is a note.

I should not read it with tired eyes, an exhausted brain. I should not read it feeling as emotional as I do.

I know better, but kick away the blankets anyway, get up, and cross the room.

Inside the bag is my ugly Post Malone hat, the game console Alec bought for us only a week ago. But not everything in here is something I forgot at the suite. There's a small box of fresh doughnuts. An expensive bottle of Zinfandel.

Alec's dress shirt that I wore when I tied his bow tie.

I bite my lips, holding in the pained gasp as I curl it into my chest, inhaling.

The last item, at the bottom of the bag, is a postcard with a beautiful picture of Laguna Beach. On the blank side, Alec has written only a handful of words.

**Gigi,**
**I know you are upset.**
**But please answer my calls.**
**—A**

His calls?

My heart drops and a frantic, heavy bolus of adrenaline hits my bloodstream. He never had my other number.

*I meant what are you doing in LA.*

*I couldn't,* he'd said. *I had to—*

Oh God. No.

*You could have talked to me,* I'd said.

His expression, so controlled. *You're right. I could have.*

The way he reacted like he'd been pushed when I told him

I'd left the Batphone here. How he quietly told me I was making assumptions about why I'd found him on my doorstep.

I trip into the bathroom, falling to my knees and checking the trash.

Eden cleaned everything. There's nothing but a fresh bag there.

A sob rips from me but when I stand, I see the Post-it note on the bowl of the sink:

> *I turned it off, but it's in your nightstand. If you throw it away again, I promise to leave it there. —E.*

With shaking hands, I move to the bedroom, pull the Batphone out of the drawer. In the time it takes to turn on, I force myself to pull in deep, intentional breaths so I don't panic. The screen comes to life.

Nothing.

Nothing.

There's nothing.

I turn, sitting on the floor, leaning against my bed, struggling against the throat-swelling sting of disappointed tears.

And then my phone buzzes in my palm. With blurry eyes, I look down at a screen that is lit up with dozens of notifications. Missed calls. Voicemails.

I check the time stamps. Barely two hours after he called and told me to "please take care," Alec called me back.

And then again.

And again.

And again.

His calls span Friday afternoon and deep into the night. They start up again before sunrise on Saturday.

Fourteen missed calls in total, all while I was at my parents' house, assuming he was on a plane, assuming he had prioritized everything above me. His first voicemail is seven seconds long. "Gigi. Please call me back. I've changed my plans and am not flying home until Sunday."

Twelve more missed calls and then his second, and final, voicemail, from late in the afternoon on Saturday. It's just over a minute long.

"Gigi." He pauses, exhaling slowly. "Right. I don't know why I keep calling when you haven't answered any of the other times. But I heard earlier today that you lost your job and am gutted. Here I am, in the thick of this stupid internet hurricane and yet I'm at an absolute standstill. Since you won't answer, here is what I wanted you to know. I'd planned to fly home to Sunny to discuss how to handle this. But I tried to leave and absolutely could not get on the plane without you. I kept hearing your voice on the phone, telling me over and over that you didn't understand. It was all a blur, but I must have been cold to you." His words break, his voice cracking. "After everything—to be accused . . . well. I was in shock." He breaks off again, huffing out another breath. "Anyway, so here I am, wandering LA, doing absolutely nothing, letting this problem fester. Retracing our steps the past two weeks and wondering how on earth it is that I could fall in love in a matter of days. But I did. In fact, I think I fell in love in a matter of minutes, with the woman sitting opposite me at a hotel bar. She was exhausted but mesmerizing, wearing a red dress and nothing else." He goes silent for a beat. "Gigi, I can't let the present circumstances rob us of the chance to see where this can go." I hear him swallow and then pull in a shaky breath. "I suppose I'll call you again when I get to London. I hope you'll answer."

I cup a hand over my mouth, capturing the sob that escapes. I could have been with him this weekend. We could have been weathering this storm together. Regret sends a staggering wave of nausea through my gut, and I have to close my eyes, tilt my face to the ceiling and suck in air.

*. . . wondering how on earth it is that I could fall in love in a matter of days.*

*In fact, I think I fell in love in a matter of minutes, with the woman sitting opposite me at a hotel bar.*

I close my eyes, remembering. Rewriting the horror of seeing the photos of us online, reclaiming that night.

*She was exhausted but mesmerizing, wearing a red dress and nothing else.*

Curiosity presses gently at the edges of my thoughts, propelling me to my feet. I search through the suitcase I'd hastily packed at the Waldorf Astoria. I rifle back through the contents of the shopping bag he left on my doorstep. But I can't find my red dress anywhere.

Retrieving Alec's shirt from the bag, I pull it on, climb into bed, and listen to his voicemail again and again and again until I fall asleep.

When I wake up, the apartment is still, sounds muted. It's a few minutes before two, meaning a miracle has occurred and I've slept much of the day away.

Outside my room, the lights are out and late-afternoon sunlight slants into the front window, turning the yellow couch a soft gold, turning the big blue chair a vibrant turquoise. The apartment is spotless. There are fresh flowers on the small dining room table, and a note that says simply: *I love you. —E.*

For the first time in days, I feel like I can pull in a deep breath.

Eden has set out a bowl of leftovers on the kitchen counter with pointedly obvious instructions.

*Step 1: Place bowl in microwave.*
*Step 2: Heat for two minutes.*
*Step 3: Carefully remove bowl from microwave.*
*Step 4: Get a fork.*
*Step 5: Use fork to put food in your mouth.*
*Step 6: Repeat step 5 until the bowl is empty.*

I've just finished step 1 when the doorbell rings. I know it isn't the downstairs neighbor telling me we're being too loud. I hope it isn't the upstairs neighbor warning me they have a water leak. Maybe Eden forgot her keys. Maybe Mom wanted to check on me. Maybe . . . I laugh dryly as I let the train of thought die an abrupt death.

But, I remind myself, Alec is going to call me when he gets to London. And that's a start.

It's only when I open the door that I'm conscious I didn't bother to comb my hair after my shower. In fact, I haven't glanced in a mirror in several days. I find myself facing two beautiful women while I've got birds' nest hair and am wearing Alec's dress shirt, a stretched-out tank top, and no bra.

I immediately recognize one of them, but she is the second to last person I expect to see there.

"Georgia," Yael says in disgust, "you look like garbage."

The woman at Yael's side smacks her lightly, and recognition hits like a slap. "Don't be mean. She's had a very shitty weekend." Sunny Kim gives me a familiar, dimpled smile, and my lungs take a nostalgic nosedive.

I look back over my shoulder. Yes, I'm in my own doorway. Yes, I appear to be awake. Yael and Sunny stare at me, waiting for me to say something. I manage only, "What is this?"

Sunny steps forward, wrapping her arms around my shoulders. "Hi."

On instinct, I lift my arms, too, tentatively snaking them around her waist. There's a familiarity to the feel of her against me. Her grown-up body still carries the echo of her younger one. "Hi."

"I realize this is a surprise." She pulls back, placing her hands on my shoulders and holding me at arm's length. "But you actually *do* look awful, G."

"I'm sure you're right." My brain is finally catching up to my eyes. I look over at Yael, who is unusually casual in a T-shirt, jeans, and sneakers. I look back over my shoulder again. Still in my doorway. Still awake. I narrow my eyes at Yael. "I thought you were on a plane to London."

"I am not," she says simply.

"But *Alec* is," I explain very slowly.

Sunny turns to look at Yael. "Can you imagine if our planes actually crossed paths midair? He would never stop lecturing me."

I don't know if it's the wrong time to point out that they

both seem very flippant about letting a distraught Alec Kim fly home to London, where he will *not* find his sister waiting for him. In fact, I honestly don't know if the average person would understand what is happening right now and I am just a mental mess, or if they are being intentionally confusing. "I have no idea what the hell is going on."

Yael rolls her eyes. "Then for fuck's sake, Georgia, let us in."


At least these two appreciate a good cup of hand-brewed black coffee. They hum into their mugs, quietly complimenting the flavor. It unspools my memories of my morning here with Alec, his unapologetic sweet tooth, the signing later that day, his proposition that I stay with him at the hotel, Yael's warnings . . .

I have to admit I don't entirely feel like Yael Miller is Team Alec right now. I don't understand her motives at all. Why isn't she with *him*? Alec may be right, and Yael may be in love with Sunny, but Yael is his personal assistant. She handles everything for him but lets him fly back to London alone in the middle of a crisis? Heat creeps up my neck.

"How are you holding up?" Sunny asks me.

"It seems like the more important question is how *you're* holding up," I say, turning my gentler attention her way.

She laughs humorlessly. "It's been a terrible few months, but I suppose the silver lining is that instead of constantly worrying that the other shoe is going to drop, the other shoe has actually dropped."

"Yes, I think even if Alec hadn't been photographed outside of the club, your and his association with Anders would have eventually come out anyway."

"Exactly." We stare at each other for several long beats, and finally our smiles break out in unison. "God, it's so good to see you," she says. "You became the most perfect version of your future self. And you're just right in front of me."

"I was thinking the same thing." My heart does a heavy, contented squeeze behind my breastbone.

With a small smile, Sunny sets her coffee down on the table and tucks her legs beneath her. We're the same age—our birthdays are only one week apart—but engulfed as she is by the cushions of our big yellow sofa, she seems so much younger. Her posture, her energy—it all feels very youthful. How could anyone hurt this person? A wave of heat passes over me, and I relate very intensely to Alec's protective streak.

"You did an amazing job with the story," Sunny says. "I'm very grateful."

I watch her, unsure what to say other than "Thank you." I want to say that I'm sorry it exploded the way it did, but if the people who are behind the crimes end up being held accountable, we'll probably all admit that it was worth it.

"We all have a bit of a mess to sort out," she says, "but I didn't want you to wonder whether it was worth breaking it. It was."

Much like her brother, Sunny has capably read my thoughts. "I know that's why Alec wanted to fly home to London," I say. "To make a plan with you about how to handle the fallout."

"He struggled to leave LA because of his feelings for you," she says, "and so I felt the need to take charge of this.

I'm sure you've noticed that Alexander's tendency is to want to shelter me from the pain of this situation, and I appreciate it. I really do. But I don't want to be coddled anymore. I don't want to be protected. And like you said, it's only so long before my own association with Josef is going to come out." She picks up her mug again. "So, not that it isn't amazing to see you for the sake of seeing you, but I have a proposition."

Thunder rumbles beneath my ribs. "Okay, let's hear it."

"Word on the street is you're unemployed." She grins. "How'd you like to put your journalist cap back on and help me make some waves?"

# Twenty-Two

Sitting across a table from Kim Min-sun, it's hard to ignore the intensity of her beauty. The newest face of Dior is all angles and precision. She speaks with careful forethought and taps shell-pink nails against her full lips when she's weighing how to best put something into words. It's easy to see how she managed to get offers from eight luxury brands in only the past two months. There isn't another face like hers out there, anywhere.

But then a smile will crash across her features, and the dramatically playful Kim family dimples appear. It's startling, in those moments, how much she looks like her brother.

"Alexander is six years older," she says. "He's always been a caretaker. He would rather die than give the impression he can't handle something."

She says all this like these qualities explain everything. Which, I guess, they do. They explain why he feels responsible for the way she was brought up, why he can sometimes be an overprotective drag, and why, on Valentine's Day this year, he stormed into a nightclub, pulled his sister's drugged and unconscious body from a VIP room, and sat on a bathroom floor with her in his arms until she was able to stand on her own feet and leave with him.

They explain, too, why he let the press beat him into hiding this past weekend, after a British tabloid posted photos of him escorting a cloaked woman out of the notorious club Jupiter. With Jupiter under scrutiny for being the site of a string of alleged sex crimes, the photos quickly went viral.

"He would rather let the world think that he'd committed a crime than tell the world what happened to me," she says. "I wasn't ready to talk about it, but there is no way I'm going to let this destroy the best person I know."

I watch Sunny read the draft of the article, and then her focus tracks to the beginning, and she starts again, slower now. A three-hour conversation has been distilled down to this: eight thousand words detailing what happened that night at Jupiter, what she remembers, what Alec has told her, what he did for her, and even my connection to their family dating back twenty years—to be emailed out tonight to whoever wins the bidding war. Sunny insists I get paid for my work. I insisted the money be donated to sexual assault survivor funds. Yael reminded me that I'm unemployed, and we settled on donating half. Yael is currently fielding calls in my bedroom from the final contenders: the *New Yorker*, *Vanity Fair*, *The Atlantic*, *GQ*.

Sunny finishes reading and sets my laptop down, her eyes shining. "You did such a good job, Gigi. I can't believe you did that so fast."

I can't, either. "I guess I was motivated. I really need the world to fall over itself to apologize to Alec."

"Well," she says, "and to you."

"I care a lot less about that."

Sunny smiles at me, tucking a strand of hair behind her ear. "I've never heard him sound lovesick before."

"He called me all weekend," I tell her. "I left the phone he gave me here because I thought he left. I was a mess, too. Everything's a mess."

"I really hope you two can work it out." She studies my face. "He needs this in his life. He has such good friends, but I want him to have a person. A *you* person."

I nod, swallowing down the nauseating wave of worry, longing, and regret. "I hope he calls as soon as he lands. Is it going to worry him that you're here in LA?"

Yael comes in before Sunny can answer, and it's so disorienting to see her smiling that I can't look away. She catches my stare and dials it up. "Yes, Georgia, I have teeth."

"I figured they were sharp and retractable."

This makes her laugh, and the sound is unexpectedly playful. "Here. This is your contact at *Vanity Fair*." She hands me a piece of paper with several lines of her predictably tidy handwriting. "They're waiting up for the story. It'll run online at 9 a.m. Eastern and an extended piece can make it into the June issue if you get it to them by noon tomorrow. They'll handle copyedits but will call you if there's anything more substantial."

I have no idea how they're managing that, but I'm not about to ask. I look at my phone. It's just after 8 p.m. Even if Alec left midday, it will still be several hours before he lands in London. There isn't any point waiting up for him.

I open my email. Type in the name Yael handed me, along with a brief message, and hit send.

Yael rocks back on her heels and pats her flat stomach. "I'm starving."

Sunny stands, stretching. And then she walks over to Yael, puts her arms around her, and stretches to kiss her chin, answering one of the thousand questions I've had today. "Then let's grab some dinner," she says. "Gigi, you wanna come?"

It feels crazy to turn down the opportunity to have dinner with my childhood best friend and the newly grinning, formerly surly assistant-bodyguard I've been dodging for the past two weeks, but no matter how hard they work to convince me to join them, I fear that with this article sent off, my adrenaline will immediately drain and I will actually pass out into my plate. There are many good eats to be found in London, but Mexican food is usually not one of them, so I give them directions to my favorite local taco joint and see them off.

When the door closes, I fall back against it, staring down the short hallway to the bedrooms, debating whether I should feed myself or just go right back to bed. My stomach growls, making the decision for me. When I finally reheat the leftovers I'd stowed back in the fridge, I can't get them in my face fast enough. I am famished.

Teeth brushed, with Alec's dress shirt and my favorite underwear on for pajamas, I'm sitting in front of the television trying to process the insanity of this weekend, and as soon as I am able to calm my mind for the first time in days, I realize . . . I don't know how I'm going to handle being away from Alec. The thought loops in my mind every few minutes: *You squandered two whole days.* And now I have no idea when I'll see him next.

I know it's useless because he's on a plane over the Atlantic, but I text him anyway.

I miss you.

I put the Batphone down, but it immediately vibrates on the couch next to me. Startled, I pick it up. Alec has replied.

God, I miss you, too.

A delighted laugh breaks free. Right. It had never occurred to me to text him earlier, that some people actually spring for the Wi-Fi on planes. I didn't know you called me this weekend.

Yes, outside your apartment this morning I realized you had no idea that I'd been calling, and calling. . . .

Are you almost home?

Not really. Hours away still.

How's the flight?

More importantly, how are you?

I'm better. I listened to your voicemail.

And? he asks.

My heart feels ten sizes too big for my body. A heart this big could pump an ocean of blood. AND I really wish I'd taken the Batphone to my parents' place.

Well, I think you know I agree.

That last phone call really messed me up.

I know. I can't tell you how sorry I am.

I close my eyes, fighting these omnipresent tears. Finally, I get them under control. I wish you hadn't left this morning.

What do you wish I'd done instead? he replies.

I bite back my smile as I type. I wish I'd invited you in.

I told you if I came in, I wouldn't want to leave.

If you came in now, I wouldn't LET you leave.

I nearly jump out of my own skin when the doorbell rings barely two seconds after I've hit send. For a fraction of a second, I consider putting pants on but . . . awareness comes at me sideways, making me unsteady as I stand and walk to the door.

With a shaking hand, I pull it open to find Alec, clean-shaven, hair combed off his forehead, in a gray button-down shirt and dress pants and holding a wilted bouquet of flowers. "I've been carrying these around for a few hours," he explains. "Sunny wouldn't let me come over sooner, and you wouldn't come out for dinner."

I make a muffled sound of shock from behind the hand I've clapped over my mouth. He's been here this whole time. Of course. Alec wouldn't leave for London if Sunny was headed to LA. Sunny wouldn't come to LA if Alec was headed to London.

And Yael would never leave either of them hanging like that.

*Can you imagine if our planes actually crossed paths mid-air? He would never stop lecturing me.*

"You were never on the plane!"

"I— Whoa," he says, immediately distracted by my outfit. "What are you—"

I hurtle myself into his arms, knocking the flowers to the ground and making him take a few steadying steps backward to catch me. He's here. I squeeze him so tight, eyes closed, sacrificing every wish I might get from here on out in gratitude for having him here on my doorstep.

His arms go all the way around me, holding me tight, and he lets out the quietest groan into my neck. He feels so good against me I can't breathe. Everything inside seems to gather at the center of my chest and then explode outward in a pulse of relief and longing so that I feel my heartbeat as ten pulses in my fingers, ten pulses in my toes. He is solid and warm. He smells like soap and the soft citrus of his shaving cream. His laugh vibrates against my face where I'm pressed to his neck.

I never would have been able to get over him.

"Gigi," he says, his voice a deep vibration, "look at me."

I can't. I press my lips to his neck, his jaw, and then kiss like a madwoman all over his face.

Alec laughs at the onslaught, carrying me inside like I'm a rag doll hanging from his shoulders, and shuts the door behind us. Reaching down, he adjusts his grip around my waist and lifts me up, carrying me to my bedroom.

Once there, he lets me slide down his body until my feet hit the floor, and then he bends, cupping my face and setting his lips on mine, kissing me with a passion that obliterates my ability to think about anything other than the feel of him. I make fists in his shirt, pulling him right up against me.

But Alec finds my hands, coaxing my fingers open. "Let me see you," he says against my kiss, and then steps back.

He reaches out, adjusting the collar of his shirt on me, dragging his gaze down the length of my body and back up. Fire follows the path of his eyes and I feel it like sweet, tiny pinpricks all along my skin.

His neck flushes red.

"Do you blush like that when you come?" I ask, throwing his own teasing words back at him.

His laugh is a distracted, forceful exhale. I reach up, unbuttoning the shirt, watching the inky black of his pupils expand into the deep brown of his irises. The shirt falls to the floor and he reaches up, rubbing a finger over his bottom lip. "I like your underwear."

"Thanks." I slide a thumb under the elastic at the waist, snap it. "Yael got them for me."

He coughs out a laugh, eyes bolting to my face. "You're going to give her credit?"

"She picked them out."

"They were *my* idea."

This reminds me, and I hold up an index finger. "I have an important question for you."

His attention has drifted to my breasts. "My answer is yes."

"You have my red dress, don't you?"

He nods, distractedly. "Stole it. Never planned to return it."

Laughing, I reach for his hand, placing it on my hip and guiding it up my body, over my breast. My smile fades as longing spreads like steam through my veins. His fingers immediately mold to the curve, his eyes falling closed. Back and forth his thumb strokes across the peak. I need his pinch, his tongue and teeth. Arching, I press into his hand.

He swallows before speaking. "I really thought this weekend—this morning—that I might never touch you again."

When he opens his eyes, I'm already watching him, and the way his expression clears at the eye contact is so pure, his expression so ardent, I feel myself falling deeper into love as if it's a physical movement. It isn't just a feeling of passion and tenderness and admiration; it's feeling like the Gigi in love with Alec exists in an entirely new plane.

Alec slides his hand up my neck and steps to me.

My heart drops in my chest when his mouth touches mine again. A single kiss and then another, and the patience he takes seducing me with his lips tells me he knows we have a world of time to devour.

But, as usual, my body doesn't care.

I send both hands into his hair, coming right up against him. The pressed fabric of his dress shirt provides maddening friction against my skin. A cool button presses into my breast. Once again, I am almost naked, and he is fully dressed.

His tongue feels like sex in my mouth, tiny flicks and tastes, teeth dragging against my lips, tugging. I would tease him like this if I could, but I can only chase. I'm forever the frantic greed to his focused patience.

"Are you going to tease me for hours?" I ask, urging him with me toward the bed.

"I'm sure going to try."

At these words we both go still, eyes meeting as the painful echo rings between us. With his hands on my hips, he walks me the last few steps to the bed, coaxing me down, coming over me. The fabric of his dress pants is soft against my thighs, but he holds his hips away, hovering carefully above me.

"I'm not proud of how I acted on Friday," he says.

"I just didn't know what to do," I tell him. "I wanted to apologize, to fix it, to be there for you, but you gave me absolutely no way in."

He nods.

"Is that always how you react to a crisis?"

Alec shakes his head. "Remember how you once said I would need to be with someone who is very chill about things? I don't think I let myself believe you were really that person. I felt like a live bomb. I was panicking. I didn't want to add to your trouble."

I shake my head. "My choices affected you. I own that. I wanted to help you. At the very least I wanted to weather everything with you."

"I understand." He smiles. "If we're doing this, we're doing it. That means you're willing to give me the benefit of the doubt if you hear rumors, and I'm not going to shut you out again."

I reach up, running my fingers through his hair. "Deal."

That focused gaze makes a full circuit of my face. "I love you."

It's dark in this room—night sky, my curtains drawn— but at these words, I feel like I'm lit up inside. "Yeah?"

"Yeah." He smiles, and I reach up to gently poke a dimple with my fingertip. "Is it too soon?"

"Yes. But I want to say it, too," I say.

"You don't ha—"

I press my fingertips to his lips. "I'm gonna save it. Surprise you with it."

Alec laughs. "Spring it on me?"

I pretend to smoke a cigar. "Yeah, see. Unexpected like."

He finally settles over me, subtly flexing his hips into mine. Alec speaks the next words into the tender skin just beneath my jaw. "I bet I could coax it out of you."

Goose bumps break out along my skin, and I snake my hands between us, tugging his shirt free, unbuttoning. "I bet you could."

He pulls back and looks at me with a wicked gleam in his eye, shrugging out of his clothes. I glide my greedy hands over the smooth skin of his torso, and it occurs to me that I might not want to dare the man who, even under normal, non-making-up circumstances, enjoys making me beg.

First with his fingers, then with his kiss, and then with his body moving with disciplined focus into mine, he does get those three little words out of me. He makes me say them, swear them, makes me beg him to believe them. When he guides me over him, I say them again through a smile, staring down at the unmasked adoration on his face. And I scream them into the pillow when he fucks me hard from behind. I promise him I truly do when he rolls me onto my back again and pushes slowly into me, his arms caged protectively around my head.

Sweaty and tangled in the sheets, we tumble in a thump from the bed to the floor, where he braces over me, reaching between us to find his way back deep into me and slowing down to the smallest movements, his lips resting over mine, sharing my breath. My hands are woven in his hair; it's damp from exertion, and he kisses me so deep, groaning quietly at how good it feels. Alec's palm slides down my side, fingertips teasing along my hip, cupping my thigh, and bringing my leg higher around his waist.

"Do you love me when I'm deep like this?" he asks me.

I whisper into his mouth that I do, more than anything. Tight and urgent, I'm so close already, impossibly, with the promise of an unbelievable weight rolling down my spine, ready to obliterate.

"I think I'm starting to believe you." Sweat beads his top lip as he stares down between our bodies. I'm desperate for the salt of his skin, the wet, messy slide of his kiss when he's on the verge of falling to pieces.

Out in the apartment, we hear the front door open and close, and the sound of Eden dropping her purse and keys on the hall table. That means it's after two in the morning; we've been kissing, playing, making love for hours. Alec stares down at me, cupping a hand over my mouth, and only now that I can't make a sound does he give me what I want: the fast snaps of his hips until my pleasure sears through me one last time, sending my fingernails sinking into his back. He arches away, face tilted up as he bites a white streak into his lower lip, coming with a quiet groan.

We stay like this, catching our breath as Alec stares down at me.

"You okay?" he asks, shifting so he can reach up, move some sweat-slicked hair out of my eyes.

I nod, cupping his neck.

"Let's get you up." He kicks away the sheets wrapped around his legs, and I groan, already sore. Alec wordlessly helps me up onto the mattress, where I collapse, and he follows, turning me and tucking me into him with my back all along his front. With his hand on my breast and his breath on the back of my neck, we crash together into sleep.

■   ■   ■

Morning sneaks in through the small cracks in my curtains. I'm pressed into the solid comfort of Alec's chest, and pull away, gazing up at his sleeping face. Squinting, I roll over and reach for the phone on my nightstand. It's just after six.

My article will be up.

When I bolt upright, Alec stirs, sending a drowsy hand up my spine. "What is it?"

"The article went live at nine Eastern. Seven minutes ago."

He pushes up onto an elbow, leaning his sleepy face on my arm. We watch it load, and my heart scales my windpipe. There are already hundreds of comments. Silently, we read my story together. And then again.

When we're done, Alec whispers a quiet, "I mean . . . this is perfect."

He takes my phone and lies back down to read the story a third time.

I'm afraid to look outside this room to see the reaction from the rest of the world. When it comes to my relationship with Alec, it doesn't matter to me what anyone else says about this. We have a bond that exploded out of nowhere and deepens every time he touches me. I love him in the frantic grip of pleasure and in the soft, yawning light of morning.

But when Alec hands me my phone back and grabs his own, we stare at each other for a quiet, surreal moment. It might not matter to our hearts what people think, but it does matter.

"Do you think it's safe to open Twitter?" I ask.

He grins, generously offering two irresistible dimples. "Is it ever?"

It's true that he and I exist far beyond the reach of the internet, but my career hinges on this article being well received, and his hinges on people believing what Sunny has to say. I kiss him once, eyes open and clear, before looking. After only a couple minutes of scrolling, I can't help the boasting laugh that escapes. Alec is trending again, but this time he's receiving an outpouring of love.

I swipe up, watching the fast scroll of hundreds and hundreds of tweets. "This is wild. Do you see all of this adoration?" I pause to read a few and frown. "You have a lot of marriage proposals." Looking at him, I point to my screen. "There is a person here who has offered to carry your baby if you are so inclined."

He ignores this. "I already have a few requests for interviews."

This makes me laugh. "Uh, I bet you do."

A text from Eden pops up on my phone. I hear you laughing in there. I'm assuming the crushed flowers I found in the entryway last night mean that there's a man in your bed.

Giggling, I text her back. Some random guy showed up. Good timing. Needed a rebound.

Does that mean Alexander Kim is single? Now's my chance.

I laugh, and then a new alert pops up on my screen. It's a follow request from @GigisBottomLip.

"What are you doing?" I ask, grinning over at him.

"Starting my fan account."

Tossing my phone to the side, I launch myself onto him and let him pull that bottom lip between his. He nibbles his way down my neck and blows a raspberry into my shoulder.

"I'm not sure I'll be able to walk today," I say.

"I'm going to be limping," he agrees.

"You know what would loosen you up?" I ask, pressing my smile to his cheek.

"What?"

"A nice hot shower." I hook a thumb over my shoulder, and he rolls over onto me, already laughing at what he knows is coming: "You're more than welcome to use mine."

# Epilogue

Sunny, Yael, and Alec stay in LA for three more days to handle the hurricane of publicity that follows the publication of the *Vanity Fair* article. When he isn't fielding interviews, Alec is with me at our old suite at the Waldorf Astoria; he insisted on rewiring my association with the space, painting over those final shitty moments. I guess I did my best to block out the sensation of the sunlight coming in the bedroom, the brightness of the walls, the chill of the sheets against my skin, and the way they heat when Alec slides into bed with me every night because being back in the simple opulence is both a disorienting shock and deeply nostalgic.

Perhaps unsurprisingly, the siblings are invited back to the same talk shows Alec visited only a couple weeks before for *West Midlands* promo. Except this time, he sits on the couch beside his sister, talking about the Jupiter scandal, sex abuse, his willingness to sacrifice his career for her privacy, and Sunny's bravery in coming forward and talking about an event of which she has virtually no recollection.

It's emotionally draining for them both, and that—combined with Alec's and my inability to go anywhere without getting mobbed by photographers—means that we spent most of our free time in the suite, wrapped around each other.

When I say goodbye to him outside LAX, no hyperbole intended, it feels like my stomach is being ripped open. We don't have a plan for when we're going to see each other next—everything has been too chaotic—but we promise to make one as soon as he's home and in front of his calendar.

In theory, I should be fine when he leaves. I know Alec and I are in a solid place. My story has led to a huge investigation into Jupiter and all the major players. Legal pundits barely have anything to argue about on the news networks—they all agree Josef Anders is going away for a very long time. I'm fielding job offers left and right (including one from the *LA Times* that I politely decline). Everything in my life is objectively golden. But in the chaos of the past few weeks, I've stopped feeling like my career has to be everything. Maybe I'm wrong about Alec and me, maybe I'm being idealistic, but I don't think so.

So when he lands at Heathrow, and he calls me as soon as he's off the plane, and I pick up on the first ring, and he blurts that he can't believe he left without me, I blurt right back, "Maybe I should move there."

He flies me out a few days later and we're only four days deep into a vacation in the Scottish Highlands, planning the shape of our forever, when his agent calls with an offer for the lead role in an upcoming Christopher Nolan film. It's scheduled to begin production in Singapore in a matter of weeks.

"Our new house can wait," I say to him.

"This is the role of a lifetime," he agrees.

"It's only four months."

But four months turns into six, and the role catapults him into household-name territory. We see each other as frequently as we can, but it's hard to find blocks of time when he's completely free. He wins a BAFTA for *The West Midlands* and major award buzz follows this new performance of his; Alec soon has his pick of jobs and collaborations. But when I visit, I get him only in the tiny cracks of his free time, and when he comes to LA, his schedule is just as packed. It isn't the same being on his arm on the red carpet as it is being pinned beneath him in bed or curled up together on the couch. I'm lonely and he's homesick for me. He worries he's losing focus, and I can't dive deep on any project because I prioritize flying to see him whenever he has a free second. Even when we have time together, it feels desperate and too short.

The problem is that I don't know what the alternative is. Even if we move in together, will we see each other more often? He's at the peak of his career and can rest in a few years when he's checked every box on his professional bucket list. And I want to work, too. Not because I need to support myself anymore, but because I love research and writing, and as much as Alec is the undisputed love of my life, I don't want to simply follow him around from one location to the next. I want to have a reason to get out in the world and write about what I see there.

The solution comes one night when we're in Fiji together on a short getaway celebrating our one-year anniversary and Alec casually tells me some wild anecdotes about a man he met on his current film shoot, and how this man met his wife. Yanbin is a horror movie afficionado from Beijing and his wife, Berit, is a biologist from Stockholm, and—the best part—they *actually* met on a train to Busan. Her research takes her around the entire globe, and he travels with her in between cinematography projects with the studio that hired Alec. The stories they told about the unconventional ways they made their marriage work are better than any romance novel I've ever read.

So I write a piece for *The Guardian* about them. A simple human-interest story. But then I start receiving letters from other couples. At first, maybe a dozen every week. Some of the stories are so unreal they make me gasp or cry or laugh hysterically. I write another feature about a transgender couple from Malaysia who wrote to me, and who I meet for an interview. After that story runs, the letters begin arriving by the hundreds every week.

I become obsessed with these unlikely and engrossing real-life romances, enamored with the people in every letter. Sometimes I even find the most unexpected points of connection between couples across the globe. All the love stories are touched by the same magic: right place, right time. I decide to write a book, compiling my interviews and their letters into a series of interwoven missed connections and found soulmates. Because I can work from anywhere, I can travel with Alec wherever his next role takes him. I write in a fever all day, and every night, wherever we are, I sleep wrapped around him. For months we are blissful nomads, living in Charlotte, Stockholm, Toronto.

While exhilarating, it's also exhausting, so when Alec gets the offer for a big-budget BBC production, he takes it.

Tonight, after a celebratory dinner with his parents, Sunny, and Yael, we curl up in bed in a London hotel and agree it might be time to buy a home here.

"And while we're at it," he says, sending a warm palm up over my stomach, across my breasts, and down again, "maybe we should get married."

I almost die on my first day back in England. It's the most prosaic version of near-death—an American stepping into oncoming traffic in London—but I can't really blame it on drivers on the opposite side of the street because I wasn't even watching for cars.

I was staring at the number 14 on the blue door of a flat in Holland Park. I was absently waving in thanks as my taxi driver pulled away from the curb and growing breathless thinking how long the flight felt—how it felt longer than even that first unending trip back from London nearly two years ago now—and whether it was stupid of me to come a day early to surprise Alec when he's probably working his ass off to get our new place ready.

My limbs feel disorientingly electrified; my heart is beating so hard it's pushing insistently against my windpipe. I guess there are times in life when we realize even in the moment that something transformative is happening. If I think about it, so many of my moments with Alec fall into that category. Like our first elevator ride, or later that night when he said to me, *Whatever we want*, in that deep, resonant voice while his thumbs massaged my palm. The evening we stood together in front of an infinite number of Alecs-and-Gigis reflected back to us and shared a thousand glimpses into our forever. His smiling lips on mine in front of the entire world just after he was told he won an Oscar. The moment I sent in the completed draft of my manuscript and Alec did a drumroll on the desk with his hands, or three weeks ago and the surprise appearance of him at my doorstep in LA with a bottle of champagne and a hard copy of the bestseller list. And now, the day we're finally moving in together, two weeks before our wedding. After all this time, we have a home base.

The thought sings to me as I cross the street: life will throw curveballs, and things won't always be this easy or straightforward, but this love—our love—is the rare wonder that comes along once in a lifetime.

He's in the front room—our new living room—directing two men where to put a sofa, his face turning toward the window as he gestures. He sees me, smiles in relief, and then it registers.

Alec is a blur of movement behind the thick glass, and then he is sprinting out the door and leaping down the three steps and into the street where he meets me halfway. Horns blare and cars swerve, but he lifts me up, his strong arms banded around my middle. Traffic slows and stops when they realize who and what they're seeing, but for better or worse, Alec has never given much thought to who might be watching us.

"Finally," he says, resting his lips on mine, "it begins."

# Acknowledgments

August 2020, I was on vacation from my writing gig and decided to . . . write. (There are obvious problems with extracurricular variety when your hobby is also your job.) I am intensely lucky that I get to write full-time for a living, and I love every second of my day job, but I hadn't written something impulsive, no-expectations, and just for myself in ages. There's a unique type of freedom in writing a side project—one that is understandably harder to find when you're writing for an established readership. Here, I was possessed with Gigi and Alec; their story rolled right out of me. It's the most satisfying kind of flow for a writer, and I hope it has been a book you, sweet reader, got lost in.

I am so grateful to this project and Kate Clayborn for being the reason I look back on the summer and fall of 2020 and feel sweet nostalgia instead of the hollow, existential panic I know so many of us experienced. Alec would not be here were it not for you. So much pain came out of that year, but you were—and continue to be—a bright spot of joy in my every day.

Having a community that sustains its support and energy is worth more than gold to a writer. I am indebted to my wonderful friend Susan Lee for her feedback but also her enthusiasm. Your fangirl smile buoys everyone around you; you are such a gem. Thank you to my sweetie, Erin McCarthy, for the long texts while you were reading, and the continual excitement you've had for this since you read it nearly two years ago.

I had zero expectations that the Word doc I was calling *Side Piece* up until like five minutes ago would turn into an actual book. I sent it to my agent, Holly Root, with a *this-is-really-steamy-but-maybe-could-be-a-thing?* email, and she didn't even blink that I put this entire manuscript out of nowhere into her inbox during the biggest dumpster-fire portion of the pandemic. She did the Holly Root thing where she was like "Cool" and sold it. Thank you to the Pocket and Gallery Books team: Hannah Braaten for loving this book just the way I'd hoped you would, Jen Bergstrom for stepping up and getting behind this without hesitation, and Mackenzie Hickey for always being the brightest and most enthusiastic star. Min Choi designed this cover, and to put it simply: I am obsessed. I asked for something very specific, and this came back, and it was one and done. Honestly, I'm not sure if anywhere in publishing a cover process has ever gone so smoothly or happily. Enormous gratitude to Andrew Nguyễn, Aimée Bell, Lauren Carr, Eliza Hanson, Jen Long, Christine Masters (my queen, you miss nothing), Emily Arzeno, Caroline Pallotta, Abby Zidle, Sally Marvin, and the entire Gallery team. When I call you The Dream Team, it is not an exaggeration. Jen Prokop, thank you for your always amazing editorial notes. I love you and I am sorry I made you read first person present tense.

Kristin Dwyer of Leo PR is the master strategist, friend, champion, and, of course, PR rep. She is indispensable and one of a kind. I want everyone to have a Kristin (but she also brings out the Gollum in me and I'm not even ashamed).

To my book community who read early versions, blurbed, or delighted me with your own words, I am so grateful for your enthusiasm and love: Ali Hazelwood, Helen Hoang, Sarah MacLean, Rosie Danan, Rachel Lynn Solomon, Tessa Bailey, Sonali Dev, Kate Spencer, Sara Whitney, Katherine Center, Erin Service, Katie Lee, Cassie Sanders, Catherine Lu, Molly Mitchell, Monica Sánchez, and Gretchen Schreiber. Thank you to the readers who requested early review copies and bombed their feelings into my DMs. Thank you to the Bookstagram, Goodreads, BookTuber, and TikTok creators who took time to make videos, posts, and reviews for this book. It really means so much to me!

To my family, you are the very nucleus of my joy. I hope the eleventy thousand quesadillas I made during the pandemic adequately expresses my fondness for you, you adorable goobers.

And to you-know-who, we always save each other for last. You know what they say about the best, and it's true. You are.